Fractured Shadow

Aurelia Ashburn

Aurelia Ashburn

For all the girlies who fantasise about unhinged, sinfully dark and depraved fictional men chasing you through a forest.
This book is for you.

Aurelia Ashburn

This book contains content that may be disturbing and traumatising.

It mentions topics including necrophilia, sexually explicit scenes, strong language, violence, murder, torture, primal play, breath play, voyeurism, hematolagnia (blood play), hematomania, NCR, CNC, coercion, somnophilia, stalking, kidnapping, human hunting, abuse, restraints, degredation, fisting, DP, DVP, PTSD, drugging, light recreational drug use, self harm, m/m, mmmm/f (reverse harem), Stockholm syndrome.

(Sorry, there are no unhinged masked stalkers. I can promise plenty of unhinged and questionable immoral behaviour however.)

If any of these are a trigger I advise you not to continue. If you are colour blind and your red flags are green, and trigger warnings are more of a snack for your reading pleasure, then I hope you feast away.

Happy reading Dark romance lovers.

Aurelia Ashburn

Kira

1

A sinister smirk played on his mouth with wicked intent and a promise of danger. It was everything I shouldn't want, but fuck, if I wasn't thinking straight. Every fantasy was playing out before me. I was almost willing to bind my own hands, drop on my knees, with mouth open, waiting, pleading to be used for his own depravity and pleasure. My own twisted desires I kept hidden from the outside world were begging to be unleashed.

Below the hood, which shadowed the upper half of his face, his hungry eyes glowed bright, boring deep into mine as though he was extracting the thoughts from my mind and replaying them over in his own head.

A deep groan rolled through his chest as he inched closer, weakening my knees and drenching my underwear with that one sound. I was a goner the moment he caught me in his web. An eager sacrifice at his mercy, bound with an apple in my mouth as an offering.

"You look so sweet and innocent, like butter wouldn't melt in your mouth," he purred.

The deep timbre of his voice caressed my soul, flooding my

core with warmth and holding me prisoner with the truism of his words.

"But, I know better. I have no doubt you are actually a filthy whore, begging to be destroyed. If I were to put on a mask and tell you to run like your life depended on it, you would make it five metres before I found you naked, splayed out on the forest floor with your dripping pussy on display begging me to destroy it."

"Yes," I let out a breathy whisper, not denying how appealing it sounded and how desperately I wanted him to use me just as he depicted.

"Good girl," he purred.

My knees buckled under those two words.

I panted as he wrapped a hand around my throat with enough pressure as a warning, but not enough to cut off my oxygen.

"More," I begged, wanting to see stars.

He raised a knife to his face, running it back and forth across the stubble on his cheek, increasing the pressure on my throat with his fingers, giving me what I wanted. Sticking out his tongue, he licked the sharp edge of the blade, slowly dragging it down the meaty flesh. Blood welled to the surface of the muscle, filling his mouth with crimson. He leaned forward, his tongue moving from my chin, to up over my mouth to my nose, before thrusting into my open mouth, letting me taste the copper of his blood.

I could have just about come from that act alone.

He shoved his knee between my thighs as he assaulted my mouth with his own, and I ground against it unashamedly, desperate for the friction.

Darkness began clouding my vision when his hand began tightening at my throat to the point I was losing consciousness. My pulse thrummed loudly in my ears, matching the racing beat of my heart and the throbbing between my legs. I ground down harder against his thigh, my orgasm building. I was so close but was losing the battle as my eyelids fell closed heavily on their own and I passed out before getting off.

I shot up in bed, gasping for breath with my hand at my throat. With a thick layer of sweat coating my body, my pussy was wet, throbbing with need.

Shit, it was just a dream.

Throwing myself back into the pillow, I groaned. Saddened that I was back in reality instead of being tormented by an unhinged man literally of my dreams. I really needed to stop reading before bed

Grady

2

Her creamy flesh was painted with a rainbow of colours. Purples, yellows, greens, blues and pinks adorned her like a living canvas. But the prettiest of the colours was the scarlet, which flowed like a river breaking the banks, dressing her in a gown of her own blood cascading over the myriad of bruises kissing her skin.

"Beautiful," Kyden stepped back, admiring his handiwork with a sound of contentment.

Sticking out his tongue, he licked the blood clean from the knife he had just used to slice open ribbons of her flesh below her clavicles. He was a master of his work, every slice made with precision.

The woman's terrified screams had long since become nothing more than a hoarse, breathy whisper. It was melodic, the hoarseness from her pleads of mercy making her throat raw and tender until the rough and abused sound of her vocal cords began haemorrhaging, stealing all sound until it became nothing but a breathy and silent cry.

Her chest heaved rapidly, her remaining eye glossy and puffy, painting her face with black tears from her mascara. She was a masterpiece. Like an RJ Derby canvas.

"Beg," Chris's deep voice rumbled from the shadows at the back of the room where the spotlight didn't reach. Ever the voyeur and dominant, he told us what to do for his own perverse satisfaction. "Beg for us to make it stop."

Her bottom lip quivered. "P… please," her lips moved, but no sound escaped.

Trent tsked, shaking his head slightly in disappointment. Stepping forward, pinching her chin between his thumb and index finger, he tipped her head up to meet his face. "Now, now, now. I think you can do better than that. Don't you?"

"Please," she sobbed silently. Her forced voice barely made a slight whimpering sound, breaking above a whisper. "Let me go?"

Trent turned his head, looking over his shoulder ah Chris with a raised brow. "What do you say? I think she needs to be punished some more. That wasn't nearly convincing enough."

"Grady?" Chris said, snapping me from where I stood, fisting my erection with a frantic motion. Fuck if this doesn't make me hard. "What do you say to making her beg some more?"

I couldn't restrain the laugh that bubbled from my chest stepping up next to Trent with my dick standing at full attention in front of me. I saw him side-eye it, so I gave him a playful wink and kissy lips. His eye-roll and lip-curl he returned was for show–I knew how badly he wanted my cock. It was magnificent, even if I do say so myself. T-man was still in the closet though, so I wasn't going to push it and make him uncomfortable.

Turning my attention from Trent to the woman. I cocked my head to the side, watching the woman's remaining eye widen and her head shake vehemently. Her head shook back and forth rapidly, her mouth silently saying, "no, no, please no," over and over.

It was comical to see in a way, as if someone had muted the volume on my favourite show. Or like a goldfish blowing little bubbles under water.

I popped my mouth a few times mocking her, unable to help myself. The woman clearly had no sense of humour; her mouth pulled down with a whimper, and her chest bobbed in rhythm with her sobs, making her breasts bounce.

"Hmm," I mused, glancing up to Trent, who stood six-inches over me. Fucking giant, he must have slept with his feet in nutrient-rich potting soil or some shit as a kid, 'cause that shit wasn't normal. "What do you say, T-man?

Pleasure or pain?"

He smirked. Slowly, half turning his head and cocking an eyebrow. "Both."

Kyden snickered behind us. Yeah, he was enjoying this. This was the point where our subject was finally broken and accepting of what would befall them.

"Good call."

I snatched my hand out, grabbing her by the throat and squeezing firmly. Her shaky breath caught, eyes widening as though her life was flashing before her eyes. It was only a matter of seconds that passed with her face tight in fear before the muscles relaxed and her head lulled forward against my hand, exhaling one final breath. Her entire body fell slack as the fight left her, and she hung lifelessly from the restraints at her wrists.

"What the fuck?" Chris and Trent shouted in unison. Chris was on his feet but stayed at the back of the room, waiting to see if this was merely a diversion to prolong the inevitable death that was to come.

I moved my hand to tilt her chin up, her eyes half-mast. The pupil in the eye that still sat in her head dilated and unfocused. Not a single breath of life fell from her gaping mouth. That was something that had never happened before.

"Huh, that was anticlimactic," I murmured, dropping her

face with disappointment.

Blowing heavily through my lips so they vibrated, I stepped back, waiting for something else to happen. I had no idea what, but this felt like some kind of prank. Like, let's see if we can fuck Grady up today and make him snap. I was kind of lost as to how to react. Were fireworks going to suddenly burst from her ass, lighting up the room and everyone jumping out and yelling, *'Surprise.'*

I had to admit that would be pretty cool. Especially if the fireworks exploded her body, coating us all in her guts, it would be like an unintended dress-up party.

Kyden ripped her head back with a fistful of hair, checking her pulse and examining her eye for himself, then turned his sight on me with a glare. His right eye twitched with restrained rage.

"You killed her?"

Well, shit! This wasn't a prank. I scratched at my cheek with my bloodied gloved hand, staring at the body with a grimace. I didn't know what to say—I hadn't done it on purpose.

"Fuck!" Chris snapped, storming up beside us, his penetrating glare locked on me. "What did you do, Gray?"

Swinging my head to Chris, I narrowed my eyes. Yanking a knife from Kyden's belt, I held it between us. "You really wanna try me right now?"

They all knew better than to piss me off, especially when we hadn't had our fill of suffering. I became defensive—swing first and *not* apologise later. And now I was disappointed that there were no fireworks. Adding that this particular subject had taken longer than usual to hunt down and apprehend, so we were all on edge right now. Not to mention I was hornier than a succubus standing outside of a brothel.

I sighed, looking down at my hard dick. *Sorry, big guy, you are going to have to hold that thought for a little while.*

Chris's nostrils flared, jaw ticking with how tight he clenched his teeth.

"Fuck!" he repeated, laying a punch into the ribs of the deceased woman with a sickening crack, spraying us all with a splatter of the flowing blood, the impact causing the body to swing from the momentum of his hit.

The tension in the room was so thick you could cut it with a knife.

"Now what?" Kyden asked, sauntering to the back of the room to take a seat in Chris's chair and reclining back with a yawn, coming down from his high of spilling blood.

I made a disgruntled noise. At least one of us got our fill.

"Now, we go in search of another sub to get a release before we turn on each other." Trent exhaled heavily, looking directly at me as if it were my fault this one died so easily.

Pft, the poor woman looked so sexually deprived and subservient that her heart probably gave out from all the excitement and she couldn't handle it. I mean, not that I blamed her. If I were tied up with four gods standing before me threatening me with a good time, I think I would spontaneously combust too.

Ah, that sounds like a wet dream.

Kira

3

I had long ago resigned myself to the knowledge that I would end up alone, most likely with a dozen or so cats for companions. Not that I didn't want a partner—I would love nothing more than to have someone greet me at home each day after work, someone to join me on impromptu picnics or trips to the beach, to challenge me to be better and allow me to lower the walls I've built around myself. Walls that prevent anyone from getting close enough to love me again.

But after losing Ninny, I quickly realised there was no one else who could ever love me so unconditionally, for no reason other than choosing to, because I was worth it to them.

And seeing the chromosomes that exist left me pondering if there was really any hope. I may be jaded and judgemental when it comes to the opposite sex, but it was not without reason. It is a forced combination of unreal expectations of men set by authors who leave the entire male population lacking in retrospect, and the winning sperm of the XY chromosome that plague the planet, thinking they are God's gift to women. Not to mention the backwater town I choose to reside in severely limits the available options in the dating pool. I can opt for the few drunks who frequent the bar from open to close. They reek of stale cigarettes and alcohol, which leeches from their pores, and the majority of them are also old enough to be my grandfather. I really don't have 'daddy kink,' so they would be out of the equation, regardless. Then there are those whose only ambition in life is to get laid or get high.

Don't get me wrong, I have considered a fling with one of these less-than-desirables once or twice, just to get the urge out of my system. But I have a distinct feeling that I would be left more unsatisfied than if I just took matters into my own hands using my vibrator on the verge of a flat battery.

Any eligible bachelor that had any remotely attractive attributes—whether it be a job, semi-domesticated, or his own teeth, (yeah that one is a tricky one to find in this town)—is quickly snapped up and held under lock and key by the extroverted women in this town.

I have never bothered attempting to approach any fresh blood that is stupid enough to venture into this town. I don't exactly have a lot going for me to begin with. Sure, I have a job, have my own place, and have a small amount of savings. I'm self-sufficient, not needing to rely on anyone. Not that my biological family accepts me anyway; I am more of the black sheep. My ancestry is a mix of indigenous Australian and British. My birth mother basically disowned me shortly after I was born when my father returned to his country, leaving me to be raised by the elders in our community.

Sure, *'raising me'* is a bit of a stretch. Once I was able to move around independently, I was pretty much left to fend for myself—surviving on whatever scraps I found lying on the ground amongst the garbage, or a few who would toss me their leftovers out of pity. If it weren't for one of the volunteers who would come through the camps to treat any injured and provide sanitary items and basic necessities, I would have died.

By the age of three, the volunteer I affectionately named Ninny—because I couldn't pronounce her name, Samantha—fought the system and fostered me. She gave me opportunities I never would have received if I had remained and survived the life I had been born into. Although I highly doubted I would have survived much past my third year if it weren't for her intervention. Ninny put me through school and taught me resilience to handle the harassment I received there. I loved her dearly. She was, for all intents and purposes, my mother. She never treated me as anything but her own daughter, and I loved her with all my heart.

If only I had more years with her before she passed away, just one week after I graduated high school, from a brown snake bite. Ninny brushed off seeking medical attention, claiming that because it was a juvenile, it wasn't as venomous. If only she had known otherwise. I never fully recovered from her death, especially when not a single soul came to her funeral. It showed the ugly side of the community, shunning her even in death for taking me in and giving me a life. That event in itself changed me. I just don't know if it was for the better or worse.

With a heavy sigh, I pushed away the memory, leaning back against the wall. I looked around the small cafe, people-watching while I waited for my coffee order. The usual suspects who comprised of the mayor's wife, the police sergeant's wife and his mistress, the local busybody who knew everyone's business before they did, and the town's local Karen who complained about every insignificant issue, all gathered around the largest table in the centre of the room, sharing their morning gossip.

I rolled my eyes and sighed when I heard my name mentioned in hushed whispers, followed by all their eyes all turning to me. It was always the same nonsense— how I didn't belong here, and I was trouble because of my heritage.

Puh-lease. I know for a fact that the mayor's son slips

roofies in underage girls' drinks at every party he attends, and that his best friend is taking Karen's husband's dick up his arse each afternoon.

But I'm the one considered trouble because I'm of Aboriginal descent and I dare to mind my own business and keep to myself.

Psht, yeah, okay.

"Kira. Latte and blueberry muffin."

I walked over to the counter and collected my order, offering a polite smile and thanks to Bridgett before quickly dispelling from the cafe.

In my eagerness to leave, I missed the fact that there were four men on the other side of the glass door, about to enter the cafe. I slammed straight into a hard wall of muscle, my fingers tightening around my cardboard cup, expelling the hot liquid all over me, scalding me from breast to navel.

"Shit. Fuck. Sorry. Fuck. That's hot." I flapped my dress in front of me, attempting to cool my flesh from the scalding beverage.

My arm was gripped by a large hand, which held my elbow firmly, putting a stop to my flapping.

"Are you okay?" The deep timbre of the voice made me involuntarily quiver.

I finally looked up to meet the face of not only the voice but the three very distinctively intimidating out-of-towners behind him. The man holding my arm hostage studied me with concern, but there was also a hint of curiosity and interest. Or at least that's the lie I told myself, while I had no doubt I was drooling as I looked up into the dark blue, almost grey eyes which stared back at me. His sharp jaw was covered in a dark five o'clock shadow matching his thick hair, giving him that sexy, tall, dark and handsome look. No, that was an understatement of just how beautiful this man was. It was dangerous how attractive he was.

And that voice? I was going to need to change more than just my shirt after this encounter.

"Are you okay?" he asked again. With my arm still in his grasp, he had begun running his thumb gently across my skin, sending a line of goosebumps flickering across my flesh. Goddamn. How can a simple motion drag out such a strong reaction from my body?

I blinked, realising I was staring and hadn't responded. Coming back to Earth from the fantasy world built by every wet dream and romance novel I'd devoured. I couldn't help but wish I would one day find myself in just this kind of situation.

I stammered. "Ah, yeah. Sorry, I was distracted. I didn't spill my coffee on you, did I?"

I took my time looking over every square inch of the man, undressing him in my mind, imagining his wide frame naked, with lean muscles on display. I wondered if he was tattooed under the sleeves that hid his arms from view.

His mouth kicked up at the corner, his eyes grazing down over my disastrous attempt to keep the wet fabric of my top off my body, only to realise I had it pulled out so far that the v neck was giving him a full view of my breasts.

Fuck my life.

I hastily dropped it back down, and it stuck to my skin, feeling all kinds of uncomfortable. Then I remembered that I was wearing white, and beneath my now transparent top, I wore the most unattractive granny bra to ever grace existence.

Please kill me before I humiliate myself any further.

"No, you didn't make me wet, but by the looks of you…" He raised one single brow with that smirk still playing on his lips. "You are well and truly drenched."

"You have no idea," I murmured, not meaning to say that aloud.

Squeezing my eyes tight, I internally cursed when I heard the rough laughter from all four men, clearly aware of my innuendo. I blushed so hard, I swear I was lit up from space in a beacon of embarrassment. I slapped a hand over my face in humiliation—or tried to, but only ended up smooshing the bag with the muffin against my face. Yeah, this was going from bad to worse.

I pulled my elbow free and stumbled back a step. "Have a nice day and sorry for …" I waved my hand at myself, keeping my eyes down, then quickly turned down the footpath away from the men eager to put distance between us.

"Wait," one of the men called out. His tone was a demand rather than a request. I stumbled over my step, then glanced over my shoulder, unable to help myself from obeying. A man with dirty blonde hair and a troublesome look about him tilted his chin up. "What's your name?"

I smiled, "Nunya."

He frowned, tilting his head to the side, assessing what I said, silently sounding out the name on his lips.

"Nunya business," I added, widening my grin, then continued down the road with my empty, crushed cup and muffin still in hand, the sounds of deep laughter echoing behind me. Leaving behind every reverse harem fantasy I've read about, feeling wetter than just where I inadvertently spilled my latte.

When I returned home, I had just enough time to quickly change from my black work slacks and white cotton top into a fresh set of the same outfit, while scarfing down my muffin. Unfortunately, my underwear had to withstand the day as my punishment for procrastinating doing laundry throughout the week. Thankfully, I had enough time to quickly throw a load in the washer on my way out, so I wasn't left commando tomorrow. I still smelled faintly of coffee, but there could be worse ways to smell. The locals proved that deodorant was more a suggestion and not a requirement.

I arrived at work with two minutes to spare, sans my usual fifteen minutes. It made me feel out of sync not having time to mentally prepare myself for my shift. As a result, I messed up several times, earning a verbal berating from my employer about the logistical implications and potential consequences of carelessly displaying prohibited items. Technically, the items are not prohibited, at least not anywhere else, but in our community, with the growing problem of backyard chemists cooking up drugs, I had been continually reminded not to allow particular products to be sold to certain individuals. Nothing was stopping them from purchasing said products via a third person, or over in the next town over, so I found the entire endeavour rather redundant.

Trent

4

"Any with potential?" Grady asked from beside me, eyeballing the gaggle of women who were not so subtly eye-fucking each of us as we waited for our order in the cafe.

They all had makeup caked on so thick it transformed their faces, morphing their aged skin and lack of facial structure into the deceptive facade meant to fool men into believing they possessed natural beauty.

I have no personal objection to women wearing makeup. Correction: I have no problem ruining women's makeup. There is something about finding a pure angel wearing mascara and bright coloured lip, then making a mess of that perfection. Smearing their lipstick over their faces as they suck cock, they cry, whimpering with tears spilling, painted, black lines down their cheeks as they gag, choosing my pleasure over air like a good little slut.

But none of these women comes close to that particular little fantasy. One was deep-throating a straw, wrapping her tongue sloppily around it trying to force eye contact with

Kyden. He wasn't even looking their way, too lost in his own head, staring blankly into space.

Grady caught the woman's attention and began thrusting his tongue between parted fingers and wiggling his eyebrows. The woman bit down on the straw with a smile, so her thick makeup cracked around her eyes, as she undressed him with her gaze.

Grady chuckled darkly, pushing his tongue into his bottom lip.

"No," I said sternly, shaking my head to make sure he got the hint before he approached the table. "They would be the type of women who would cause issues."

Not that they would put up a fight. It was the quality of the accessories they donned that screamed money. We didn't need anyone with money or power pulling resources to search for them before we'd had our fun.

"Doesn't leave many options from what I've seen. Just the dark girl at the door and the one at the counter," Chris whispered, jutting his chin in the direction of the barista. He usually sought out our subjects, leaving me to approach them, but since our last endeavour, he has been hesitant.

I glanced over at the young girl who was busying herself frothing milk for our coffee. Her name tag read Brittany. I scoffed. Yeah, she looked like Brittany too. Long blonde hair pulled up into a perfectly sleek ponytail, manicured nails, fake lashes. She looked to be barely fifteen.

"Too young," I dismissed. And not to mention that she looked to be too much trouble to be worth it, regardless. Our morals may be slightly skewed, but we still respected the fact that any girl underage was off limits, as were mothers with young children or pregnant women.

"Move on to the next town then?" Grady suggested with a devious grin. "Unless you want to hunt down the little Chocolate drop? She looked like she would come willingly. I could practically hear her purring when you touched her." Grady paused, chuckling to himself. "Cum willingly, fuck, I'm funny."

Fucking hell, he had already given her a nickname. Meaning, he was zeroing in on her as a potential subject.

Kyden snorted, joining us back in reality from his little daydream. "Ah-huh. She would be easy."

"No," I shook my head vehemently. Something about her intrigued me. I don't think I could fully commit to our carnal desires with her if she found her way into our web. She was… different. The moment I laid eyes on her, I knew that I wanted to play with her one on one. "We'll hit the pharmacy on the way out to grab a few essentials, so we are prepared and move on to another town."

Grady, Chris and Kyden all gave a nonchalant shrug before grabbing their orders from the counter as our names were called. Not that we ever gave our real names. We usually avoided stopping at places with security cameras too, finding most of our victims in backwater towns that were behind with technological advances and security. The type of towns that rarely made the news, and no one gave two shits about. The less evidence there was to trace back to us, the better.

The pharmacy was only up the road, but we decided to move the car closer rather than lug questionable items through the street. We didn't want to draw any further attention to ourselves for what we had planned once we found our victim, and we had already attracted more than enough stares to make me uncomfortable about stopping here to begin with. It's probably fortunate we didn't take someone from here.

"Well, fuck me. Fate's playing her hand. Trent, see who it is?" Grady said from the back seat. "You sure she doesn't have potential?"

My eyes instantly locked onto the girl who spilled her coffee all over herself in front of the cafe. She had obviously changed her clothes and was now standing in front of the pharmacy with a deep scowl on her face, hands on her hips, muttering a string of curse words as she paced back and forth in front of the pharmacy window. I couldn't help the smirk on my face as I watched her catch sight of me behind the steering wheel as I pulled up to the curb in front of her. She quickly reigned in her momentary outburst, smoothing out her expression. Her hands twitched at her sides as she looked up and down the street, chewing her bottom lip, then darted inside the pharmacy—but not before casting a lingering glance over her shoulder, locking eyes with me. I gave her a wink, watching the surprise on her face, which she returned with an unsure smile. That smile sent blood rushing straight to my groin. She was going to be mine; she just didn't know it yet. I wasn't allowing the others to have a piece of her for what they had planned.

"Leave her. I have other plans." I mulled over in my mind all the ways I could watch her come undone at my mercy. And I had a feeling she would play along willingly.

Chris turned his head to me from the passenger seat with raised brows. "Other plans that include us? Or are you going off script and performing a little solo act on your own? Because you know I am the one who orchestrates and details every decision we make to cover our bases. The last thing we need is to be caught, and I promise I will not go down because of some half-cocked, spur-of-the-moment decision you make with your dick."

"Other plans as in, we will find what we want in the next town," I snarled between clenched teeth. Fuck me, I was tied up in knots. How can one encounter undo me so easily?

Grady

5

"What do you mean by other plans? Either she's *our* target or we move on," I snapped. "She'd be an easy grab too. I reckon she wouldn't take much convincing to come and sit on your cock if you whipped it out for her. Hell, with the moon eyes she gave you, you could more than likely ask her to be our next subject and she would bind her own hands and jump in the boot."

The way she eye-fucked Trent and then turned her focus on the other three of us, I had no doubt she would be fun. It had been too long since we had found a girl who was turned on by the act of violence and being inflicted with pain. Yeah, we love their screams, but it was so much better when they were followed with moans of pleasure. We tended to drag out the suffering, making the end game so much fucking hotter.

Trent's jaw tensed. "No," he growled, looking over his shoulder at me. "Now drop it. We get what we need and move on."

Rolling my eyes, I slumped back in my seat, muttering

curse words as I stared out the rear window, watching the lifeless, vacant stares that echoed in the eyes of all the locals as they meandered listlessly along the dilapidated streets. If I didn't know better, I would swear the zombie apocalypse had taken root in this town. There was nothing here worth our time except the Chocolate drop who caught Trent's eyes. Maybe mine too, if I had to admit it. Okay, I admit it. She wasn't his usual type. She was pretty, I guess, for a half-caste, especially because her eyes stood out. They didn't match the rest of her features. Her eyes were so blue, they were like crystals that were lit from behind. Oh, they would look so pretty filled with tears.

My dick hardened at the thought of making her hurt, just so I could see the tears well there and watch the radiant sparkle back through them.

Settle down, big guy. I will pay you special attention later. Trent and Chris lost their shit when I'd whip him out and give him the love he deserved. I think they were just secretly jealous that their dicks weren't as pretty or big as mine, though.

"I got the list," Chris grumbled, opening the passenger door and climbing out of the car, slamming the door closed with force.

Obviously, I'd missed part of the conversation while I was

stewing. It wasn't as if my input on whatever they discussed would have been taken into consideration anyway. I was more the muscle in our little operation. I got to do the dirty part of the job—the cleanup. Not that I minded. Messy was my specialty.

"Gotta take a slash," I informed the car, not expecting a response and not really giving a shit either way. "Back in a few."

I climbed out of the back seat and stomped towards the sign indicating public toilets down the side of the pharmacy. There was a narrow walkway, shrouded in darkness thanks to the height and close proximity to the buildings on either side. The walls were covered in graffiti over the peeling paint and filth that was likely to be decades old. The path lifted in areas where weeds had pushed through the concrete, making it uneven beneath the leaf litter and garbage that had blown down here from the street. At the end of the path, the filthy, desolate building containing the toilets looked as if they hadn't been cleaned in a decade. The ground was covered in a thick sludge by the entrance, and judging by the dark, decrepit interior, it wasn't going to be any better.

"Ahh, fuck this," I groaned, walking down the side of the building.

I yanked out my cock to piss on the side of the building

instead of venturing inside. It only added to the filth that already existed, not just on the facilities, but in this godforsaken town. There was fuck-all actually going for the place, from what I had seen. It made you wonder why a person would willingly choose to live in such a miserable, soul-sucking place. If hell existed on earth, it would be pretty close to where I stood. Any life we would have taken from here would have been doing them a favour. Nah, then again, they might have fleas.

With a final shake, I tucked myself back in my pants to walk back to the vehicle hastily.

A gust of wind blew through the narrow laneway, blowing the collective litter my way.

"Fuck this shit," I grumbled, trying to dodge the onslaught of random shit that was attacking me, hovering in the wind.

Minding my step over the uneven path, I noticed discarded syringes littering the ground, ones that I hadn't seen on my way through here, buried beneath the litter.

Yeah, fuck that shit. I repeated in my mind for the hundredth time since we pulled in here.

I hate to admit it, but Trent was right about one thing—we needed to move onto the next town immediately.

With some quick side steps and jumps, I cleared junkie lane, kicking a discarded beer bottle across the road. I stepped back onto the footpath in the street, which suddenly seemed as clean as homosexuals asshole ready to be rimmed. I shuddered involuntarily, feeling all kinds of dirty from my little side venture to relieve myself, wishing I had just taken a piss on the car tyre instead.

When we get to whatever lodgings Chris has hooked up for us, I'm planning on getting hammered and maybe even high, just to try to wipe the memory of this shithole from my mind.

Chris

6

The pharmacy was pitiful. It was barely even stocked with essentials. A single set of shelves jutted out from one wall, holding only some basic first aid items and hygiene products. On the opposite wall, there were health and beauty products, but nothing beyond what I could find at a supermarket. Behind the counter, locked in a caged display, were other pharmaceuticals, like basic analgesics and aerosol deodorants—but from what I could see, it was vastly lacking.

What the fucking hell is going on in this town? Bugger this, we can get what we need elsewhere. It was time we hightailed it from here before we found ourselves being the innocent victims of a missing persons report or late-night documentary. Who knew what weird shit went down here.

"Hi. Can I help you with something?" A soft, lyrical voice asked from behind me, making me turn instantly on the spot. I had intended to tell the woman to fuck off and storm out, but instead, I was pleasantly surprised to come face to face with the girl from outside the cafe.

I raised a brow and gave her a small smile. "Nunya, right?"

She smacked a palm over her face with a slight shake of her head. "Yep."

"Are you closing down?" I asked, gesturing to the lack of stock.

She frowned and glanced around, obviously confused by my question. Then, realisation hit. "Ah, no. We keep the majority of our stock behind the counter for safety and security reasons. Although we are still restricted as to what we can stock. What do you require? I would be happy to assist you with your needs."

Oh, little girl, those are the wrong words to say to me.

I leaned down until I was face-to-face with her, invading her personal space and testing her. There was a noticeable difference between my six-foot-two and her height, which I estimated to be five-foot-five. She didn't flinch or back away, maintaining eye contact almost as a challenge to me, even when I moved my mouth to brush against her ear. She didn't react.

"What I would like is to take you away from this hellhole of a town. Come with me," I said low enough for only her ears.

As I pulled back, I saw her swallow deeply. Her face turned so her nose brushed mine with a gasp. I had to resist the urge not to nip her pouty lower lip.

"Believe me, sir, there is nothing I would love more," she said straight-faced, but her tone suggested that I had gotten under her skin, finally earning a reaction. Then she stepped back, tilting her head and looking me over with such scrutiny that I felt self-conscious under her gaze. What the fuck?

"Besides," she frowned, then scrunched her nose, which was fucking adorable. "I really don't think I'm your type. If you are wanting something particular, then perhaps you should try the next town over; there will be a lot more options available to you."

I blinked rapidly, trying to understand the meaning behind her words. She looked around, then to the rear counter, where the male standing behind the counter was glaring in her direction.

"The pharmacy there is well-stocked and carries the prohibited items we are not allowed to sell without a written script in our community," she explained, her voice louder after clearing her throat.

Right. So, she was trying not to get into trouble for fraternising with customers. I gave her mock trigger fingers and clicked my tongue. "Gotcha."

What the fuck was I doing?

She looked at my hands, then my face, shook her head with

a smirk, and turned her back on me, walking behind the counter at the back of the store. I was left standing there like a total tool, my fingers still sticking out in front of me.

"Yo, bro. You practising your ... moves or some shit?" Grady called out from the doorway, with his head tilted, frowning with his eyes locked onto my hands. I dropped my hands, mentally chastising myself for whatever that was that I had just pulled.

Without a backward glance, I stalked out past Grady to the car.

"Let's get going," I snapped, ripping the passenger door open forcefully and throwing myself in.

"Where's the stuff?" Trent asked, perplexed, looking at my empty hands and then back to the pharmacy.

"They ain't got shit in there. We've wasted enough time. Let's move on out of here." Especially after I just humiliated myself.

I pulled my phone from my pocket to start looking into accommodation, trying to distract myself.

Grady slammed his door in the back seat loudly, waking Kyden, who had been snoring soundly, already deep asleep.

"Yeah, I say we hightail it out of here. I think I caught salmonella just from pissing on the dunny wall."

Kyden let out a confused grunt, pinching between his eyes

in confusion trying to process what Grady had said while in his sleepy state.

"Salma what?" Trent muttered, equally as confused. "The fuck, Grady?"

I laughed. "I don't even want to know what the fuck you did down that laneway, you sick fucker."

"Well, if we stay here any longer, we will be catching some STI just from breathing the air. Roll out T-man." Grady slapped the side of Trent's seat twice with his palm then reclined back with his phone in hand. He looked up with all three of our eyes trained on him. "What?" he asked, looking up between each of us with a furrowed brow.

I shook my head with a sigh and turned to the front, my eyes catching the girl inside who was watching us with curiosity from behind the counter. She would have been a good target, too. It's a shame I buggered that up. Not that she actually said no.

"You do know the difference between an STI and a gastroenteritis bacteria right?" Kyden queried, still stuck on the salmonella comment.

Trent started the engine and was rolling back out from the curb, ready to leave this shithole. "With Grady's questionable sexual escapades, it wouldn't be a surprise to any of us if he caught one from the other."

"What does that mean?" Grady snapped, sounding on edge.

Grady being on edge in a confined space was troublesome. If he exploded, he would just as soon embed his blade in the side of Trent's neck as he would pommel his fist through the glass, then try to wank off with his bloodied hand for lubrication. He took unhinged to a new level.

"It means," I offered for Trent, who was smirking at riling Grady up. "That you would probably mutilate a live chicken, then fuck someone's arse with its drumstick while still warm, then suck them off or eat them out."

Grady smirked, settling back in his seat, rubbing his hand along his jaw as if contemplating the very idea. "Fuck, why does that make me hard?" he said, confirming what I was thinking.

"Because you're a sick fuck," Kyden murmured, his eyes already closed, ready to go back to sleep, with his arms crossed against his chest and his head leaning on his shoulder.

"Says the man with a fixation on cutting our victims up and drinking their blood." Grady shot back.

Kyden half-opened one eye to look at Grady. "Yes, because the idea of fucking someone's arse with a chicken leg is so much more normal." Kyden muttered groggily, sounding as if he were seconds from sleep.

Grady laughed deeply. "I wouldn't use its fucking leg. I'd insert a whole chicken up there… alive!"

With his hands, he made a fist with his open palm, while biting down on his bottom lip and making grunting noises for emphasis.

"Can we stop talking about chickens? Fuck! I'm starving, and suddenly the idea of fried chicken at the drive-through is becoming less appealing by the second." I complained as my stomach protested on queue.

"No chicken," Trent agreed. "But I could go for some Mexican."

"Aw, are you still thinking about that sweet little chocolate drop back there, T-man?" Grady said. "You can always turn around and we can pick her up. Chris tried showing some moves, and it looked like he scared her off. Maybe you'll have better luck."

"Shut the hell up, Grady." I rolled my eyes, focusing on my phone, refusing to comment and confirm or deny anything.

Trent frowned, flicking his eyes to me, then glanced up to the rear-vision mirror to glare at Grady. "She isn't Mexican, you ignorant moron, and I already told you that she isn't what we are after."

I flicked a quick peek over my shoulder to Grady, who was trying to hide a smirk behind his thumb that rested on his lips, with his hand curled into a fist at his chin. What are you up to, Gray?

Trent

7

"You know…" Grady drawled, his face suddenly uncomfortably close to the side of mine as he leaned forward from directly behind me.

I tensed at the close proximity of him breathing down my neck. The asshole knew it too, and I swear he did just to make me uncomfortable. I hated that he chose to sit there. The prick would just as soon stab me as he would fuck me. His unpredictability always left me uneasy. If he weren't so good at cleaning up any evidence we left, he wouldn't be part of the team. Well, maybe there was more to it than that, but that is what I told myself.

"I think you're bullshitting us. Got your eyes on her for a little *one-on-one*. Gone soft on us, T-man? Want to make love, slow and gentle? Kiss all her boo-boos? Whisper sweet words in her ear while she comes on your cock and confesses her undying love?"

I half spun in my seat, coming nose to nose with the psychopath. If we weren't stopped at an intersection, I would have run us off the road.

"Fuck up. We both know that no one in this car does sweet and gentle, Gray. We will find our fun in the next town. That. Girl. Was. Not. It." I reiterated, sounding way too defensive even to myself.

Grady snickered, his face still hovering uncomfortably close to mine.

In my periphery I saw his hand move. Expecting his knife to make a sudden appearance, I readied my hand to cut him off. The flicker of a lighter came up instead. Bringing it between our faces, with his free hand he plucked a cigarette from the air, settling it between his lips. His eyes crinkled with amusement, knowing full well he was taunting me.

"Light it and I'll piss on you while you sleep, Gray," Chris warned, without looking up from his phone. "No smoking in the car."

The sad part was that Grady would probably actually get off on being pissed on. His tastes ran a little more on the depraved side than the rest of us. Just to prove my point. Grady rolled his eyes with a chuckle, lighting the cigarette despite the threat. Turning his head to face the side of mine he blew a puff of second-hand smoke in my face from his slightly parted lips.

"Bloody hell, I'll never get the smell out," Chris spat,

winding down his window, waving his hand in front of him in an attempt to clear the lingering scent, all while his focus remained on the phone in his hand.

Grady huffed out an amused sound, filling the cab with more smoke as he brought the cigarette back to his mouth. Twisting my head from the road, I bared my teeth then bit into the end of the cigarette, burning my tongue in the process . I spat it back in Grady's face before returning my focus back to the road. With the vile flavour of tobacco and ash lingering on my tongue, but the small satisfaction in ruining Grady's fun was worth it.

"Sit the fuck back so we can leave, or I'll tie you to the roof racks naked, coated in oil, so you cook under these fucked up temps." Forty-two degrees celcius was the expected temp today, with ninety percent humidity with no expected relief in sight. God, I hated summer.

Grady pulled the remainder of the cigarette from his lips, tucking it behind his ear with a wide grin, then kissed the tip of my nose. I swatted him back, missing as he fell back in his seat laughing like an insolent child, knowing that it was an empty threat.

Kyden yawned loudly, having been woken from his brief nap in the backseat. He looked around through hooded lids, oblivious to the tense drama unfolding in the car. He would still be asleep again in seconds, provided Grady didn't pull his annoying shit on him. Then again, Grady treated Kyden with kid gloves. We all did, really. But Grady was particularly attentive to Kyden's sleeping habits. It was obvious he cared for him; I just couldn't pinpoint the reasoning, considering the only time they seemed to interact was in the brief few hours that Kyden was awake each day. Even then, their conversations seemed forced at times.

"Any particular requests for accommodation?" Chris asked, breaking the tension.

"Other than the usual?" I gave a one-shoulder shrug. The usual being no close proximity to neighbouring properties, four bedrooms, a garage or basement, and a concealed street view. We never stayed anywhere longer than a week, so creature comforts weren't a big deal.

"I want my own bathroom and a king-sized bed this time. None of that one-bathroom, single-bed bullshit," Grady whined. Then, he muttered quietly to himself about the last bed being so small that he had to sleep with his knees bent over the edge, so his feet could sit on the floor.

I flicked my eyes up in the mirror, catching Grady crossing his arms like a petulant child pouting. I had to bite back a laugh. None of us had bothered to inform him that it was a child's toddler-sized bed, and there was another room with a double in it. Kyden had stayed sleeping on the couch each night, and Grady never ventured into Chris's or my room, which each held two doubles, so he was unaware that there were other options.

Chris gave me a side glance, biting down on his lower lip. "Should I tell him?" Chris whispered to me out of the side of his mouth, fighting his own laughter.

I shook my head, silently chuckling. At least not while we were in the car and I was behind the wheel, anyway.

I turned on the stereo as a distraction, streaming one of the local radio stations, which played a mix of newer and *old* music. Their definition of "old" was music from the 90s, which didn't sit well with me. At what point was the music I grew up with considered "old"? After several of the *newer* songs played, I cracked the shits, not wanting to listen to garbage that was perforating my eardrums and ruining any hope of enjoying music anymore. I turned off the stereo, opting for the uncomfortable silence instead .

The air was rigid in the cab as we drove from the backwater town to the next one, an hour and forty-five minutes over. Grady was conspiring something. His face contorted as he chewed on his mouth with narrowed eyes while staring blankly out the window. Chris was hunched over his phone, tapping repeatedly and writing notes down on a small notepad. Kyden's soft snores were the only noise over the sound of the quiet hum of the engine and tyres rolling over the poorly maintained roads. The uncomfortable silence only aggravated my mood further. Chris looked up a few times, watching me white-knuckle the steering wheel, then would flick his eyes to my face. Opening his mouth and closing it, he wordlessly went back to the phone before repeating the action.

"If you have something to say, spill it," I gritted out between clenched teeth."

For a man who was domineering as he was when it came to his sexual endeavours and obsessive need to be in control, he could be rather dubious at times.

"Ahh, want me to drive?" he offered hesitantly, looking at my hold on the steering wheel.

"No!" Grady and I both snapped in unison. Unable to prevent the smirk on my face, I let go of some of the tension.

"You sure? I mean, I don't mind getting behind the wheel …"

"I think I'd rather walk barefoot, dosed in petrol, over hot coals," Grady drawled from the back.

"That's a Saturday night for you," I said, looking at him in the rear-vision mirror. Grady's grin told me I wasn't wrong.

"Fuck you both. There's nothing wrong with my driving,"

Chris scoffed.

"Firstly, the fuck, Chris? That's a line even I won't cross," Grady gagged.

"Secondly," I added. "We want to actually arrive in one piece."

"What is that supposed to mean?" he snapped back defensively.

I glanced over, giving him a look that clearly said, *really?* "Do I really need to elaborate?"

"Apparently," Grady deadpanned, leaning forward, his head appearing between the seats.

I swung my elbow narrowly missing his head, earning a chuckle from him. "Get in the back."

I was rewarded with a pocket knife being slammed into my left tricep for my effort.

"Fuck!" I growled. Yanking my arm forward across my chest, tightening my grip on the steering wheel with my right hand. "Don't distract the driver. First rule of being a passenger." I ground out.

"First rule is put on your fucking seatbelt," Grady argued.

"Then put on your… Ow…!" Chris yanked the knife from my arm and tossed in the back on the floor at Grady's feet.

Grady bent forward, headbutting the back of my seat, picking up the weapon. "Cheers, bro."

"Don't give it back to him," I admonished with a glare.

"You should know better than to try to hit him," Chris dismissed with a shrug. "I have us booked at an Airbnb," he said, changing the subject. "The owners are out of the country for six months and are fine with us hiring it on a week-to-week basis. The property is on the outskirts of town, sitting on twenty-hectares, so neighbours won't be an issue."

Well, that was a plus.

"And who did you put down as being the tenant this time?" Grady asked with his fat head back between the seats. I sighed indignantly.

Chris smirked. "Lola Cruz. An international student who is looking for somewhere to get away while on summer break from uni. She has impeccable references and has also been known to house sit, with her profession listed as a housecleaner and an avid interest in wildlife."

Fake I.D., bank accounts, and rental history have never been an issue to forge for our master hacker. Plus, he has covered our arses on more than one occasion, falsifying documents and alibis so we don't get caught being the serial killers that we are. Hey, everyone has a vice. Ours just happens to be a little more liberating and frowned upon than old Bob and Jane's weekly keys in the bowl get together up the road.

Kyden

8

We settled into whatever Airbnb Chris had found on our way to the next town, which was just under two hours away from the last place we considered as a potential stopping ground to find a subject. Alas, the low population, inbreeding and polluted town water—an inherited effect on every generation that existed there—meant that there were no viable options outside. Well, besides the one female who Trent had rather strongly shot down as an option.

We stopped at a few drive-throughs before hitting our stop, grabbing a mix of Mexican, burgers, Chinese and pizza. Or at least, that is what I was told when Grady woke me and gave me a brief rundown.

The incessant arguing between Trent and Grady made me regret ever opening my eyes and allowing my body to rouse from the peaceful sleep my body was embracing. My head pulsated in pain, their voices echoing through it like an empty chamber, robbing me of coherency as I fought through the ailment which forced my exhaustion.

Stumbling inside, aided by arms curled around my side, I didn't bother to glance around too much as I was led to a bench.

I was too fucking tired and not mentally inept to deal with whatever shit the others were yacking about when they all pulled up around the bench beside me. My name was mentioned a few times with questions I hadn't answered, but my mouth was unable to move enough to form a response. It required energy that I didn't possess. My stomach was growling with hunger at the scent of food. I knew I had to force something into me before I fell asleep again, so I wouldn't waste away—it could be a day or two before I woke up again, given how tired I felt.

I opted for the first things I laid my hands on, digging through the bags dumped on the bench. Pushing away from the bench, stumbling through a hall with a wrapped burger and a beer in my hands, I found my way to find the first bed I came across. I didnt give a flying fuck if this was the best bedroom or the worst; a bed was a bed. I would, and have slept anywhere. Fuck, I wished I'd stayed in the car as the voices rose behind me in heated discussion. I slammed the door behind me. The pounding in my skull eased by the slight reprieve as their voices muffled behind the wooden barrier.

Fractured Shadow

My hypersomnia was always triggered when we traveled without being about to release our pent-up urges. Instead of my usual twelve to fourteen hours of sleep a day I required, the travel in the car increased that up to eighteen to twenty hours. I would sometimes wake briefly, mid-way through our travels in an almost zombie state, not conscious of my actions and would be directed to use the toilet or have water forced into me. I was grateful for that.

Now that we had a temporary base, I could let my condition take over, meaning at least I'll get a couple of days to sleep it off while the others hunt down our target. Then, my inner maniac can come out and allowed me to get the fucking release I needed in order to go back to normal sleeping habits. Normal for me anyway.

Stumbling into the room without taking it in too much, I settled back on the bed, which was covered in an absurd amount of oversized pillows and really small blankets thrown at the end. Fuck knows what they were used for.

Maybe the owner had a weird foot fetish, and midgets slept at the foot of the bed, sucking their toes while they slept or some weird shit.

Nothing surprised me in the slightest anymore. I had come across some seriously fucked up fetishes people were into. At least mine wasn't that off kilter, a little blood play never hurt anyone–until they ran out of blood, anyway.

I bit into the burger, straight through the paper, which had soggied from the fats and sauces dripping from the inside. Too fucking exhausted to give a shit to unwrap it, but also knowing if I don't eat something, it would only make me sleep longer and possibly slip into a coma.

Chewing mindlessly as the oozy insides poured out onto my face, down my arm, and no doubt onto the ridiculous pillows, which actually felt fucking amazing to lay on, like I was floating on a cloud. I hooked the beer under my belt buckle, using it to lever off the cap and spilling it over my crotch in the process. I brought it to my mouth, downing a couple of gulpfuls to wash away the greasy film coating my mouth. My body was so fucking heavy, I was now moving in slow, practised motions, knowing I was gonna pass out soon.

I dropped the burger onto my chest, feeling it leak into my shirt as I fumbled in my pocket for my pocket knife. If I dug it into my thigh it should be enough to keep me coherent enough to at least finish the beer. My body had other ideas. Before I could stab it into my flesh and flood my body with adrenaline, I passed out, feeling my beer spill from my hand, soaking the bed, with the knife resting limply in my hand next to me.

Grady

9

"He out?" I asked, hovering at the doorway of the room where Kyden was lying.

Trent was bent over the bed, a towel in one hand and an empty beer bottle in the other. He straightened at the sound of my voice, moving to the side, giving me a view of a deep-sleeping Kyden, who was looking like a fucking toddler who had just fed themselves for the first time. By the looks of it, he didn't get more than two bites of food in before passing out. Half of his face was smeared in sauce and gravy, and I could see uneaten food and a piece of paper still sitting on his tongue. Fuck, I think he ate more of the paper than the actual food inside. The poor bastard was beyond knackered.

If Trent hadn't found him first, I probably would have licked his face clean, then eaten whatever was still in his mouth, while I tongue-fucked him. But Trent was already here, and now he was wiping his face gently, removing any remnants for me to indulge in later. Fucker! I wanted to choke him out for that alone.

"Yeah, he's getting worse." Trent turned to me with a furrowed brow, snapping me out of imagining all the ways I could inflict retribution on him for stealing my fun. "We might hang here at this place for a bit to give him a chance to recover before seeking out the next subject. I know the last one didn't exactly go to plan, and none of us were able to really enjoy it, but…" Trent looked back to Kyden. The very fact that he was considering Kyden's welfare over his own urges helped me simmer down the building rage inside.

I nodded in agreement, walking into the room fully to give him a hand stripping Kyden from his boots and filthy clothes. We usually take it in turn caring for Ky when he gets like this. It is something that I particularly enjoy on a personal level, and I have no doubt Ky enjoys watching the videos I record of me *tending* to him when he rouses. It was something we kept private between the two of us, our own dirty little secret so to speak. The secrecy only made it so much more thrilling.

"Fucking dickhead." Trent reached down and pulled a pocket knife slick with blood from Kyden's limp hand, then began lifting his shirt to see the extent of the damage. I leaned over Kyden's lithe body, seeing where he had cut his hip, unknown if it was intentional or not.

"I thought he was past self-mutilation." Trent shook his head, sighing exasperatedly.

I gave a shrug, doing my best, *shit happens, not much you can do about it,* reaction. "He usually stabs his thigh to keep himself awake. This was probably accidental."

"What?" Trent's head whipped to me with concern, quickly morphing into anger. "How long? How long has it been going on Grady?"

Okay, so Trent didn't buy it. I needed to work on my deflection skills. That kinda pissed me off as much as his tone. I let out a breath, clenching my fists, so I didn't reach over and rip the fucking open blade from his hand and swipe up his inner wrist for speaking to me in that tone. I know I would regret it later if I did. By later, I mean after I had fucked his bloodied hand with my fist curled around his dead one. "Look, T-man, it's not my place to say."

Trent growled through clenched teeth, demanding an answer. "How fucking long has he been doing this, Grady?"

One breath in. Hold. One breath out. *Don't kill the fucker.* Another breath in. Hold. Release. "Five months," I finally admitted through clenched teeth, keeping my eyes trained on Kyden and the dark circles that permanently settled under his eyes. Then, so I didn't accidentally kill Trent, I took a few more deep breaths, holding them as I counted in my head.

"Fuck." Trent moved to the end of the bed and began unlacing Kyden's boots to remove them. "Fuck. Fuck. Fuck."

Look at him exploring his vocabulary. I figured it was as good a time as any to let him know how bad Kyden actually was, because I wasn't a total heartless bastard, and even though I wouldn't admit it to his face, Trent was better with the first aid side of things than I was.

"Check his toes aren't infected. There was a strange smell in the backseat on the way here. Dunno if the back seat needs a hose, or it's his feet."

Trent paused midway through slipping off one boot. Closing his eyes for a beat and breathing heavily through his nose, he carefully continued removing it. "Why?" he asked hesitantly.

I rubbed the back of my neck and grimaced. "He, ah, began ripping out his toenails as an outlet when we got too long between hits."

Trent didn't say anything else as he exposed Kyden's feet with a sad frown, examining the reddened skin on his feet while I moved to unbuckle Kyden's belt and remove his pants.

When we had Kyden stripped to his trunks, I had to concentrate on the most disgusting thing I could think of, which happened to be cutesy rom-coms, so the big guy in my pants would deflate. I couldn't very well focus on Kyden's needs when my own were forcing out all rational thoughts for what sat below my belt. Plus, Trent was still present.

We cleaned up Kyden's wounds, applying antiseptic and bandaging his feet, then rolled him over to pull the soiled comforter out from under him. We settled Kyden partially raised on the cushions, and we covered him with a fresh blanket from the other room. He didn't stir while we manhandled him. Then again, he never did. He was the perfect living corpse. Better than any sex doll on the market. Warm, unreactive and malleable. I could do anything the fuck I wanted to him, and he wouldn't react. Well, not until he woke, then it was game on bitches.

Trent left to collect a bottle of water and some snacks so we could leave them for Kyden when he woke, while I gathered the dirty washing.

I actually hated seeing him this way. He had lost a significant amount of weight from not being able to eat properly before passing out. It worried all of us how much worse he was getting. We were going to have to set up a feeding tube if he couldn't get more nutrients into his stomach other than semen, because that one was guaranteed, and I don't think he could survive on that alone. Or could he? I mean, essentially it was pre-baby, and cannibals live off human flesh…..

65

Chris

10

I had been checking the local community and buy, swap, sell pages on social media, trolling for an indication of where would be a good place to find our next victim.

Our last plaything was too weak and died before any of us could even fuck her. Well, fuck her while she was alive, anyway. Grady fucked every hole in her corpse while she was still warm, and by every hole, that included her eye socket after Kyden had scooped one of her eyes from her skull. Then before he buried her in a shallow grave, Grady fucked her cold, dead corpse and set it alight, wanking off to the scent of burning flesh.

I preferred my dick being buried in something with a pulse. Sinking into the slick warmth of their body while it's entirely at my mercy. There is something about watching the fear in their eyes as I hold my hand around their throat, tightening slowly, watching as they gasp for breath, knowing you could end them at any time. Having them beg with their eyes, their mouths silent pleading; having them willing to do anything I ask of them, to please me. Their cunts tightening in fear, squeezing the most intense orgasm from my cock every time before I release them and allowing them precious air. I loved the feeling of control over our subjects, having them at our whim, restrained and vulnerable. There was nothing else that compared, and no one strong enough to withstand our levels of depravity to fully sate all of our urges, leaving us in need of a new target each time one dies.

I adjusted my pants, my cock straining uncomfortably. Just the thought of hunting down our next sub had me hard; it also hadn't helped that I never got the chance to sink into our last two. My balls were so blue it was past the point of manageable discomfort now.

I pulled my hand free from my crotch when Trent stalked out from where he and Grady had been assisting Kyden. His face was laced with a concerned scowl, causing an uneasy feeling in me. I wasn't convinced Trent's mood was entirely a reaction from Grady's presence, something was wrong with Ky.

"All good?" I asked, my voice coming out strained as I reached over and grabbed for another slice of pizza across the table. The movement caused my pants to pull taut against my painful erection. Fuck, I was going to have to find someone to sink into soon; my fist just wasn't cutting it.

Trent didn't look up, keeping his eyes downcast. He just shook his head, dropping a bloodied knife on the bench, then began rifling through the bags we brought in, before disappearing back down the hall with water and a few packaged snacks in his hand.

I raised my brows, eyes focused on the blood coating the blade. Had Kyden been self-harming? Crap, I knew our last outlet hadn't exactly gone to plan, but I had assumed that he would have at least had enough of a fill seeing the way he had bled the sub.

Worry clouded my thoughts as I considered how best to approach the conversation we were going to have to indulge in regarding this issue. Kyden was a concern for all of us. If we didn't think of the little shit as our kid brother, we would have cut him loose. We are all aware it's a matter of time before his self-destructive tendencies result in his inadvertent death.

Grady stumbled into the kitchen ahead of Trent, dumping an armful of washing into the sink before snatching a beer and cracking on the edge of the counter. I glanced at the washing, then at him, where he sat perched on the arm of the couch, all from over the top of my laptop, deciding to keep my lips sealed. I'd rather not have the glass bottle in his hand smashed against my head for demanding he remove the washing from its current resting place. Despite how much it made my eye twitch and my urge to move it to the laundry.

Trent dropped into the chair beside Grady with an open bottle of scotch in one hand, half-full glass in the other.

"We need to talk," Trent finally relented, looking like he wanted to do anything but talk.

"About the kid?" I asked, trying to sound casual, despite being desperate to wring information from him. Kyden was far from a kid, only a year younger than Grady and me, and a few years younger than Trent, but we had taken him under our wing with a protectiveness ever since he had stumbled into our lives.

Trent gave a single nod as he sipped on his drink.

"We're not cutting him loose," Grady snarled, his grip tightening around the bottle in his hand.

I watched him closely, waiting to see what he was going to do with Trent sitting so close. Trent didn't seem concerned, however.

"Wasn't going to suggest it," Trent dismissed offhandedly. "I was going to say, we need to convince him to see someone, maybe get medicated."

"You and I both know he isn't going to go for that. He hates quacks." Grady scoffed, taking a swig of his beer and dropping the empty bottle on the ground before snatching the glass of scotch from Trent's hand and downing it. "'Sides, once he sleeps off his hypersumania, he'll be right as rain."

"Hypersomnia," Trent and I both corrected at the same time. Grady shrugged, holding the glass out with a grunt to Trent for a refill.

"It isn't the hypersomnia that is the issue, Grady. His self inflictions are becoming worse. Once slip and he will bleed out before we realise he isn't just passed out." Trent disagreed.

"No, he won't," Grady said, assuredly tapping the glass to the bottle. Trent poured some scotch into the glass before drinking from the bottle and hissing in response.

"You don't know that," I argued.

"Actually, motherfucker, I can, and do know that," Grady deadpanned. "He is a fully qualified doctor or some shit."

I snapped my head back in surprise. Trent was also caught off guard, his face wearing the same look of shock, the bottle frozen, half extended to his mouth.

Grady laughed and snatched the bottle from Trent's still hand, tipping it to his own mouth as he stood.

"Fucking priceless." Grady muttered behind the neck of the bottle before tipping it back.

"How the fuck do we not know this?" Trent asked, finally dropping his hand as he eyed the stolen bottle in Grady's grip.

"You never fucking asked," Grady responded, walking to the kitchen area and grabbing a foil-wrapped burrito.

I exchanged a questioning glance with Trent before we both looked over to Grady, whose cheeks were already bulging with food while he still tried to bite into more.

I didn't know what to do with this revelation. I knew Kyden was pretty handy with first aid, but never imagined his skillset went as far as Grady had mentioned. In fact, we knew bugger all about Kyden in reality—he was a fairly closed book. "What else don't we know?"

"Yeah Grady. Like, how the fuck do you know so much about Kyden? He's not exactly a conversationalist?" Trent asked accusingly.

"Only because he sleeps more than a cat," I added. "It isn't exactly like we can get all deep and personal when he sleeps more than he's awake."

Grady snorted, "I clockim andang ey hawks ooee."

"Swallow, then talk." Trent rolled his eyes as if talking to a child.

Grady grinned maniacally, baring his food-covered teeth and waggled his brows at Trent, who dropped his forehead into his palm with a look that conveyed, *why do I bother?*

We waited while Grady took his sweet ass time and finished

the remainder of his meal, taking more bites before finishing his previous one, just to drag out the suspense. The bastard smirked, wiping his mouth on the back of his hand. Crossing his arms, he leaned back against the counter, sticking his tongue in his cheek, then sucked his teeth.

"I said," he grinned, dragging it out. "I fuck him and he talks to me. Well… after he returns the favour to me, when he wakes." Grady's eyebrows wiggle suggestively.

My eyebrows hit my hairline at his admission. Shock stealing my words. Silence hung in the room, which only enticed Grady's smug satisfaction, eating up our responses or lack thereof.

"Nah, you're full of shit," Trent dismissed, waving him off with a laugh.

I watched Grady carefully as he held that expression without wavering.

"He's not bullshitting," I said, as Grady met my stare with a knowing grin. "It's more than a casual fuck between you two, isn't it?"

Grady cocked his head to the side, chewing on the bottom corner of his lower lip, contemplating his words carefully. "In a way…"

"How can he be a doctor? When we met, he was basically a teenager," Trent scoffed, still not entirely convinced.

"He told me he finished high school when he was twelve. He's some genius with a huge IQ or some shit. He was given a scholarship to study at any uni he wanted and decided on medicine. He aced all his studies or something, and has a few different letter thingies to his name, making him a qualified doctor in different areas. At least that's what I think he said." Grady scratched at his chin thoughtfully. "But 'cause he has that sleeping thing, he can't actually work." Grady shrugged. "His two biggest kinks are somnophilia and hematomania, which explains his blood play, and I'm more than happy to fulfil his fantasy to fuck him up while he sleeps, so it's a win-win for both of us."

"The fuck is any of that?" Trent asked, reaching for his phone on the table to Google.

Reeling from the influx of information, I held onto the last bit of information. "So, you have no issue relaying the names of sex kinks, but you struggle with remembering medical conditions, which I might add is one that attributes to the sex kink?" I queried.

"Let's not forget that salmonella is in fact *not* an STI," Trent added with a chuckle, as he tapped away at his phone.

"Grady already admitted that it can be an STI, when he is involved." I smirked.

"Fuck you!" Grady snapped, throwing the scotch bottle at

my head. I ducked just in time; it smashed on the wall behind my head, spraying my back with glass.

"No thanks. We discussed this in the car. Incest is not my thing," I taunted.

"Want me to knock you the fuck out?"

It wouldn't be the first time he had. In fact, it had only been a week since he had caught me in the temple with his fist, giving me two hours of sleep, and a blinding headache to contend with when I woke.

"I'd rather be awake in case you try to shove a live chicken up my arse, maybe I should go outside and find a possum for you to use on Ky."

Grady's face turned scarlet as he launched across the room with a fucking knife in his hand, ready to inflict damage on me. He wouldn't do irreparable or life threatening damage, didn't mean it wouldn't hurt though. And where the fuck did the knife come from?

Trent jumped to his feet, grabbing Grady around the middle, pinning the arm with the weapon pinned to his side. Trent is the bigger and stronger of the three of us, even so, he struggled under Grady's scrappy and frantic fight he put up.

"Calm the fuck down, Gray," Trent demanded. "And you." He looked at me. "You know better than to shit-stir him."

I did know better. We all did. Only I'd had a lifetime of

dealing with it. Didn't mean that sometimes the eggshells we walk over around Grady didn't get turned to dust occasionally.

Grady's chest heaved, his pupils dilated in his rounded eyes, nostrils flaring, he bared his teeth.

"Sleep with one eye open, Chriso," Grady spat. "And if you fucking dare step foot in Ky's room, I'll find something bigger than a possum for you." I know it wasn't an empty threat. Grady had on more than one occasion used creatures in his fury. Trent, not four weeks ago, woke up with a shingleback lizard attached to his semi-hard cock while he was sleeping. He was fucking lucky it didn't bite it off. He hasn't told us if it did any lasting damage, but sometimes we see him walking funny as if the pain still exists.

"Chris," Trent barked. "Apologise."

I gave a questioning look to Trent for having the audacity to make a demand of me. I should have ripped him a new one for it, but I understood the reasoning. Trent's eyes flashed for a split second when he concluded his mistake and gulped, but to his credit, he managed to retain his composure. Great, I had to placate Grady's sensitive feelings.

"I apologise for imposing that you wanted to expose Ky to beastiality."

Grady grunted, lowering his lips, his jaw hardened, then he

stopped fighting Trent's hold. Trent hesitantly released his hold on Grady when he dropped the knife to the floor, then stepped between me and him, forming a barrier.

Stepping back two paces, Grady took an unopened six-pack of beer and a bag of take-away, then disappeared down the hall to either a spare room or Kyden's. Either way, I wasn't going to go and find out.

Trent

11

Chris was buried deep in research the following morning, making a list of possible areas where we should be focusing our attention, with local hangout spots and hidden areas where couples would hookup away from prying eyes. He had already been up for some time judging by the empty mug he kept reaching for, and the abandoned half-eaten piece of cold Vegemite toast in front of him, long since forgotten about.

He reached for his cup, holding it in the air wordlessly when I walked to the kitchen, turning on the kettle — a silent request for a refill.

"Any perspectives?" I asked, taking the cup from his hand as I peered over his shoulder, eyeing the social media page he had open with dozens of women's faces on display.

"Yeah, possibly," he craned his neck to look at me, then back to his screen, clicking on a picture of a young female with a hopelessly sad look in her eyes. "I keep coming back to this one. She seems desperate and lonely. In the past six months only one person liked one of her posts, so I don't think she would be missed in a hurry, giving us a chance to stretch it out and have some fun."

I reached over, clicking through the pictures she had shared. She was dark-haired, not pretty but not unattractive either, just average. Easily looked over. No distinguishable features or tattoos that I could see, and no photos taken with family or friends. In fact, the only photos other than selfies were that of her dog and the beach.

"She made mention that she was going hiking on the weekend and asked if anyone wanted to join her. Twenty-six people saw the post, but like all the others, there were no reactions or comments. She works casually at the supermarket. An hour ago she wrote, *'Another day another $. Ugh, openings suck ass.'* I planned to head over there in an hour to check her out, and perhaps strike a conversation to get a feel for her. "

"Good work." This girl had definite potential, which spiked my heart-rate with excitement.

I slapped Chris on the back, making my way back to the kettle, which had finished boiling. "Want company? I'll stay out of view."

He peered over the laptop at me, then at the hallway, before returning his eyes back to me again. "As long as you are accompanying me and not …." *Grady.* He didn't need to finish. Grady was likely to become too excited and drag her from behind the counter in front of witnesses.

"Let me caffeinate and shower, and I'll be good to go."

Chris nodded in response, writing down more notes as I placed the fresh coffee down in front of him.

"Do you ever think about stopping?" he asked out of nowhere, with a deep frown gazing down at his laptop.

I paused with my mug halfway to my lips, unsure if I had heard him correctly. "What do you mean?"

He let out an exasperated sigh, running his hand through his mussed-up sandy blonde hair. "I mean, at what point do we walk away from this?" He waved his hand around in front of the notes strewn across the table in front of him and the laptop screen. "I just … it's losing its appeal. I'm not getting the same kick anymore. I feel like it's barely taking the edge off. I want… fuck. I don't even know what I want anymore. Everything feels like too much of a pain in the ass, that it's taking the high out of it."

I walked over, placed my coffee down on the table opposite Chris and sat. I needed a moment to process this. I sympathised with what he was saying. In truth, it had been a while since I had felt the thrill. The same stale routine of capturing our victim and playing out the same scenario had become a monotonous routine that wasn't entirely hitting the same way.

"So you need more?" I asked.

Chris didn't respond, he just stared blankly at nothing in particular. I had a thought that had been lingering in the back of my mind for some time. "Or we can change up how we go about it. Let you start instead of sitting back and watching and making demands."

Chris's face pinched, looking troubled. He was staring at the screen in front of him like it was personally offending him. "I miss how it was. When we made a game of it. Now Gray and Ky take the lead, and the majority of the time they kill the girl before we even get our fill, or there's not much left for us to even work with."

I nodded in agreement. Chris's tastes ran a little more vanilla and less off-kilter than Grady's and Kyden's; they complimented one another with their depravity. Chris tended to lean more towards voyeurism and domination, with a sexual perverse for degradation and praise. I complimented Chris's desires. My fetishes also involved degradation, as well as fisting, and turning pain into pleasure.

"Let's say we make our next target a hunt?" I suggested, finally revealing the thought I had been hanging on to, snagging Chris's interest. "Go back to where it started. Win them over, have a little fun, then give them the chance to escape." I chuckled.

No one had ever escaped, but it was amusing to let them think they even had a chance. "It might be the incentive we all need to regain the balance between us again."

Chris looked past me to the hall where Grayden and Kyden were still hauled up, contemplating the idea. I could see his mind ticking over. If Grady weren't his fraternal twin brother, we would have cut him free long ago. But there were just some connections that ran too deep.

"Fuck it." He slapped his hand down on the table, stood and knocked several sheets of paper onto the floor. "Sounds good to me. I'll go grab the bows from the boot and check the strings."

"See if the knives need sharpening too," I suggested. "Kyden got a bit carried away last time trying to remove the femur, and three blades ended up being used to dislodge it from the muscle and tissue. Just leave them out for Kyden to do when he wakes."

Chris harrumphed in recollection, then strode through the front door just as Grady made his presence known. I rolled my eyes in response, twisting so I wouldn't give him my back.

"Morning", I greeted.

"Mmm," he grunted, going straight to one of the open spirit

bottles and taking a mouthful.

"Starting on the alcohol early today, I see," I spat out, unable to bite my tongue.

Grady flipped me off and stalked around the counter. Before I could comprehend what he was doing, I found myself wearing the remaining water left in the bottom of the kettle.

"Fucking psychopath," I yelled, the hot water scalding my skin. It burnt like a motherfucker, but I was glad it had cooled considerably between the time I had boiled it, and the distance it flew through the air, before landing on me.

Grady grinned like a Cheshire cat, leaning back against the bench as he took another swig of booze. "Hot for me, T-man?"

Guess it was one of those days.

I curled my hands into fists and breathed through my nose to rein in my control. Then, before I completely lost my shit from being in his presence too long, I strode down the hall, slamming my door shut to quickly shower. One of these days Grady wasn't going to be the last one standing.

With the precarious Grady and Kyden situation, I couldn't help but wonder how much longer we could keep doing this. Sure, when we find our target, there is a balance that works between the four of us. We all contribute different attributes that allowed us to work seamlessly, all finding that different release we each crave. But it's the moments in between like these that tip the balance.

Kyden

12

"What the fuck do you think you are doing?" I yelled, storming into the kitchen, wrenching the Karambit from Chris's hand, and cutting open his palm in the process.

The wanker was running the edge of the blade back and forth with a jerky motion along the side of a flat-edged stone. A flat, fucking edged stone, so the corner was damaging my baby.

"I'm sharpening your blades, you crazy bastard," Chris snapped before feeling the sting in his palm and hissing. "You fucking cut me."

"I'll do a lot worse than that if I ever catch you sharpening it again." I warned through gritted teeth.

"What was I doing wrong?" he asked, flabbergasted, cradling his palm in his other hand.

Rifling through the pack that held my gear, I retrieved the stone I was after and held it up in front of me. "Firstly, on a curved blade you use a curved stone, and you don't rub it back and forth like you're trying to get it off. You need to glide it at an angle in one direction."

Trent groaned as he walked in, taking stock of the situation. "Uh oh, Sir is being told he's a bad boy."

"Don't," Chris warned, swinging around to face down Trent, with a glare that would make any normal fully grown man backpedal. But not one of us is normal, so Trent just shrugged it off and made his way to the kettle for his fifth or sixth morning coffee.

"How many of my knives have you fucked the edge up on?" I snapped, unable to help myself as I saw the jagged edge of my kukri.

I'm not going to cry. I'm not going to cry. I breathed back deeply through my nose then let it out through my parted lips, to reign in control so I didn't snap and ram the blunt tip through Chris.

Gathering up the equipment from Chris, along with my knives, I moved it all to the far end of the bench away from him to protect my babies, leaving him to check over the bows and arrows. No one touches my knives but me, and he bloody knew that.

"Seriously, what is the big deal, Ky? They will still cut."

I let my jaw fall open, unable to form words. I brought my hands out in front of me, mimicking the action of wanting to throttle him. In my mind, his face was turning scarlet as he was deprived of oxygen, his hand battering uselessly at me, before his eyes rolled into the back of his head and he ceased struggling, falling limp in my grip. The image in my mind cast a sense of satisfaction through me until I looked down at the kukri again.

"No big deal? No. Big. deal?" My mouth opened and closed wordlessly.

I don't want my knives to *cut*. I want them to glide seamlessly through the dermal layers, slowly, opening the flesh and tissue up with precision, not hack at it like an apprentice butcher breaking down his first side of beef. I wanted to watch the blood cells gather between the smooth layers, and emerge together, swimming to the surface and flowing freely, escaping their prison. I did not want to watch them pool in uneven globs through jagged flesh, and chaotically spill from the rough, jagged flesh. It was unsatisfying.

"*No big deal,* he says. No big deal. No big deal?"

"Okay, who broke the kid? He's stuck on repeat," Grady chuckled, coming in through the front of the house, then paused when he saw me protectively hovering over my knives. His eyes moved back to Chris with raised brows. "You touched his knives? You fucked up, bro." he tutted.

Chris dropped his head, "I did *not* fuck up."

I picked up my wounded kukri, running a finger along its edge. It hooked my skin, causing me to poke out my bottom lip sadly at the loss.

Grady gasped, shaking his head slowly as I assessed the damage. "Ohhh, Chriso, you royally fucked up. You don't touch the edges of Ky's knives, ever."

"Yeah, yeah, I know," Chris finally admitted.

I know how much it hurt him to admit he was wrong, but it didn't matter. He hurt my weapons, and that was a huge no-no, just like fucking with his laptop was off limits. fuck, "I don't give a flying fuck Chris, you crossed a line," I snapped, holding up a machete towards him.

At least he had not attempted to sharpen this one yet. I couldn't not get a little stabby if he had touched the edge on this. It had to be a perfect canter on the edge so it glided effortlessly through soft tissue.

"I should take my kukri to you and show you first- hand the difference between the hack job you did and what a well cared for blade can do."

"Hey, easy up, Ky. Chris was only trying to help," Trent placated, forever trying to be the peacekeeper for everyone but Grady.

"It isn't helping if it means five times as much work for me to try and get an edge back on it. I honestly don't even know if I can."

Grady came around behind me, wrapping his arms around my waist. He rested his head on my shoulder. "I'll get you a new one, Peaches."

I shook my head. It wouldn't be the same. I had a sentimental attachment to this one. It was the first blade I had used on a victim.

It carved into her flesh without resistance. I can still visualise the way her skin parted, exposing the layers of tissue and muscles. Her blood complemented the untarnished new blade like it was made for her.

"Maybe we *should* let Kyden wound you with the knife you fucked up so you learn your lesson not to touch ever again." Grady glared.

"Oh, piss off," Chris rejected, throwing his hands in the air, "I said I was sorry."

"Actually, you didn't," Trent pointed out, not taking Chris's side for once.

"Your exact words were, *it's no big deal,*" I said, waving my damaged baby at him.

Chris mentally chastised himself. Sucking in a deep breath, he looked at me. "I'm sorry, Kyden. I should have known better than to touch your knives. I was only trying to help as a surprise, so Trent and I could share with you what we had been discussing." I could see how much it hurt him to apologise.

"I think a non-fatal wound or amputation of maybe …a finger would suffice as an apology," Grady mulled over, rubbing his chin.

I turned my head to Grady. "I'm not cutting…."

Grady pressed his fingers against my lips. "Shhh, the grown-ups are talking."

Turning back to Chris to finish the conversation, he kept his fingers pressed to my lips. I nipped his fingers hard, drawing blood. Grady spun me so quickly that I didn't have a chance to react, gripping my throat with his free hand, forcing me back against the wall with his fingers still held captive between my teeth. I smiled around the appendages when I saw just how turned on he was by it.

"Oh, for fucksake, you two, can you quit it until we have finished?" Chris groaned, whacking Grady on the back of the head as he walked past us, back to the table.

Grady, however, was shamelessly grinding against me, biting along my jaw, showing just how badly he wanted to *finish,* right now.

"Gray, put it away before I turn the hose on you," Trent warned.

It wasn't an empty threat either. Despite the fact that the

action would flip Grady's switch and he would be out for blood, it never prevented any of us from taking drastic action against Grady's uncontrolled sexual urges at times. He was like a horny dog that humped everything in sight.

"Cock blockers," Grady murmured, releasing my throat at the same time as I released his fingers from my mouth.

"Later," I winked at him. I planned on having Grady do a handstand and force him to hold it while I sucked him off. Better yet, we can sixty-nine that shit.

"I don't like that look on your face, Kyden," Chris pointed at me. "No stabbing me in the back or conspiring until after we have our subject."

I rolled my eyes. "Yes, sir." Knowing full well it would trigger Chris with the bratty response. What can I say? Being around Grady has influenced me to release my inner brat that I didn't know I had.

Trent

13

I volunteered to check out the local cafes and eateries, then play the tourist role and scope out some attractions of the town. My task was to get a feel for the local vibe and see if I could uncover anything–or anyone–of use.

The only problem was I wasn't doing any of those things. Instead, I found myself turning the car away from the town, heading back to where the girl who was consuming my thoughts existed. I watched her from a distance, thankfully she didn't see me. Her attention was elsewhere as she walked along the leaf-littered street, blissfully unaware that her life would soon change drastically. For now, I stayed hidden, observing and learning as much as I could.

Dressed in an outfit identical to what I had last seen her in, I knew she would be on her way to work at the pathetic excuse for a pharmacy

She carried herself with slow, practised steps, effortlessly avoiding the damaged sections of the footpath without glancing down—proof that she had walked this path so often, she knew it by heart. Seemingly lost in her own mind, an array of expressions flickered across her face, as if she were lost in deep thought. It was pleasing to watch, especially because it wasn't forced. This was her in her natural environment. She had such an expressive face, one that I craved to know what it would look like experiencing moments of both pleasure and pain.

Her posture shifted, becoming slightly rigid. With a forced smile, she waved, her mouth moving in greeting to a couple approaching. But the couple, upon seeing her, deliberately diverted their attention, ignoring her presence. The action noticeably deflated her demeanour—her face fell, and her shoulders slumped, defeated. Something about that small gesture made me see red. She didn't deserve to be treated that way.

I briefly considered following the couple who had dared show her such disrespect, just so I could teach them a lesson. But I wasn't ready to pull my focus from the woman who had become the object of my obsession.

With a dark cloud over her head, she walked sadly, her shoulders slumped, head down, doing everything to avoid drawing attention to herself. She stepped into the cafe where I had met her just two days ago, at the same time of day. If she was a creature of habit, at least I knew where I could find her in the future. I made a mental note.

No matter what it took, she was going to be mine. In the back of my mind, I had laid claim to her the moment those big, beautiful eyes looked onto mine.

I moved the car up the street, positioning it so I could track her movements more closely from inside the café. But my attention was suddenly drawn to a man berating a woman. He manhandled her, demanding she get into the car. The fear in her eyes was unmistakable from where I sat, and it triggered urges I had been holding back with minimal restraint. Pinching and twisting my scrotum, forcing tears to well in my eyes, I caged my desires so I wouldn't react.

People ignored the altercation without a single glance as they passed by, as if it were an everyday occurrence. When the male slapped the woman, throwing her to the ground, and then yanked open the passenger door, my interest peaked.

Was this a kidnapping? What was this, amateur hour? Surely he isn't dumb enough to kidnap someone in broad daylight, with so many witnesses drawing attention to himself ... unless it's a DV situation?

Dragging the woman across the pavement by the hair, he forced her into the car, but not before slapping her across the face.

When my subject stepped from the cafe with a small white bag containing a bakery item and disposable cup, I was torn between following the couple who snagged my attention and my desire to learn more about her.

Deciding I could return the following day to continue my investigative stalking, I followed the couple, curiosity getting the better of me as they drove out of town. There was no need to maintain distance—it was the main thoroughfare in and out of town. Behind me, there were three or four other vehicles. My only concern was the possibility of dash cam footage being used to identify our vehicle. I might have to get Chris to switch plates again.

Not too far out of town, the vehicle began to slow, then indicated to turn down a dirt side road that was lined by overgrown trees and thick heavy underbrush. I pulled over to the edge of the road just before the exit, allowing the vehicles behind me to pass as I watched dust rise into the sky from the car I was following. When it was clear that no one else was driving past, I turned down the side road, following the car into an open clearing with a small house that looked as though it were undergoing renovations. It was surrounded by thick vegetation, concealing it from view from the road. The side road turned out to be a private driveway.

Pulling in behind the car in the driveway, I was immediately confronted with the male. He stormed over to my door yelling incoherently, saliva spraying from his mouth, his hand pointed in my direction. I waited until he was beside the passenger door, which sat open just a smidge. Pushing it out forcefully, I slammed it into him, jumping out as he stumbled back in surprise. Before he could recover, I had him by the scruff of his neck –using his own weight against him, I propelled him to the ground, face down. I knelt down on his back, taking his struggling arms in my hands and pulling them behind his back.

"Get off you asshole. If I owe ya money, I'll pay it tomorrow. I'm good for it," he yelled, with a hint of fear in his voice.

"I'm not interested in your money." I told him.

I saw the female climb out of the car, looking wide-eyed and afraid, taking in the interaction but making no move to escape.

"What do you want then? I ain't got much," he grunted, still attempting to fight me off.

"Did you abduct the woman?"

The males' struggling stilled. Looking over his shoulder as best as he could, his face pulled into a confused frown. "What? Who?"

I ripped his head back by his hair so he was forced to look at the woman in question. "Her."

"That bitch is my good for nothing, wife." He spat on the

ground. "Doesn't do a goddamned thing she's told, and gives shitty head. You want her, then take her. I don't give a shit. She's more trouble than she's worth."

The woman chewed on her lower lip, curling in on herself anxiously. "Is anyone else in the house?" I asked her.

She shook her head in a quick motion.

"Are you expecting anyone else?"

Again, she shook her head.

"Does he abuse you?"

Her eyes widened again. She gulped, looking down at the piece of shit under me, too afraid to answer.

"She gets what she deserves," he sneered.

With his head still raised with my hand fisting his hair, I slammed his face into the ground four times forcefully.

"That's not what I asked," I spoke calmly.

Looking back at the woman, I asked again. "Does. He. Abuse. You?"

She nodded, rubbing her arms, which I noted were coated in a myriad of bruises. Shit, that was a pretty sight. Nope, get your head straight.

"Do you have somewhere else to go for a while?"

"Yes," her soft voice finally broke.

"Go inside, pack your belongings and leave. Don't look back, and you will never have to see him again."

The woman's chin trembled, a shuddering whimper fell from her lips, as tears cascaded from her eyes.

"Thank you, thank you." She sniffed, wiping her face on the back of her arm, then darted inside.

"Still with me, dickface?"

He groaned incoherently.

Hmm, I may have smashed his face too hard against the ground. Standing, I grabbed him by the collar, dragging him across the ground to the side of the house. Inside I could hear the distinctive sounds of cupboards being opened and closed, and feet shuffling around quickly as the woman hurriedly packed, seizing the opportunity that I had presented her with.

Dropping the man's body on the ground, I dropped the heel of my boot into the side of his head until I heard the crunch of his skull cracking. Satisfied he wouldn't be waking anytime soon, if at all. I perused the property, debating what to do with his body. It took no real consideration the moment I saw the septic tank, just beyond the hills hoist.

"Perfect for a piece of shit like you."

Was killing a man for harming a woman contradictory? Probably. The main difference between us was the method in which we went about it. Dickface abused his victim out in the open, flaunting his mistreatment of her. Whereas we preferred to keep that side behind closed doors, hidden from public spectacle, with no notable connections between us and our chosen subjects.

Deciding to wait until the woman had left, I abandoned the body and made my way to the front door. I came face-to-face with the woman just as she was exiting, her arms laden with her belongings, crammed into plastic bags and a suitcase.

"He will find me, he always does. I don't know if I should leave."

I cut her off with a simple raise of my hand. "I will take care of him permanently. But you need to disappear and never return. Can you do that?"

The woman nodded, looking around fearfully, as if she expected her abuser to spring from behind her and punish her for her attempted escape. He wasn't coming after anyone in his current or future state. "Yes, my sister lives interstate."

"Very well, can you drive?"

"I... I have my own car," she said meekly, then clicked a fob in her hand, opening a garage door and revealing a small hatchback.

I took half of her poorly packed luggage and assisted her by loading it into the back seat of the small car. She offered a small thanks without making eye contact, and quickly jumped into the driver's seat, pulling out and hitting the accelerator like her life depended on it. If only she knew just how true that was in my presence.

Once the woman had left, I retrieved a drop pick from the garage. Walking to the rear of the property, I levered open the septic tank lid; I was hit with a waft of raw sewage. I quickly ducked my face into the crook of my elbow, gagging as the scent of methane smacked me in the face. What the fuck had these people been eating? That didn't smell healthy.

The opening was large enough that with a little persuasion from my boot; the male squeezed through the opening , disappearing into the sewage with the lid being replaced quickly, sealing him in his tomb.

Walking through the house, I found myself pleasantly surprised, given the piece of shit that had lived here. It was clean and organised. The bathroom and kitchen had been recently renovated, though the grout between the tiles hadn't been filled yet. In the bedroom, a main exposed beam held a chain that descended to a boxing bag. I smiled wide, having other ideas for the chain. Removing the boxing bag, I tossed it aside, then tested the strength of the chain, adjusting it to its full length.

Happening across that couple could not have been a better circumstance, this was almost too perfect.

After I had participated in our group activity with the next subject, I would return here with a particular person of interest that was consuming my thoughts. But first, I needed to taper these urges or I would be likely to take things too far with her, and I had no intention of destroying her. I wanted to keep her. Permanently. I just hadn't figured out how I was going to do that yet.

Kira

14

For the past two days, my mind continually recounted the interactions with the mysterious men—the ones I'd encountered outside the café, then their unusual appearance later at work. My pulse quickened at the recollection of their touch, the timbre of their voices and the rich masculine scents they carried. They were alluring, yet being in their presence screamed red flags and danger. They demanded attention, drew it to them like a moth to a flame. I had no doubt they would incinerate any woman – or man, for that matter – who fell into their trap, luring them with the promise of forbidden desires being unleashed with just a glance, only to leave them forever changed, whether it be for better or worse.

But as I seemed to have no self-preservation instincts and was an utter glutton for punishment, I couldn't help mulling over the words one of them had said to me. "What I would like is to take you away from this hellhole of a town."

I wanted to jump up and wrap my legs around him, and ask

him why we weren't already gone. Instead, I dismissed him, letting him know I wasn't good enough. Too late to go back now. Maybe one day, I will have the opportunity to meet another Mr. Tall, Dark and Dangerous.

I sighed, pushing the image of their dangerous personas from my mind as I slowly walked home under the fading light of dusk, heading toward the empty house awaiting me at the end of the street.

As usual, the townspeople turned the other way or feigned distraction rather than be seen associating with me as I passed. God forbid I were born culturally offensive to them, as though I had a choice in the matter. The mob of my people had disowned me because of my sperm donor of a father, and for being 'stolen' from them by Ninny. More like rescued and given opportunities. The whitewashed town had disowned me, considering me one of the problems that tarnished their perfect image. They conveniently forgot that the native lands they settled on were inhabited long before any of them arrived. In fact, the local town hall had been built over a sacred burial site.

I was used to never quite fitting in. My mind drifted back to the men—particularly the one I ran into with that sinful smirk. Were they passing through? What I wouldn't give to climb in the back seat and disappear from here forever. I highly doubted my disappearance from this town would raise any alarms or suspicion, anyway. If anything, there would be relief that there was one less indigenous person daring to live on their own native lands.

But I couldn't leave. With Ninny gone, nothing was tying me here but her memory, and for some reason, I couldn't let go of it. The house where she raised me and gave me a home was now in my name. It was the last piece of her I had left, the only proof that I had ever been wanted, that I had belonged somewhere.

Chris

15

Unable to sleep after restlessly tossing and turning for half the night with my mind racing. I was teetering on the edge of losing control, from not being able to release my pent up aggression and urges. The result was nowhere near as detrimental as what Grady or Kyden's would be, but nonetheless, it was something I had no control over.

I decided to forgo lying to myself any further and left the room, seeking something more productive to do. After mindlessly tapping away on the laptop for an hour, checking over my notes and fine-tuning a plan I was orchestrating, I decided to step outside for fresh air. The humid tropical night air was suffocating and heavy inside, even under the fan. Outside fared no better, but there was a distinctive scent of rain in the air, with the promise of relief to the discomfort of the relentless heatwave.

I was startled when the glowing ember of Grady's cigarette moved through the night air after he inhaled. I hadn't even noticed the smell when sniffing the air, catching only the faint hint of petrichor. I had been too lost in my head. Taking another breath, I realised it wasn't tobacco he was smoking. The marijuana only came out when his demons were bad.

"Can't sleep?" I asked, watching the glow move through the air back and forth from his mouth. I wondered how long he had been sitting out here.

"Do I ever?" he deadpanned. "What's eating at you?"

I ran a hand down my face and collapsed into a chair. "Overthinking."

A huffed grunt escaped Grady in silent agreement. "Any luck with the next sub?"

"I think I have her nailed down. I have just been fine-tuning the details. I will do some recon tomorrow."

We sat there in comfortable silence, surrounded by the sounds of nature, interrupted only by the occasional moment of flatulence from Grady.

Eventually, he let out a heavy sigh. "Look, you know I wouldn't have actually done any lasting damage, right? Like, I wouldn't have killed you or some shit. I mean, you're the only family I have left."

I looked over in the direction of where Grady sat in the darkness. Even though I couldn't see him, I could picture the way his forehead scrunched and the way his mouth tilted down to one side as he battled his emotions and feelings of guilt

"I know Gray. I understand just how much you struggle with control. But at the end of the day, you wouldn't intentionally end my life, I trust you… for the most part."

He exhaled a ragged breath, "yeah." He cleared his throat. A moment later he made sounds like he was opening his mouth to speak, then snapping his mouth shut again. Finally he spoke, "I just needed you to know, you're my brother and have never turned on me, no matter how fucked up I am. I uh, it means a lot."

I smiled into the dark, enjoying this rare moment. "Love you too, Gray."

He let out a strangled laugh, flicking the joint butt into the air so it landed somewhere out on the curved driveway. "Night, bro, I'm …" he let his voice trail off, not needing to finish the sentence.

"Night Gray," I answered. "Oh, and the day after tomorrow, we are hunting our sub down, so don't wear yourself out, or hurt Ky too much tonight."

Gray made a devious noise. "No promises. Maybe you should cuddle up with Trent. You both seem to have a lot of built-up tension between the pair of you."

I scoffed. "Never happening."

Trent's idea of foreplay always involved a fist disappearing into holes that weren't designed for them to fit into. Not one part of that appealed to me. Not to mention that even if I were inclined in that way, it would never work with two domineering males both fighting for control; we would only end up in a bloody punch-up.

Gray disappeared inside with a chuckle, leaving me alone again with my thoughts.

Grady

16

The best part of the Airbnb—other than the fact that there were full-sized beds and my own bathroom (*thank fuck for both*)—was that it sat on twenty hectares of uninhabited land, with a four-thousand-square-metre patch of grass at the rear of the property, surrounded by thick scrub. Which meant I could sharpen up my aim with the trusty bow and arrow I had slung over my shoulder. I had planned on letting go a few rounds on the target I had set up on a mannequin I found in one of the back sheds on the property, but *nooooo*... Trent was worried it'd draw too much attention if someone heard me discharge it.

Fucking pussy. There was no one around for kilometres.

Setting myself up, I licked my finger holding it in the air, checking the direction of the wind. Perfect—nothing more than a subtle north-westerly. Stretching my shoulders, I knocked the arrow in position, lining it up with my target. It was one of the few times I could fully focus my mind.

On an inhale, I pulled back on the string, correcting my

line, then let the projectile fly on an exhale. The whistle of the steel arrow careening through the air brought a rush of satisfaction, only to be trumped by the *thunk* it made as the point sunk through to the shaft, in the centre of the mannequin's head. It didn't have quite the same effect as the sound of hitting flesh did, but nonetheless, still a rewarding noise. A satisfied grin spread across my face. I was fucking awesome.

"Bullseye motherfucker. You're dead."

Once the mannequin was full of more chewed up, gaping holes than a brothel, and no longer resembling what it once was, I decided to go inside in search of food, then try to catch some Z's after having not had an ounce of sleep all night.

Kyden's delectable ass played no part in the reasoning for my lack of sleep either. Okay, perhaps I may have spent a few hours buried deep inside of him, but it was purely for mental health reasons. Nobody likes a moody fucker with balls that were so big they basically had their own zip code from not ejaculating enough through the day.

Unsurprisingly, when I eventually made my way inside, Trent had made himself scarce, and my brother was neck-deep in research, making sure we covered our bases in case something went wrong—he had a plan A all the way to

Z.

Without raising his eyes from the screen, he greeted me, hearing my heavy-footed approach, too tired to give a shit. "Hey, Gray. There's leftover Chinese in the microwave, just warmed up not long ago if you're hungry."

"You eaten?" I asked, pulling the plastic container from the microwave, ignoring the heat on my hands from the searing, half-melted plastic.

Chris shook his head, too wrapped up in his research. The dark circles under his eyes probably matched my own, but otherwise in every other way, we were chalk and cheese. He thrived on making sure everything is to plan, organised and under control. I, on the other hand, thrive on chaos, relish in the unknown, and embrace my unpredictability. My actions tended to be 'react first, damn the consequences' – that's a problem for later. And later Grady tended to not really give a shit either.

Doing my good deed for the week and earning my place in heaven, I grabbed a plate. Dishing some fried rice and satay beef onto it, I slid it in front of Chris with a fork. When Chris made no attempt to reach for the food, I decided on forcing his hand by way of a threat.

"Eat, or I'll sit on your fucking chest and force-feed you like I used to do with dog shit when we were kids," I warned.

He knew I would see through on my promise. Relenting, Chris closed the laptop and brought the plate to his face, inhaling the fragrant sauce. I emptied the rest of the beef into the rice container and began shoving it into my mouth with a fork.

"Watcha working on?" I spat rice out as I spoke through a mouthful of food, only to shove more in before I swallowed.

Chris flicked the food around his plate before collecting a small amount on the tip of his fork. "Trying to find a hunting ground on Google Maps we can use." He brought the fork to his mouth, almost moaning when the food hit his tongue, quickly diving back in for more.

"Need help?" I asked, knowing he would refuse. As predicted, he shook his head, already half finished with his plate of food.

"When did you last eat?" I asked, watching him swallow without chewing. He paused, looking at the plate, then at me. "Last night… I think… Yeah, pretty sure." He tilted his head to the side in thought. "Or maybe it was the night before. I don't know anymore."

"Fuckucking hell, Chriso. You gotta do better than that, bro." I scolded, throwing my big-brother-protective-vibe down. Big brother by seven whole minutes, but it still counts.

He gave a shrug, tipping the plate so he could scrape the last of the rice into his mouth from the edge. "Cheers, Gray." He inclined his head towards the plate, then opened the laptop back up, burying himself back into his research.

Leaving Chris with a few snacks around him, to make sure he didn't waste away, I slunk into Kyden's room, knowing full well he would already be passed out again, and hopefully dreaming of my impressive cock.

Between shooting the arrows, imagining they were being forced into the flesh, and seeing the pics of the shiela we were going to be hunting, I had a fucking raging hard-on.

As predicted, I found Ky curled up on his side, shirtless, under the blankets. He had his back to me, the bedside lamp illuminating the tattooed muscles of his bicep and shoulders, highlighting him like a forbidden piece of art—something that you could admire and not touch. I was never one to follow rules, though.

I licked the drool from the edge of my mouth, admiring him for a moment. I locked the door, kicking off my shoes, underwear and pants in one motion. Then, I pulled my top over my head, discarding it amongst the floordrobe. Pulling back the covers, expecting to have to remove Ky's trunks before I took my fill of him, I was pleasantly surprised by what awaited me.

"Ky, you bad boy. Were you waiting for me?" I groaned when met with his naked ass pushed out towards the edge of the bed, waiting for me to take him. I sunk my teeth into my bottom lip, quickly retrieving my phone from my pants pocket, all while oogling Ky's taut, peachy ass. He was delectable.

Setting my phone up so it was leaning against a vase on the dresser at the end of the bed, perfectly angled so it captured the scene, I hit record.

Making my way to the side of the bed he was facing, I stroked my cock with one hand. I dropped down to my knees on the edge of the mattress, taking in Ky's perfection. He was so fucking pretty yet masculine, with full lips and dark long lashes that framed his grey eyes. He had a strong jaw that was covered with thick stubble. He was sexy without even trying. I had to remember to send his parents a thank-you card for those genes. Maybe a gift basket too.

Leaning over, I pressed my mouth to his. Biting down on his lower lip I sucked on it, pulling on it between my teeth I let go, then moved my mouth down along his neck and chest, leaving a trail of purple marks as I sucked and bit into his flesh, all while he lay there, none the wiser.

When I got down to his flaccid dick laying against the sheet, I tugged on it, hard, squeezing and digging my nails into the underside of his foreskin until it began hardening under my touch, knowing how much his body craved the pain, even when he was out like a light.

"Such a good sex doll. I know how much your body craves me even when you can't respond."

When he was rock hard and weeping. I pulled on his foreskin, stretching it out over the head of my cock, so I was seated inside with his cock.

"Fuckucking hell, I love wearing your skin," I groaned, running my hand back and forth over our joined cocks. "Next time we do this, I'm going to pierce your dick. I want a barbell right on the end, so it rubs against me while I get us both off."

The thought of it alone had my balls tightening. "Ah, fuck."

Increasing the speed and firmness of my grip, I jacked us both off until my cum was spilling out from under Ky's foreskin.

Lightheaded and breathing heavily, I let my semi drop between my legs, then worked Ky until he came, painting the sheets with his release. A small moan rolled through his throat, but otherwise he was entirely unresponsive.

"Such a good boy," I said to the camera, blowing a kiss.

Moving up by his head again, I smacked my dick against his face. It made a satisfying *thwack* sound, with the last drops of cum leaking out, splattering across his cheeks.

Reaching down his body, scooping up our combined release, I shoved my fingers into his mouth, forcing our semen onto his tongue and down his throat. Nutrients and all that.

"Look how much you love being a cum slut, holding it in your mouth, savouring the taste."

Gargling saliva at the back of my throat, I brought it forward in my mouth, pressing my mouth against his lips I held open, I spat the wad in his mouth, then mixed it together with my finger. Sitting back, I admired the glistening combination pooling on his tongue, then pushed his mouth closed, pressing my lips against his before walking around the other side of the bed. All while my fingers were trailing across every inch of his naked body. He really was too good to be true.

Settling my body in behind him, I ran my fingers through his crack and found his tight little hole—it was slick, already lubricated.

My jaw dropped open in surprise. Looking at my phone, knowing he would see my reaction, I spoke to awake Kyden.

"Bad, bad, boy. I should deny you my cock for being such an eager little fuck doll." I tsked, then brought my hand down hard on his ass repeatedly, until It bloomed in a deep shade of crimson and the skin welted with raised handprints.

"Fortunately for you," I said pointedly to my phone, "I can't say no to your corpse. Look at you lying here, waiting for me to defile you. *Disgusting.*" I shook my head in faux disappointment, then smiled darkly. "Just the way *I like it*."

Lining my dick up, I pushed in, my eyes rolling back in my head at the sensation of his tight warmth, circumferencing me. Nothing felt better than being buried deep inside of him. It was like coming home; it was the happiest place on earth. I don't care what anyone says, my happy place doesn't involve a talking mouse, it's in Kyden's sphincter.

"If. You. Didn't. Feel. So. Fucking. Good." I grunted between thrusts. "Then. I. Would. Deny. You. My. Cock." My release came too quickly. I wasn't ready to be done taking advantage of him yet, plus he needed to be punished.

"Now," I said, panting slightly, I pulled myself free and leaned over Kyden's face then looked back at the phone. "Because you're such a needy whore, eager to have your ass stretched out, I'm going to fulfil your wish." I held up my hand, wiggling my fingers, then made a fist and gave my best menacing grin. I had watched Trent do this enough times on our subs to know just how to proceed. "I'm going to fuck you up so hard, you won't be able to sit for a week."

Kyden

17

I woke up with the usual heaviness after a long sleep –my throat was dry, stomach aching from hunger, body sore from lying in one position for countless hours, and my arse feeling like an elephant had climbed out of it.

Wait what?

I clenched my ass cheeks. The stinging pain brought a smile to my face.

"What the fuck did you do, Gray?"

Through blurry eyes, I fumbled around the nightstand, my hand knocking against a bottle of water. I grabbed it, then reached around blindly until my fingers brushed over my phone. I popped the lid off the bottle and began downing the water. It did little to sate the unquenchable thirst, but I needed to hydrate. I unlocked my phone with biometrics and tapped on Grady's message I knew would be waiting for me.

♥ You can thank me later 😜

I grinned with anticipation, pulling my body up in the bed with a wince, feeling a crusty layer of what I can only assume was cum, covering most of my skin.

I grabbed for the second bottle of water, opening it as I hit play on the attached video. The moment Grady came into view, my heart did a stupid little flutter in my chest. I watched him taking in my unconscious form. When he pressed his lips to mine, my cock sprang to life, standing at attention with that sentiment.

I watched with rapt attention, stroking my aching length as Grady defiled me, using me for his own pleasure. Fuck, it made me feel so much for the man who would do this for me. Knowing how much I got off on that, he abused my body as he wished without my consent, with no limit to what he could do to me. I trusted him wholeheartedly.

"Now," Grady said, as he pulled his beautiful thick cock from my arse, leaning over my face, then looking back at the phone. "Because you're such a needy whore, eager to have your ass stretched out, I'm going to fulfil your wish," he held up his hand, wiggling his fingers, then made a fist, giving his best menacing grin.

I gulped, clenching my arse and feeling the lingering ache. My cock throbbing painfully in my grip. I was panting heavily, knowing what he had done and about to witness it.

"I'm going to fuck you up so hard, you won't be able to sit for a week."

"Oh fuck," Those words made my balls tighten, and I came all over myself, barely even touching my dick. Ropes of cum kept flowing from me as Grady began working his fingers inside of me, moaning deep. My chest was heaving breathlessly as I finished. I was still hard.

I kept watching as Grady thrust his entire fist inside of me. I felt the phantom thrusts as he worked my ass in the video. The ache intensified with the sound of his fist punching into my gaping hole, his groans pushing my body to the edge again, seeing how much he enjoyed fisting me. The lust on his face was replaced with pure satisfaction as I came in my sleep, urging his own release across my back. I was seconds from spilling again and had to look away, holding back so I wouldn't ruin the built up to my second orgasm. This one was owed to Gray and this video. This was being kept in the vault for my spank bank.

I found Grady waiting for me in his room looking fresh from a shower, with damp messed hair, in nothing but a pair of cotton shorts which were sitting low on his hips, exposing every inch of his tanned, toned flesh. His chest, arms and up his neck, covered in a myriad of skull tattoos, making him even more appealing to gaze upon. He was sex on legs, and he knew it.

A knowing grin spread across his face as he turned to face me with a joint pinched in his fingers.

"Do your worst," he challenged eagerly, inhaling deeply on the joint before tossing it aside and spreading his arms wide in acceptance of whatever I wanted to do to him.

I kicked the door closed behind me with my foot; the motion made me just aware of how sore I was. Standing before him naked, in nothing but the dried cum from countless releases he had left on my skin, I could feel the heavy desire pulsating from him.

Between my legs, my cock was rock-hard, standing proud, begging for attention, and leaking from the tip. Grady licked his lips, eyeing the precum with thirst. I wrapped my hand around myself, running it slowly up my shaft, pinching the tip and gathering the fluid in my fingers and sucked them clean.

Grady let out a whimpered moan, his tongue poking out, imitating my own in a licking motion.

With my favourite knife held loosely in my other hand, I flicked it between my fingers, taking a step closer to Grady. He pushed his shorts down in one swift movement, kicking them aside hungrily, caressing me with his eyes. His tongue darted out, moving across his lower lip when he focused on my cock again.

"Just remember," I said, taking measured steps, closing the distance between us. I pressed the knife to the side of his face, sliding it down to his neck without breaking the skin, earning a deep moan from him. "You started this."

Chris

18

We all piled into the 4x4, in our usual seats — Trent driving, me in the passenger seat, and Kyden and Grady in the backseat. At my feet were our basic grab kits, which included rope, chloroform, knives, guns, cuffs, gags, blindfolds and syringes filled with ketamine. Because you can never have too many back-ups.

Grady was whistling some annoying fucking tune from the back seat, tapping on his leg with the palm of his hand out of sync with the melody. His body bopping along, completely mismatched to whatever rhythm he thought he had going on.

Beside him, Kyden was flipping his knife absentmindedly between his fingers, while stuffing his face with processed carbs and sugars, readying himself for the high. He kept adjusting himself in the seat with a wince, as if sitting was uncomfortable. I guess warning Grady to take it easy on him was seen as more of a challenge than a suggestion. I didn't want to know the details, but whatever happened had them both grinning like Cheshire cats last night when they emerged from Grady's room. Grady, noticeably, was sporting a few blood-soaked gauze patches taped to his abdomen, chest and bicep, however.

Trent sat behind the steering wheel, his face tight and focused, no doubt mulling over my plan and running through every possible scenario in his mind—both best and worst case. His hands clenched and relaxed absentmindedly on the wheel as he chewed on his cheek.

In the passenger seat, I was double and triple checking the grab kit while keeping an eye on the subs' social media accounts, looking for any changes or updates in her plans.

We all had a role to play when the time came. Women naturally swooned over Trent; there wasn't a female we had encountered who didn't feel his pull. He was the bait to attract their attention. When the time was right, and they were distracted, I would swoop in and *run* into Trent, pretending I hadn't seen him for some time, then introduce myself to the potential sub. It was an act we had used numerous times because it seemed the most effective. When the coast was clear of prying eyes, I would reach out to shake hands with the sub, effectively to farewell her, then I grab her hand, pulling her close and I would use the body's own natural pressure points to render her unconscious.

The next steps involved Grady, our in-house master of shibari, to tie them up, then Kyden, who was proficient in dosing the correct level of whatever drug we are using, ensuring they stayed unconscious long enough to move them onto the next location.

We had played it out so many times that it had become a well-rehearsed routine—so flawless that no one ever doubted or questioned it.

Pulling up near the car park of the hiking trail, we positioned the car so it was hidden, but close enough to the trail that we could transfer a body without having to drag it too far. We sat and waited, having arrived an hour earlier than the sub had posted. Trent, our expert stalker, casually meandered through the car park, dressed as a well-seasoned hiker doing a last-minute check through his backpack.

"She's early," Trent said, sounding muffled through the earpiece.

He was probably scratching across his face so it wasn't noticeable that he was talking to someone through his hands free.

I gave Grady and Kyden a nod indicating it was time to move.

"Coming up behind," I said walking across the carpark, looking like a lost tourist with a map in my hand. I was pretending to study it with keen interest, all while watching our potential sub discreetly.

Trent had already begun walking along the path ahead of the sub, well out of sight. She stood at the entrance of the walking trail, looking back and forth along the car park, with a deflated expression. Then, she snapped a selfie, faking a wide smile, before typing something on her phone. After tucking it into her pocket and casting one final glance around, she hiked up her tiny bag higher on her shoulders and began walking behind Trent.

"Subs on the move," I informed everyone, waiting one full minute before starting on the trail behind her. I checked her newest post on social media, where she mentioned that anyone still keen for the hike should meet her at the lookout. I almost felt sorry for her.

"Following from the east." I updated everyone, as I took my first steps.

"I'm watching from the south," Grady said.

"Eyes from the north," Kyden added.

"Paused to literally smell the flowers," Grady grumbled a short time later. I could hear the eye roll and head shake from here.

"On the move again," Kyden informed us, with an excited tone.

"Causing interference," Trent said quietly.

"The old untied shoelace act?" Grady asked, with amusement.

"Mm," came Trent's response, not elaborating further at risk of giving himself away.

I increased my pace to close the distance. Before I reached the target or before Trent intercepted her, a high-pitched scream cut through the air.

"Trent?" I asked. Wondering if he had gone off script.

An annoyed sound came through at the accusation."Not me," he responded.

"Who has eyes?" I asked, pausing my steps. No response.

I ran ahead, not sure if I had a backup if all else failed, from plan A all the way down to plan Z.

The woman had detoured at some point; she had ventured off-track, having slipped out of Grady and Kyden's sight. By the time we reached her, she was lying unmoving, sprawled out on her back, her unfocused eyes staring into the sky. A river of crimson soaked the ground beneath her head, her head having landed heavily on a jagged rock.

Did she trip?

"Fuck!" Trent yelled, ripping at his hair with his hands. "Fuck."

Kyden said nothing, mesmerised by the flow of blood,

having his perverted needs somewhat being met.

I glanced around quickly, making sure there were no witnesses to link us to her death. Looking back down to the female, I jumped back when a snake slid past my feet, earning a bellowed laugh from Grady, as he came up to the scene joining us.

He took stock of the scene before him, whining, "She's already dead? Can I at least fuck her mouth?" He indicated to her parted lips.

"No, we aren't getting involved with this, and it's not ours to clean up," I snapped.

My fists clenched at my side, with the urge to punch something. This wasn't how it was supposed to go. All the time spent searching, stalking and planning was wasted.

Grady poked out his bottom lip and crossed his arms unhappily.

"Fuck," Trent repeated, clearly just as frustrated. We all felt it.

"Let's move out and regroup before we're seen," I suggested. "Follow Grady's path south, back to the car, so no one puts us at the scene."

One by one, we all follow back mindfully, walking without leaving a trail. Tensions high. Moods soured. Urges unsated. It was a precarious situation we would have to remedy

ASAP.

My steps were heavier than usual as we moved through the shrub, the bitter taste of failure in my mouth. Every crack in the ground beneath me felt like it was echoing my frustration. This wasn't just about the loss of a sub—it was about everything we had planned and were in need of to feel like we all had some control. And now it was slipping through our fingers.

Trent

19

How did I find myself back here so soon? I had planned to wait—wait until after we'd all had our release, so I could indulge in my unrestrained urges without the risk of compromising her. But now that option has been stolen from me. From all of us. I didn't want to risk going too far, losing control, and finding myself unable to restrain myself when the next encounter with the woman who consumed my every thought inevitably happened. I was obsessed with her.

My mind kept circling back to the girl from the café as I aimlessly drove, my thoughts wandering far from where I was supposed to be—scouting potential hunting grounds for our next sub. Instead, I was hunting a female I had deemed off-limits. I ran a hand down my face, frustrated, as I slowed the car to the posted speed limit of fifty, as my tires rolled past the welcome sign.

"Welcome my arse!" I scoffed.

Nothing about this town was welcoming. It should come with a warning sign in its place.

My eyes drifted back and forth across the street, searching—though I didn't realize it—looking for a hint of long, light brown hair and piercing blue eyes.

Realising how absurd this obsession was becoming, I knew it was too much of a distraction, especially with our next target already claimed. I spun the car in a U-turn, determined to get back to my original agenda.

But as fate—being the fickle bitch that it is—would have it, none other than the dark beauty who had been consuming my thoughts since our first brief encounter stepped into view, as if she were seeking me out. Her steps faltered as her eyes locked onto mine, her jaw falling open in surprise. I slowed the car to a stop beside her on the sidewalk. Rolling the passenger window down, I leaned across the seat. She smiled, a blush creeping across her cheeks as she tucked a strand of hair behind her ear.

"Oh, uh, hi," she said sweetly, the rough sound of her voice, a melody that could raise the dead—and by the dead I mean my dick, which now stood at attention, wanting to poke its head out and greet the throat responsible for the sound.

She was so much more enticing than I remembered, my memories not doing justice to the reality before me.

"Fancy meeting you here. Should I be worried that you have more coffee hidden on you to get me to take my clothes off?" I Joked. *What the fuck was I saying? Shut up, you fool.*

Her mouth dropped open. She frowned at me as if I were a fucking idiot. I didn't blame her one bit. "What? No. I, uh, it was an accident…" she stammered. I laughed, unable to help myself.

"Would you care to join me?" I broke the awkward silence, my nervousness creeping into my voice. "I was about to take a tour of your town, and a little local knowledge would be … insightful."

She rolled her eyes, glancing up the street. "That would take less time than it would for me to climb in the car and do up my seatbelt."

Her sassy remark forced a chuckle from my lips. She bit her lip, a faint blush creeping across her cheeks, leaving a beautiful pink stain.

"Then perhaps … just the privilege of your company for a while?"

She frowned, staring at me cautiously. *Yes*, I wanted to say, *I am as dangerous as you think – maybe worse.*

I raised my hands defensively. "I assure you, I will be a perfect gentleman for as long as you are in my company within your town's limits," I encouraged. It was when we left the town that she should be afraid of me.

"Fuck it," she relented with a grin, opening the door and

sliding into the seat. She turned to me. "Hi, I'm Kira."

"Kira," I said her name like it was the most beautiful word to ever grace my lips. It is an absolute pleasure finally knowing your name. It is as beautiful as you."

She scrunched her nose disbelievingly. "You don't have to lay it on so thick. You already have me at your mercy in your car."

I smiled widely, my tone taking on an edge of warning. "I am very much aware, Kira."

"What's your name?" she asked, completely missing the hint of danger in my voice.

"Trent." Why, in all the four corners of the earth did I give her my real name?

"Trent." She repeated, making my dick jerk at the sound of my name on her lips. "I like it. So what brings you to this hellscape?"

I grinned at the truth of her description.

You, I wanted to say. "Work."

"And what exactly is it you do for a crust?" she pressed, eyeing me closely as I drove through the back streets of the town.

"I take people's lives and carve them into something unrecognizable. I use my special talents to mold their minds so they understand the true value of their lives—how brief their existence is. Because no matter how bad they think things are before I meet them, it can always get worse."

"So, you're like a life coach?" she teased.

"I offer a specialised form of therapy." I smiled inwardly at my own personal joke.

"It must be nice to find your niche and know exactly where you fit in," Kira murmured, looking down at her fingers that were twisted in her lap. She was so preoccupied that she hadn't even noticed the fact that we had left the town and were headed away.

"Niche is a rather fitting description," I said, my voice low. "What is it that you want from life?" I asked. She was difficult to read.

She paused, as if trying to search for an answer. "I don't know," she admitted after a long moment.

"Okay, try this. What do you enjoy? What sparks your interest?"

"Outside of reading, not a great deal," she sighed. "I never had the opportunity to find out my full potential. I strived to be…" She waved her hands in the air trying to find the word

.

"A sheep?" I offered.

She blew out between her lips with a scoff. "Pretty much. I wanted to blend in, so I made myself fit into the little box that was considered acceptable and expected."

"And if I break apart the box, remove the top and walls. Then what might I find?"

"A confused woman who feels like I'm under the spotlight because of my heritage, too afraid to move from under the spotlight."

"Maybe it's time you stepped out of the light and edged into the shadows. Leave all you know behind you and walk amongst the unknown."

"I'm afraid to want more," she admitted softly, wringing her hands together with discomfort.

"But fear isn't what is stopping you. You don't know genuine fear, not yet anyway."

I saw her head whip to me in my peripheral vision, then quickly scan our surroundings. She was finally acknowledging the fact we had left the confines of "hellscape" as she so eloquently put it. I glanced over at her briefly before returning my attention back to the road, waiting for her reaction.

"Where are we?" she asked, her voice cracking at the end. That small, subtle shift in her demeanour ruffled the monster caged inside of me.

"Going on an adventure," I replied, my tone calm and collected.

"No," she said quickly, her voice shaking. "Can you please take me home now? I, ah, it's been really nice talking to you, but I need to get back. I have… stuff I need to do."

"You aren't going anywhere, Kira." I looked her in the eyes with a cold gaze. "You made the mistake of trusting me, and now I am going to show you first-hand just how proficient my life coaching skills are."

With my eyes back on the road, I reached into my coat pocket, uncapping the syringe.

Kira began screaming, her words a frantic blur as she demanded I stop the car. I could smell the adrenaline flooding her system, her genuine fear now unmistakable, and it thrilled me.

"Now, now," I said soothingly, my voice calm as I swung my arm out and injected the syringe into her neck. Her nails dig into my arm, drawing blood, as a barrel of expletives rolled from her tongue. "Don't waste all your energy, beautiful. We haven't even gotten to the fun part yet. I don't want you ruining your voice before you've had a chance to use it screaming my name."

Seconds later, her hands relinquished their fight on my arm; her body slunk forward, unconscious. With the seatbelt the only thing holding her upright. I withdrew the syringe in her neck, briefly glancing at the deep mark it left when she attempted to fight me off—a reminder of her fight. I was not pleased by the abrasion I was forced to mark her skin with, but she had left me no other choice.

I hoped she would forgive me once she discovered just how pleasurable it was to become mine. No matter what it took, I would make her see reason. She belonged to me.

Trent

20

Pulling up in the driveway behind the previous inhabitants' sedan, I did a brief scan to make sure the woman's car wasn't tucked away somewhere around the property, ensuring she had not returned. The house appeared to still be locked up, with no visible lights on, so I took that as a good sign.

I brushed Kira's hair back from her face, pressing my lips to her forehead.

"You will forgive me when you see what I can give you."

With one final press of my lips to the tip of her nose, I climbed from the car and made my way around to collect her in my arms.

Her body slumped lifelessly in my arms. She was lighter than I expected, which concerned me. I would take care of her now and make sure she ate properly. But first, I was going to introduce her to my world. Show her just how good we can be together—no matter how long it took her to realise she wasn't going anywhere.

Reaching the front door, I dug around in my pocket, finding

the house key I took from the male who was now decomposing with the sewage, like the piece of shit he was.

I walked straight through to the bedroom, laying her down on the bed.

The house was stuffy, and there was no fucking air-conditioning, only ceiling fans. Opening the windows and cranking all the fans to high, I adjusted the length of the chain I had left hanging from the ceiling to compensate for Kira's height, or lack of.

Returning to where she lay sprawled out on the bed like an offering, I couldn't help but feel thankful that Kyden had demanded we stop for coffee and food the day she ran into me. We were intending to do a visual sweep of the area for potential suspects, but that yielded only a discouraging number of possibilities. Disregarding the beauty before me. But none of that mattered now, not with her here before me. She was utter perfection.

Against the white bedspread, her darker skin created a stunning contrast, making her stand out like a shadow in the light behind her. It only highlighted her, drawing my attention effortlessly. Not that she needed any help in that department.

Subtle movements of her fingers twitching informed me that the low dose of sedative was wearing off. Retrieving the cuffs from the bag I had left here, I snapped them around her wrists until they bit into her skin. I was going to make her realise that there was immense pleasure to be found in pain.

Lifting her back into my arms, I inhaled deeply, pressing my face into her hair and savoring her scent. She didn't wear perfume, as far as I could tell—her natural scent had a sweetness to it that needed no enhancement. Delicious.

Hoisting her arms up with one hand, I attached the cuffs to the chain with a shackle, then gradually let her weight drop down. Her feet met the ground with her legs bent slightly, not bearing any of her weight. A small moan rolled from her throat at the discomfort of her wrists, rousing her from the sedative.

"There you are, beautiful. I have been waiting to see your gorgeous eyes."

She blinked slowly as her vision came back into focus. Her brow furrowed as she attempted to gain her bearings. Her head rolled from side to side with murmured confusion as she questioned what was happening.

I ran the side of my index finger down her face, across her silken skin and along her jaw, then pinched her chin between my fingers, forcing her head to look at me.

"Tell me, Kira, what is your deepest, darkest desire?"

Reality came slamming back into her in the blink of an eye

as she thrashed against her restraints, snarling at me. "You piece of shit. You kidnapped me."

"I did."

"Let me go this instant," she demanded, swinging a leg out to kick me. I moved just before she connected. There was more force behind her attack than I had been expecting.

"Now that wasn't very nice," I tutted.

"Drugging me and chaining me up isn't very nice either," she retorted, swinging her legs out to kick again, this time connecting with my kneecap, causing me to fight back a grunt of pain.

I couldn't wipe the smile off my face. Finally, he found someone willing to fight back with gusto.

"I warned you about me," I reminded her.

She had the nerve to throw her head back and laugh, confusing the hell out of me by the response.

"And here I thought it was some act. The dark and mysterious vibes trying to sell how dangerous you are to entice me to want you, just so you can get into my pants and brush me off once you got what you wanted." She shook her head with a sad laugh. "Maybe I shouldn't have been so blinded by my own desperation to realise that no one would ever actually want more than that from me."

Her self-evaluation threw me off balance. How could she

possibly think so little of herself? From the moment she had thrown herself at me, I had been enamored. She held a magnetic pull I couldn't deny, devastatingly beautiful in a way that was uniquely hers. There was a fire behind the mask she wore—a fire I'd caught glimpses of in our two brief encounters, moments where it slipped for just a fraction of a second. That was why I decided she would never leave my side. I would make her see the reality of who she truly was.

I reached out, pinching her cheeks between my fingers and yanking her face toward mine. "You will never degrade yourself like that again, do you hear me?" I growled, my teeth clenched as I hardened my gaze on her. She met my stare, eyes burning with defiance. The nerve of her.

"You are more than what you let yourself believe, and you will prove to me just how much you believe in yourself," I said, my voice low and commanding. "Now convince me you know your worth."

"No. I am noth…"

I released her face from my grip and slapped her cheek, sending her head whipping to the side. A shocked gasp fell from her lips.

"You will learn to love yourself. I will punish you every time you dare to run yourself down, or think less of yourself.

Either show me your pride or face my wrath until it has been drilled into you. Only I hold the power of your degradation in my hands—so when I call you a needy little whore, know that I mean I want you for who you are and I know without a doubt that you want me too, so I had better find your cunt dripping for me."

Her chest heaved as she clenched her jaw, emotions and thoughts flickering across her face so fast that I struggled to predict her response. I honestly didn't know what I expected, but when she spat in my face and sneered, I found her continued defiance … enticing.

Pressing my nose to hers, I held her stare, waiting for her to break first. But this girl—she had nerves of steel.

"Tell me your worth," I demanded. Tell me anything.

My eyes flicked back and forth between hers, but she bit her tongue, fighting me even on eye contact, refusing to blink—break first. She was unyielding.

Relenting, I gave in. "Fine, you made your choice."

Pulling a strip of fabric from my pack pocket, I tied it around her mouth, forcing her silence. She fought against the gag, swinging her head back and forth, but I have had years of experience and had it tied off firmly before she could stop me.

"If you won't freely give me what I ask, then I won't allow

you to speak when you choose."

She didn't make a sound as I stepped around her. Her eyes followed my every step intently, unwavering, as though she were the predator and I were the one who was her subservient prey. I didn't like that. It was unnerving.

I pulled the blindfold from my pocket, securing it over her eyes and cutting off her sight. A frustrated sound rolled from her throat, giving me a small bit of satisfaction.

I traced my fingers along her clavicle, down between her breasts. Her sharp, short breaths were fueled by a mix of rage and arousal. I watched as her abdomen and ass clenched when my fingers moved to grasp her breast—squeezing firmly.

A needy whimper fell from behind the gag. She would deny just how much this was turning her on if I could only manage to get her to talk. So, for the moment, I would prove to her just how alike we were, how much she loved being a willing submissive.

I released her breast, my hand dropping lower down her abdomen. Sliding my hand inside her underwear, I cupped her cunt, pressing my hand firmly against her flesh.

She was so fucking aroused that slick warmth coated my fingers before they sunk into her. I groaned, matching her own moans at the connection.

"You like that? Being restrained and letting me force myself on you? You're a sick fucking bitch. I bet you would take my fist and still beg for more, you needy whore."

I curled my fingers up, forcing two straight inside of her, proving just how badly she wanted it, sliding them in and out slowly.

Her muffled moans rang out from behind the gag. The rocking of her hips on my hand to gain friction and seek pleasure hardened my cock.

"Fuck!" She was so much more responsive to my methods than I could have ever imagined.

I rocked the heel of my palm against her swollen clit, while my fingers rammed into her roughly. She matched my tempo with the rocking of her hips. She was already close to coming, and *fuck*, I was about to come too, with no contact.

Before she could get off, I withdrew my hand. Her muffled cries of protest pleased me.

Finally, we were getting somewhere.

Raising my hand into the light, spreading my fingers, I watched her glistening arousal cling like a web and coat my hand.

I put my index finger in my mouth and tasted her. I moaned at my first taste of her. Ambrosia. I knew she would taste like my new favourite flavour.

I yanked the blindfold off, watching her blink a few times until stunning eyes came into focus, before settling on me with a glare.

Oh yeah, she was shitty that she didn't get off. I smirked at the venom in her gaze; it was such a fucking turn-on. Holding my cunt-smeared fingers up in front of her, I ran them down her face, smearing her mascara with her arousal.

Fuck me, that's a sexy look.

"I can't wait until mascara runs down your pretty cheeks from gagging too much on cock. I'll make sure you keep it applied at all times for those moments. There is no bigger turn-on than knowing I'm ruining perfection with my cock."

She yanked against her restraints, screaming incoherent, muffled obscenities from behind the gag. There were definitely a few threats of violence in there. I chuckled.

"Don't worry, your mouth will be just as much of a mess. I promise deep red lipstick will be smeared across your face in time, then I will paint you with my cum, and you will thank me for my gift."

I ran my hand down the front of straining pants, palming my erection at the thought. She tracked my movements, her eyes widening when she caught sight of the outline of my cock.

"You like what you see?"

Her eyes flicked up to my face with a glare before redirecting her attention away. I laughed walking behind her. Grasping her by the throat, I wrapped an arm around her pelvis, pressing my hips firmly against her ass. Her breath caught by the action, and she stiffened briefly before subtly pressing back against me. She could deny how much she wanted this to herself, try to lie to my face, but her body betrayed her. She was just as fucked up as I was.

"Soon enough, my dark little shadow. You will know just how good I can make you feel. But first…."

I pulled her pants down in one fluid motion, stepping back and tossing them aside before she could kick me again. But she didn't flinch or indicate that she was going to fight me. We were making progress.

I approached her slowly, noting the conflicting emotions crossing her face. Unable to resist, I kissed her covered mouth as I gripped her underwear and pulled at it, trying to rip it free from her body. It cut into her body, forcing her to cry out in discomfort when the material wouldn't give way.

Well, fuck, that didn't go as planned. What were they made of?

"Shhhh," I crooned, retrieving a flick knife from my pocket. I cut her underwear free, then directed the blade up cutting through her top, then between her breasts, slicing through the lace there.

Her breathing was heavy as she stood motionless, while I held the blade so close to her flesh.

"Now be a good girl and let's see how well you take my fist."

There was the unmistakable sound of her breath hitching, and body stiffening.

Slowly, she turned her head to try to see me. There was an unmistakable expression of fear in her eyes, which widened when she caught sight of the dark look on my face. Finally, acknowledging the real me. Her head was shaking, tears welling in her eyes, making them look like fractured crystals with a silent plea for me not to do what I promised.

"I will work it in slowly, then… then, I will take your ass when you are done writhing in pleasure."

She screamed out through her gag, pleading with me–pleading for me to stop, but I knew better. I knew what she really wanted, what she craved, what she needed. She needed her options taken from her; she needed to be forced, needed to have her eyes opened, and I was going to be the one to introduce her to her own unbridled desires, without limits.

I ran my hand down her back, slowly meeting the roundness of her plump backside. I gave it a firm squeeze.

She jerked her hips away, squeezing her knees together tight, as if that would be enough to stop what was happening.

"Relax, you will feel nothing but pleasure," I assured her, pressing my fingers between her cheeks then sliding them down to meet her dripping cunt.

"You are already so receptive to my touch." I sank four fingers into her knuckle deep, holding still as her head dropped back with desire, her legs opening willingly of their own accord.

I smiled at her response to my touch, laying featherlight kisses over the side of her hips, while thrusting my fingers in and out.

She was so tight that I should have eased her into this with one additional finger at a time, but I had the feeling she would enjoy the slight discomfort of being stretched. I was right.

When her heavy breathing morphed into deep moans, I withdrew my hand, moving back around to the front of her body. I lowered the gag across her mouth, crushing my mouth against hers before she could demand I stop. I dove my tongue between her lips, exploring every inch inside roughly. She reciprocated without hesitation, opening her mouth wider for my assault, returning the ambush back onto me. I pulled back, both of us breathing heavily, her lips red and puffy and, as promised, her lipstick was smeared across her face and no doubt mine as well. With the hand I had inside of her, I ran my thumb across her bottom lip then shoved two fingers to the back of throat expecting her to gag. The slut only opened her mouth wider, her eyes smiling back at me with challenge.

I raised my brows in surprise. "No gag reflex," I noted, pulling my hands free. "Pain it is then, to spill your tears and paint your face with your ruined makeup."

She opened her mouth to protest, but I pinched her lips together between my fingers, preventing her from doing anything but grunt.

"Your first warning. Stop fighting me, or I will make you bleed. The only sound I want to hear from your lips is when you cum on my fist, then when I fuck your arse, do you understand?"

I released her lips. "But …"

"Nup!" I cut her off, holding up my switchblade I retrieved from my pocket in warning, wiggling it back and forth in front of my face. "Do you understand?"

I watched her closely as she considered the options posed. She looked straight past the blade as if it wasn't even there, her gaze bearing straight into my eyes. With a heavy scowl on her face, she gave a single nod, keeping her lips held together tightly, but I could see the clear and evident defiance in her eyes. There was a fire igniting there. Challenging and fierce. Yes, baby, fight me. I want you to fight me. It will make the highs feel so much more euphoric.

"Good girl. Now spread those pretty thighs. I want to taste you on my lips instead of my fingers."

Obliging me, she spread her legs wide, allowing her weight to pull on her wrists above her head, despite how uncomfortable or painful it was. But she never let on at her discomfort. The heavy-gauge chain whined in response to the shifting weight. She lifted her head, examining it, to no doubt ascertain whether it would hold.

While she was distracted, I dropped to my knees before her, grabbing one leg, I lifted it onto my shoulder and met her centre with my open mouth, my nose pressing into her slit against the sensitive bud. I inhaled deeply as I tongue-fucked her, smearing her delicious essence across my face.

"Fuck!" she screamed, bucking against my face, raising her other leg onto my other shoulder so my head was held captive between her thick thighs. I moaned into her as she continued writhing desperately against my face while I was sucking, nibbling and lapping greedily at her arousal. Her hips frantically gyrating against my face and her heavy panting let me know how close she was. I pulled my head back, sucking in a deep breath, and I blew on her sensitive flesh as I plunged three then four fingers deep inside of her. Then, I bit down on her clit, earning her the release that had been building up. I sucked feverishly on her as she peaked, working my hand inside her up to my knuckles as she rode out her orgasm. As she began coming down, I curled my fingers together, tucking my thumb in, slowly working my hand in and out as I licked from her opening to her clit in long strokes, before sucking her clit into my mouth and starting again.

"Please. I can't," her breathless begging told me she was close again. "No more… it's too much."

I growled against her cunt, then slapped my free hand across her ass as I continued working my hand inside her gradually. The moment my hand connected a second time, she came undone again, flooding my palm with her release and opening her up enough for me to force my hand further inside.

Her head was thrown back as she screamed hoarsely into the air, between gasping breaths. Her skin was slick with sweat and shuddering of its own volition.

"No more …" she whimpered, "it's too much."

I pulled my face away, my hand thrusting in and out, picking up speed. "You are doing beautifully. A little more,

I'm almost there."

With my free hand, I rolled her clit then flicked it, feeling her muscles contract around my hand coinciding with her moans. Then I slid my fist deep into her wet cunt up to my wrist easily as I continued my assault on her, rubbing a circular motion on her swollen clit, pumping my hand in and out of her roughly, punching her deep in her begging cunt.

"Oh, my God. Oh, my God. No, no, no, no more," she whimpered before voicelessly screaming out in ecstasy, flooding me in her orgasm—squirting across my chest and drenching me in her release. She let out a small mewl, then passed out with exhaustion, her head lolling forward.

I stood looking down at the moist claim she left on me with a grin. I was eager for a repeat performance as soon as she was capable. Fuck, I think I would push her boundaries and claim her again before she was capable. Break her in brutally, to give her a taste of what she can expect. I know she could take it. She just proved that and would probably thrive on the mercilessness of my ways.

Brushing the sweaty strands of hair from her face, I kissed her temple. She did so well; I knew she was special. A diamond that was just waiting to be unearthed. Forged under the pressures and restraints of life.

Lifting her weight into my arms, I unclamped the shackle

from her restraints with one hand and carried her to the bed, laying her unconscious body on her side. I wasn't done with her yet.

Opening the bedside drawer, I pulled out the lube, dropping it beside her on the bed, then slowly began undressing, watching the steady rise and fall of her chest and admiring her thick curves. She was crafted just for me. Created for my dark side.

I peppered soft kisses down the length of her body until I met her arse, then I sank my teeth into the meaty flesh, marking her so every time she sat down, she would think of me. A small whimper escaped her mouth, but she didn't react otherwise, still too exhausted.

Opening the lube, I squirted some into my hand, working it up and down my engorged cock as I lined up behind her. I wasn't going to prep her for anal. I wanted her tight around me.

Rubbing my dick back and forth along her crack with my hand wrapped around the end of it, I found her hole with my index finger then positioned the head against the tight entrance, pushing in slowly.

Fuck, maybe I shouldn't have forgone the prep. I was going to blow my load before I was fully seated inside. I took a steadying breath and thrust into the hilt, taking pleasure in her unconscious whimpers as I sodomised her. The feeling of being buried inside of her was unlike any fuck I had ever had before. It was beyond all expectations, and there was no way I would ever find anyone as perfect as her. I knew it at that moment. She was it for me.

As I picked up my thrusts into her ass, there was no way I was ever going to let her go even if it meant keeping her permanently chained to my bed. She was mine.

With that thought, I let out a guttural moan, pulling her body firmly against mine and spilling inside of her. I buried my face in the back of her head, closing my eyes and inhaling her scent. I was intoxicated by this woman. She had no idea how possessed I was with her.

"I'm keeping you until the day I die, and even then my soul will be connected to yours and haunt you into the afterlife. You are never leaving me," I whispered, finally feeling sated.

I relaxed into a deep sleep, still seated inside her ass with a semi-soft cock, cradling her body so it snuggled into mine. The perfect fit, as if she was made for me.

Kira

21

I woke up lying down, my hands still restrained but now in front of me. My body ached and was sore in places I hadn't expected, yet there was a strange sense of satisfaction lingering beneath it all. It was a feeling that I had never been able to achieve alone.

Part of me wondered if all of this had been one of my dreams—an alternate reality where my darkest desires were played out. It felt wrong to have enjoyed what happened. I was drugged, kidnapped and raped, for fucksake. But there wasn't a part of me that didn't enjoy every second of it, even at the beginning when I wasn't sure if my life balanced on the edge of a deranged serial killer being pissed off by my defiance. It was a thrill that made me feel alive.

I feigned sleep, feeling him moving around the bed behind me with incoherent muttering, his arms caging me in against his naked body. When he moved, I could feel his erection inside my arse. It was a weird feeling, and I was too scared to move just in case I woke him from whatever nightmare he was experiencing. When his hand grabbed my throat tightly and he began shifting his hips, moving himself in and out of me, I tried digging my fingers into his hand in an attempt to free his grip from my neck.

"Stop," I urged. "I can't… I can't breathe."

His hold was strong, and I was unable to decipher whether he was still sleeping. Still, I clawed and slapped his hand, feeling it tighten as he continued to fuck me mercilessly, grunting with frustration.

My legs kicked frantically as I attempted to arch myself away from his hold—anything to gain freedom before he killed me.

Just as my fight weakened, his movements froze. I heard his breath catch, and then he released his grip on my neck, allowing me to gasp for breath.

"Fuck," he murmured. Clearly realising what he had done in his sleep.

His hips moved slowly, sliding further into me, causing him to groan in both pleasure and regret at what his sleep-stated body was doing to me.

"Please." I don't know what I was asking for. I was still so sore, but it felt so good.

Trent let out a heavy sigh into my hair, running the hand that choked me moments ago with a slow, gentle motion from my shoulder to my elbow and back up again. His hips were still gently rocking against me.

"I didn't mean to … I was …fuck!" He rocked deep inside me. "You feel better than anything I've experienced before."

He pulled me firmly against his chest, tucking an arm under my head to squeeze my breast in his hand, the other arm came around my waist with his fingers finding their way to my still tender clit where he began rubbing, while he picked up pace again, fucking my arse.

"I'm so sore," I complained with a grimace, doing my best not to squeeze around him and make the discomfort worse.

"Shh," he kissed my shoulder, grunting in pleasure. "I'm nearly there, beautiful."

His fingers picked up pace, bringing me closer to an orgasm. I moaned without meaning to, feeling wrong for enjoying what this man was doing to me.

"That's it, baby. Show me what a good little cum slut you are. You take my cock so well, you were made for me. I'm going to fuck you so hard you won't be able to run away."

I don't know if it was his dirty words, the expertise way his fingers moved against me knowing just how to make me pliant in his hands, or if it was his thick cock inside of me, but whatever it was sent me careening into an intense orgasm. My arse cheeks tightened around him as I clenched, forcing his own release and filling me with his cum, with his endless grunts and groans lasting almost as long as the act itself. When he was done, he slid himself free from me, causing a wince from my body at being used.

"Come on, let's get you showered. I need to take care of you and wash the shit off my dick so I don't get a UTI."

I rolled onto my back wide eyed scrunching my nose in disgust. "Oh my God, I'm so sorry." I don't know why I was apologising. It wasn't as if I gave him permission or had any control over my body's natural ability to digest food.

He laughed and shrugged as if it were no big deal. "Unless you douche beforehand, it's normal. Doesn't bother me, it all washes off."

I was still screwing up my nose, feeling repulsed and embarrassed.

"Hey."

He leaned down in front of me, kissing the tip of my nose. The tenderness was polar opposite of how he had been treating me. Perhaps he just needed a fuck?

"A bit of shit on my dick doesn't bother me. I take a dump each day just as you do. It's just the leftover digested food your body doesn't need. It's already at some point been in your mouth, just in a different form. And if it really bothered me, I wouldn't be fucking your arse."

He stared at me, watching my reaction. When I relaxed my face, he cupped my cheek and brushed his lips on mine.

"Now, if you want, I can release the restraints so it's easier to wash in the shower. We both have BO, morning breath, and no doubt need a good feed and some water. Will you promise to behave?"

I nodded. I was too sore to even attempt to escape anyway, not that I was sure I even wanted to. Did Stockholm syndrome set in this early, or had I indulged in too many dark romance novels?

"I'll do whatever you want," I answered too eagerly.

He studied me, trying to see any sign that I was lying. When satisfied with my response, he unclipped the pendant on the chain around his neck and inserted it into the cuffs, releasing my wrists. I rubbed my wrists where the metal had bitten in, before standing on wobbly legs.

"The toilet's in here, behind the shower. There's a door separating it, so feel free to use it while I get started in the shower."

I nodded slowly, following him into the bathroom, feeling every bit of abuse my body had sustained the day before.

After I had relieved myself, I was flushing the toilet when I heard Trent's raised voice and a *thump*.

Shit, he was calling out to me.

I hurriedly washed my hands in the toilet cubicle and opened the door, expecting to see him on the other side. A wave of relief coursed through me when he wasn't standing there. The sound of the shower running filled the room, steam already clouding the air.

"Trent?" I called out hesitantly. No answer.

Clearing my throat, I called again.

I was just about to open the frosted glass door of the shower when panic seized me. A large hand suddenly wrapped across my face, covering my mouth and nose, smothering my breath. Another arm coming around my torso, pinning my arms to my side, pulling me firmly against the firm chest of a much larger body.

Hot breath tickled the side of my neck.

"Don't scream and you won't get hurt, pretty girl," a deep voice rumbled in my ear. "Nod if you understand."

I gave a hurried nod as I tried to breathe past the hand on my face.

"Good girl," he crooned and licked up the side of my cheek slowly, causing my body to tremble in fear.

He let out a throaty chuckle in my ear before he nipped at my lobe. "I love the taste of your fear, it's intoxicating. You will be so much fun to break."

I whimpered and attempted to pull free of his forceful grip, but he only tightened it on me.

"Don't fucking try me or I will hurt you, and that isn't what I want right now…that will come later…."

I was vaguely aware of something else being said, but with my oxygen cut off, I fell unconscious.

Kyden

22

Trent didn't know I had followed him, using a motorbike I just so happened to find in a locked shed on the side of the property. It was supposed to be an area that was off-limits, holding the owner's personal effects, but since when has that ever stopped me? Besides, if they didn't want it touched, why leave it there in the first place? I saw it as doing a service, anyway. If they were gone for months, then taking the bike for a run would prevent it from seizing up, sitting there abandoned.

I watched as he stalked and then took the girl for himself. That wasn't the deal. It doesn't go down like that. We are all supposed to share our victims. He was being greedy by not sharing and thinking he could keep her for himself.

I watched as he tormented her with his own perverse sexual urges, waiting to see blood spill. Fuck, I was desperate to see how nicely she bled. I watched through the open window as he plunged his hand deep into her gaping cunt, which he had stretched out nice and wide. His fist slick with her arousal, taking everything he was giving her like a well-trained slut.

My cock hardened, and I bit down on my lip until it bled, needing the coppery hit on my tastebuds.

"Come on, come on, rip her insides out through her cunt," I whispered to myself, freeing my cock from my shorts and squeezing the tip to the point of pain. I groaned as he all but punched his fist into her roughly, and she writhed in pleasure at his brutality.

That's it, pretty girl. You will take our torture like the little fucked-up bitch I know you are.

I slid my grip back and forth along my length, getting off on the dry friction, watching as the slut squirted all over Trent, drenching him with her orgasm.

Fuck, she was made for us. None of our victims had ever responded like that.

My vision began darkening as I came close to getting off. No, no, not yet. I gritted my teeth and tensed, fighting my body's natural response of forcing me into oblivion.

Trent had moved to unshackle her; a trail of blood ran down her wrist where the cuff had dug into her wrist holding all of her weight. That one sight was all it took to feed the monster inside me. My balls tightened, and ropes of cum exploded from my dick, spraying up the side of the paint-peeled wall below the window.

With a wave of dizziness, I collapsed on the ground in a fucking heap, with sleep stealing me.

When I awoke, it was dark outside. I was on my back lying in overgrown grass, and I could feel bugs crawling across my skin. My limp dick hanging at the top of my shorts and the feeling of something scuttering across it had me whacking my groin in a flurry of desperation before I had an unwanted visitor climb up into my urethra.

When I had finished jumping around like I had ants in my pants, literally and figuratively smacking the critters free of my body and shuddering in repulsion, I peered back into the window where my *'associate'* and our new plaything were last lingering.

The room was cloaked in darkness, but there was enough light filtered in from the full moon to illuminate their figures curled up together on the bed.

He could have at least left her hanging from the roof while he slept. At least prolong the torment and lessen the risk of her escaping. Fucking amateur.

I was reeling from the betrayal Trent had inflicted on me—on all of us. When Grady finds out, he would more than likely kill Trent. I smiled at the thought. I loved watching Grady come undone. He didn't hold back or try to suppress who he is at the core. He is unapologetically free and openly unhinged, without apology or remorse. It was the raw authenticity that had drawn me to him in the first place.

After a sordid encounter catching him masterbating over somnophilia videos, I divulged with him my own fantasies regarding the often disparaged kink. Naturally, of course, it took Grady until the first moment my hypersomnia took me for him to indulge my fantasies. Waking up and finding videos of him using my unconscious body for his every whim was erotic and a fucking massive turn-on. I usually sought him out after watching the video he left me. In return, he always let me fuck his throat raw while I rewatched the video. I would have him on his knees before me, my hand gripping his hair tight pulling to the point of pain and his palm in my mouth, bleeding from my teeth or blade, either way he floods my mouth with his blood filling that need I have in order to cum.

I needed to get back to Airbnb. The thoughts were going to send me into a tailspin of bloodlust if I waited much longer. We are one another's vice between kills. At least our next victim has already been found, so it means less waiting around and scooping for one. I just had to deal with Trent first.

Well, he was about to discover what happens when you betray us.

The front door was unlocked, creaking as I pushed it. Idiot, he should know better than to make such a reckless mistake like that; anyone could just walk in. Fuck I just have.

I paused briefly, making sure he didn't come stumbling to the door with a gun. When there was no sound of movement, I edged through the gap in the door, padding silently through the open layout of the house.

I wanted to know how the fuck he had found this place. It didn't appear entirely uninhabited. Then again, I didn't look around the perimeter. If I had, I would probably have found the owner dead, discarded haphazardly somewhere nearby to dispose of when he was done.

I stood at the entrance of the bedroom, taking in the scene before me. The girl lay naked, curled on her side with her hands cuffed in front of her. With Trent's hand resting low on her abdomen, his fingers possessively cupping the apex of her thighs, he held her firmly against him.

I walked to the end of the bed, taking in every inch of her flesh, biting down on my lip, imagining her dark skin coated in crimson.

Fuck, she will look so pretty painted in blood.

Dragging my eyes back down her body, I kicked my head to the side, withholding the sound of a laugh when I saw her ass cheeks wrapped around Trent's hard dick. I knew he preferred anal but was in denial about his sexuality. I had pressed him on a few occasions, but I think he thought I was just fucking with him rather than wanting to fuck him. At least Gray caught on to my advances, and he is everything I could have hoped for and more.

But there was still something missing as much as I hated to admit it to him or myself. He couldn't provide me with the supple and soft flesh that only a woman can. His deep voice made my balls tighten, but the sweet whimpers from a feminine voice made my hair stand on end, sending a shiver down my spine. Fuck, I loved that feeling. If I had to choose between cock and pussy for the rest of life, I don't think I'd be able to. I would rather go without either than have to pick.

Nah, scratch that. I'm greedy and have a knack for spilling blood, so I would carve my name into whoever threatened me to pick, then take both anyway.

Pretty girl began stirring in her sleep, so I stepped back behind the heavy curtain and waited for my opportunity. Soon she would be in my grasp, a cocooned caterpillar begging to be freed so she can spread her wings. Only for me to brutally tear them from her and show her just how fragile acceptance of change can make you.

Kyden

23

"The fuck are you doing here, Ky?"

Trent stepped back aghast, looking at me like he was staring at a ghost. He closed the glass shower door where he was waiting for the water to warm. The distinctive sound of the toilet flushing made both of our heads swing in that direction, reminding me I needed to be quick.

"Making sure you share," I informed him.

Before he could blink, I threw a fist, catching his temple and knocking him out cold. His body hit the shower door, making the glass rattle. I caught him under the arms before he hit the floor and dragged his heavy-as-fuck, naked body from the bathroom, dumping him on the bedroom floor.

"Trent?" her soft, uncertain voice filtered through from the bathroom. She called his name again.

I stepped into the bathroom and watched as she reached for the shower door with trembling fingers. Before she made contact, I pounced, wrapping my hand around her face with my other arm around her middle, pulling her close to me.

Her body moulded against mine perfectly as if she were created just for me.

Pushing my face into the side of her neck, inhaling her scent of stale sweat and fear, my arousal sprung back to life.

She squirmed against my erection in an attempt to pull away.

"Don't scream and you won't get hurt, pretty girl," I warned, not wanting her to waste that voice until I could make her sing with my blade. "Nod if you understand."

Her head rapidly moved up and down under my hand that was cutting off her air supply. I could feel her racing pulse against my lips on her neck, invoking the need to cut her open and spill her blood. But I didn't want to rush this.

"Good girl," I praised, noting the way she softened slightly at my words—or perhaps it was the oxygen deprivation. Either way, I couldn't help licking the side of her face slowly, tasting the saltiness on her skin.

She shuddered at the contact. Oh yeah, she was enjoying this. I chuckled to myself, nipping at her ear.

"I love the taste of your fear, it's exhilarating. You will be so much fun to break."

She whimpered and attempted to fight me, but I knew it was all an act. She wanted this, I could see it in her eyes.

I tightened my hold on her. "Don't fucking try me or I will

hurt you, and that isn't what I want right now…that will come later. First, I need to get you somewhere else and secure my very bad friend."

She had finally stopped struggling. I realised that my hold was so tight that she was unconscious. Releasing my hand from her face so I didn't kill her yet, I scooped her up in my arms and carried her to the bed. Lying her out, I brushed the strands of hair from her face, rubbing them between my fingers, taking her in. She really was exquisite and unique. With a splattering of freckles decorating her warm skin, the cutest nose, and those lips… fucking hell. She had an innocence about her that was captivating, that was until you saw the shadows of darkness dancing around behind her eyes. With my hand still tangled in her hair, I snapped a rubber band from around my wrist, pulling half of it into a loose ponytail beside her head, then did the same to the other side. I was planning on asking Grady to put them on my ball sack so I wouldn't come when he had his way with me tonight, wanting the painful edge of blue balls so when he choked on my cock when I woke up it would be a more intense release. But making my pretty girl look even more innocent with these two little pony-tails is worth the small sacrifice.

Adjusting myself in pants, I contemplated taking advantage

of her unconscious form. But I did not want to miss an opportunity to hear her cries of suffering.

Trent disturbed my pondering as he made a small noise behind me, alerting me to his waking. I wasn't having that. Pulling a syringe from my cargo shorts, I popped the cap, piercing his skin, making sure he stayed knocked out a little longer.

"Hmm, what to do with you," I mused, narrowing my eyes on the man who betrayed us—the man I considered a friend.

I unsheathed my knife, tapping it against my lower lip. I squatted down beside Trent, cocking my head in thought. I considered just slitting his throat for his deception—but perhaps that was taking it a step too far.

I tipped the point of the knife forward, running it across Trent's naked body, not quite breaking his skin, fighting the urge to flay him. I sheathed my knife before I succumbed to my urges, formulating a plan.

"You, my man, are going in time-out," I told his unconscious body. "I hope it gives you time to reflect and think about your actions."

Hoisting Trent's oversized body up, I clumsily dragged him through the house and across the gravel driveway, then remembered I didn't have the car keys. Dropping him like a sack of potatoes, I saw the gravel rash across his legs from being dragged across the ground.

"Oopsie. I don't suppose you would believe me if I told you it was an accident?" Naturally, Trent didn't respond. "Didn't think so," I sighed, leaving him to bask under the sun while I went back inside to poke through his clothes. I found two sets of keys—one set belonged to whoever's vehicle sat in the drive and the other was for the 4x4 Trent had been driving.

I made sure my pretty girl was still peacefully asleep before heading back outside.

Popping the boot of the sedan, I awkwardly hefted Trent's unconscious body up, twisting his thick limbs in and around him in the most uncomfortable way I could bend them. Then, unable to resist, I gave his exposed ballsack a hard whack before slamming the boot closed and tossing the keys on the ground.

I began walking back to the house to collect my prize when I realised my mistake. The bike I rode here sat in front of the house. I could take one of the cars, but I didn't know how to fucking drive a car—thanks to my slight ailment.

Running a hand down my face, I groaned. "I really didn't think this through."

Oh well, it's too late now. Improvise, overcome, adapt or some shit. I would just have to tie my girl to my back and take her back that way. But first, I better get her dressed and dose her with a sedative so she doesn't wake and freak out on the back of the bike.

Trent

24

My eyelids felt heavy; a dull pain radiated from my temple. Bringing my hand to the side of my face, I noted the discomfort of my limbs, which were contorted around me at a weird angle. Blinking into the darkness, I tried to recall my last memory.

"Fucking Ky!"

I did not know where I was, only that I was in an enclosed space and it was stiflingly hot. I manoeuvred my limbs as best as I could in the cramped space to relieve the discomfort. My hand brushed against a smooth, cold bar. Feeling the shape, I took stock of my surroundings and realised with growing horror that I was in the boot of my car.

"Motherfucker." Ky!

If he hurt Kira, he was a dead man.

I fumbled in the dark until I found the boot release, gasping as the slightly cooler air rushed in, offering me some semblance of freedom. My legs sent shockwaves of pain radiating up to my hips as I curled them, then stretched them out, my back stiff and sore from the cramped position, and for some fucking reason my balls were tender when I moved to sit up, putting a little weight on them. I did a quick check, cupping them to make sure there was no docking ring there, and making sure Kyden hadn't amputated one. I wouldn't have put it past him. Correction, I wouldn't have put the first one past Grady, but I wouldn't be surprised if he wasn't in cahoots on this.

My bare feet hit the rough gravel on the driveway, the sharp edges of the small stones digging into the soles of my feet as I hurriedly hopped across them, taking my naked arse inside in search of my dark little shadow. Tearing through each room, I found no evidence of either Kira or Kyden.

"Fuck!" I yelled, throwing my fist into a wall, tearing open the skin on my knuckles.

Stomping back to the bedroom where my clothes were haphazardly discarded, I quickly dressed and threw my belongings into the duffle bag, then ran to my car barefoot, ignoring the added pain from being on the rough surface again.

Tearing off up the driveway in a cloud of dust, I ripped the car out onto the main road, tail-whipping the rear end not bothering to check if the coast was clear of other motorists. Ignoring the speed limit, I headed to the Airbnb, knowing

Kyden would have returned there with the girl I had single-handedly captured.

Frustration and anxiety clawed at me as I slammed my hand against the steering wheel, the uncertainty of how long I'd been out or what had happened gnawing at me.

"Fuck. Fuck. Fuck!" I yelled over and over. The only word I could coherently form as my brain was overthinking every worst-case scenario in my head, expecting to find Kira deceased when I arrived.

Time seemed to stand still as the drive back to town stretched on longer than ever, despite keeping my speed over the sixty-k posted sign.

"Come on, you piece of shit car, go faster."

I frustratedly rammed the accelerator flat to the floor with all my strength as if it would actually increase the speed.

Chris

25

With the ultimate fuckup of premature deaths from our last two subs, I was back to square one. It was a shame too, because the last one was such an easy target. We could have had her here and been getting off before disposing of her body with no one the wiser. I hadn't even seen any missing person reports or heard reports on police scanners that her body had been discovered. Clearly, few hiked through that area of the trails.

I had been staring at the screen on my laptop for the last hour without paying any attention, zoning out completely. I had found another potential girl, but I didn't really want her. My mind kept slipping back to the girl from the coffee shop and the chemist. I knew the others had sensed the possibility there too. She wasn't our usual MO, but something about her appealed to each of us in a different way.

I tried searching for any details I could find on her through social media, the pharmacy website, the community pages, and newspapers, but there was nothing. It was like she didn't even exist.

She was a perfect subject, but Trent had voiced his opinion loudly that he didn't want her. Actually, come to think of it, he didn't; he only rejected the idea of her being *used* by us for our urges—repeatedly emphasising that.

I ran my hand down my face in frustration.

"I need coffee," I murmured to myself, standing from the chair, which had almost moulded to a permanent imprint of my arse at this point.

I did not know where Trent, Grady and Kyden had disappeared to. That in itself was enough to worry about. Especially because two of the three needed almost constant monitoring.

As the kettle came to a boil, I heard the distinctive sound of a motorbike approaching the property.

Walking to the side of the table, I armed myself with my throwing knives and gun, which was sitting next to the laptop. Keeping close to the wall, I peered around the side of the window through the sheer curtain, ready to fire or drop if shots were fired.

I kept my eyes on the two figures straddling the bike as it slowly rolled along the driveway, having to do a double-take to make sense of what I was seeing.

"Kyden?" Where the fuck did he get a motorbike? And who

is on the back? The passenger looked female. Oh no, please tell me he hasn't picked up a sub on his own. Dread filled my stomach with the repercussions that this could cause.

Storming through the front door, ready to tear him a new one for the irresponsibility—finding a potential sub without me first checking her lifestyle or considering the possible attention her disappearance would draw—I stumbled back and froze when my sight locked onto the girl he had physically bound to his back. The very same girl that had been haunting my thoughts ever since we first laid eyes on her. The one I had been quietly obsessing over, and mentally chastising myself for the humiliating interaction between us.

"What the fuck is this, Kyden? Are you trying to get caught?" I yelled, unsure exactly how pissed I was.

Not just at the reckless way he had her noticeably restrained, but at the carelessness of the fact that he isn't allowed behind the wheel of a vehicle with his condition.

The assshole gave me an incredulous smirk as he slid from the bike with the girl still tied to his back—wearing her like a fucking backpack.

"Is she at least alive?"

Kyden glanced over his shoulder and gave her a small shake. "Yeah, I think so."

Before I could ask where he had taken her from and if he

had been spotted, Grady appeared from around the side of the house. His steps didn't falter as he took in the scene, a grin spreading across his face. He jogged over and slapped Kyden on the arm, clearly amused by the human accessory he was wearing.

"Fuckucking hell, I love you, man. Have I told you that? Is this present for me?" Grady bounced on the spot, making Kyden laugh.

"Come on, Peaches, tell me it's for me." He fluttered his lashes, sporting a flirtatious grin at Ky.

"Enough!" I snapped at Grady. "First things first. Who saw you, and how soon do we need to pack up and move on?"

Kyden rolled his eyes. "Not my first rodeo, *Sir*, and Trent is the one you need to ask that."

That made Grady and I pause.

I glanced up the driveway, unease settling in my stomach. "And where is he?"

"In the boot of the car." Kyden shrugged, like it was a perfectly normal explanation, walking up the stairs past me into the house.

"Wait, what?"

Grady came to my side, scratching his head. "I feel like I'm missing a part of the story here. Not that I'm complaining, but …"

"What did you do?" I asked with apprehension.

"He's still alive… or was when I left him," Kyden said over his shoulder, stomping through the threshold, and unceremoniously dumping the girl on the ground with one pull of the rope around his chest. Leaving her on the floor where she landed, he stepped over her and walked to the fridge, ripping open the door. I stepped cautiously over her body, doing a quick visual inspection. Seeing her unhurt and breathing, I followed Kyden into the kitchen area.

"I need you to explain exactly what the fuck is going on and in more detail that a few half-arsed answers."

Kyden frowned over my shoulder, slamming the fridge shut with a beer in his hand. I turned to where Kyden's eyes were focused to see Grady unzipping his pants over the unconscious body.

"Grady," I warned. "Whatever you were about to do, don't!"

His head snapped up with a glare. "Whatever, fucker," he snarled.

Kicking the girl in the ribs as he stepped past her, he threw himself down across the two-seater, with his pants still undone and his feet resting up on the back of the chair.

I pinched the bridge of my nose with a sigh. I didn't know where to start with this shitstorm. This already felt too messy, and I hated not being in control of these situations. There were too many unanswered questions, and we still didn't know all the details of this girl and whether she was going to be an issue for us in the long term. For all we know, between Kyden and Trent, the police could already be moving in on us.

Hell, I didn't know where Trent was other than in a boot, somewhere.

After a swig of the beer he was nursing, Kyden finally spoke. "Something hadn't been sitting right with me, so I followed Trent. He seemed … off, like he was hiding something this morning. Instead of scoping out locations that he had so generously volunteered for, he actually made a large detour in the opposite direction. It appears the wannabe leader of our team had been participating in some extracurricular activities, meeting up with a subject. Enjoying a little one on one with this precious little thing, leaving us behind."

Grady sat bolt-up, swinging his legs around to the ground.

"That fucker. I'll kill him."

"No one is killing anyone…yet!" I stated. "I need to hear from Trent first."

"Oh, piss off, Chriso. This goes against everything we work together for. We made an oath to one another, and I'm sick to fucking death of the pedestal Trent has put himself on."

Grady stood in front of me, arms crossed, giving Kyden a look asking for backup, completely ignoring the fact that his undone pants had just fallen to his ankles. He wasn't even wearing underwear, for fucksake.

What did I do to deserve this?

I chewed on my cheek, knowing there was an element of truth in Grady's words. Trent had done wrong by all of us. While each of us had nothing against a casual hookup between subjects, it was the fact that he had deceived us all, and instead of completing the task he volunteered himself for, he went after a subject who had caught all of our eyes.

Pinching the bridge of my nose, I dropped back into a chair behind me, leaning forward with my elbows on my knees. I considered how to play this out.

"Look, I'm just as pissed as the both of you are right now, but going in half-cocked, ready to spill blood without hearing his side of the story isn't going to solve the current problem." I lifted my head to my twin, watching him fight the internal battle he was having with himself not to knock me back on my arse. "I want to know why he decided to go after her…" I pointed to the unconscious girl on the floor, resisting the urge to scoop her up and lay her on the couch. "And hide it from us."

Grady ground his teeth, flaring his nostrils. Biting back his thoughts, he bent over, mooning Kyden in the process, and yanked up his pants, then gave me his back, to face Kyden as he refastened them.

"What did you see?" Grady asked.

Slightly distracted, Kyden's eyes flicked from Grady's crotch to his face, then to mine, before returning to Grady. He grimaced and scratched at his cheek.

"He got his *fill* and then snuggled with her until he fell asleep. She didn't even fight to get away when she woke, if anything she wiggled closer."

Grady fell weirdly still. "He *cuddled?*"

Kyden pulled his lips into a tight line and nodded.

"Like, arms around her, tucked in close, cuddled?"

Kyden rolled his eyes. "That is the general consensus of a cuddle, Gray."

Grady turned his head to look at the girl, his surprise shifting to confusion as he took her in. "*Huh.*"

"Did he say anything to you before you threw him in the boot?" I asked.

Kyden's mouth hitched at the corner. "He asked, *what the fuck I was doing there*? I was a little irritated and knocked him out cold before he could say a whole lot more."

I leaned back against the chair, looking up at the ceiling,

hoping for some damn miracle to solve this mess. Neither Grady nor Kyden were going to let this issue go without repercussions on Trent's end, and I was in agreement… to an extent. I just had to be careful in how I let it play out. I held the most control over Grady being his twin, and Kyden would always follow Grady's lead. So now, I had to find the best solution to manipulate Grady into not killing Trent.

The loud roar of an engine closing in from the mainroad, followed by a sharp skid, had the three of us flying towards the front door ready to fight or fly depending on the company. Kyden was first through the door, bounding over our unconscious company—the main cause behind all the drama.

Trent's car came into view, flying down the driveway leaving a cloud of dust in his wake. He pulled up directly in front of the house, skidding the car to a stop with the handbrake, causing the engine to sputter as it stalled. He leapt out out the door, which was opened before the engine cut off, rushing Kyden with his fist already pulled back.

"Woah." I jumped down the steps in a single bound and stepped between him and Kyden. "We all need to talk."

"Talk?" Trent's face was red with fury. "I don't want to talk. This fucker shut me in the boot and …"

"He told us."

Trent snapped his head to me, shock and rage marring his face. "And you're on his side?"

"I wasn't the one keeping a sub to themselves," Ky interjected.

Trent attempted to shove past me, his fist pulled back again, ready to strike. I grabbed Trent around the chest, holding him back.

"Settle the fuck down," I said, in a warning tone.

In my periphery, I saw that Grady had defensively stepped in front of Kyden with a raised gun trained on Trent.

"Shoot me, you fucker, go on, I dare you," Trent challenged, lifting his chin.

"Grady put the gun down. No one is shooting anyone," I sighed.

"Give me one reason why I shouldn't fuck him up?" Grady snapped.

"Because you and I both know none of this works without him. The four of us work well together."

"Yeah, well, this shit ain't working for me right now," Grady snarled, with the gun still raised.

"Fuck," Trent struggled against me, almost overpowering me. I did the only thing I could to diffuse the situation. I hit the pressure point in his neck, knocking him out cold, letting his weight drop to the ground at my feet.

"Is he dead? Or do you want me to lay a few rounds in to be sure?"

"Put the gun away, Gray," I growled, frustration ebbing at me to take the weapon and lay a few rounds into all of them for their stupidity.

"Ky, move the girl to the spare room until we sort this shit out," I barked.

Kyden opened his mouth to object, but I raised my hand to stop him. "Not now. Let's all take five, settle the fuck down before someone does something they can't take back." I looked pointedly at Grady with the gun. "Then we can discuss all of this rationally, and figure out how to diffuse this epic fuck-up."

"This is bullshit." Grady kicked the ground and stomped inside like a petulant child.

Kyden did the creepy stare thing where he didn't blink or move. I never knew if it was his brain shutting down, forcing him to have a power nap while he was awake, or he was imagining skinning me alive. Knowing Kyden, it was the latter. I waited until he stalked off to move Kira into the spare room. I followed him inside, watching him gather her in his arms gently. He stroked her hair from her face, tracing his fingers along her cheek and then turned down the hall towards the rooms. It was a softer side that I had never witnessed from him before, and I wasn't entirely sure what to make of it.

I would check on her once I had Trent settled in his room and poured a drink or two. First, I needed some space. Night had fallen quickly while we argued, and mosquitoes had found their way inside through the open front door. I stepped outside to close it, but instead found myself wandering out onto the dark verandah.

Leaning over the edge of the railing, I let my gaze wander over the expanse of the night sky. The endless seascape of stars made me feel insignificant compared to the vast endlessness of space. The past few days—full of minor mishaps and frustrations—seemed trivial in the grand scheme of things. Annoying, yes, but just an inconvenience. And in comparison to everything we had faced together, this was nothing more than an irritating itch. At least that was the lie I was telling myself as I tried to force the idea from my mind that this girl held more of an influence over us all than I cared to admit to myself.

Kira

26

I felt my consciousness return in stages

It was difficult to fight past the heavy fog consuming my mind. I was struggling to recall how I found myself in a position that was rendering me unable to focus or think coherently.

Distant voices were muffled somewhere in the distance; I could not make out the words or recognise the voices.

Vaguely, I was aware of someone trying to shake me awake. Instead, I allowed the heaviness to consume me again instead of facing whatever predicament I was in. I needed more sleep and needed time to understand why I felt so sore and heavy.

The next time I woke, I instantly regretted the decision to open my eyes. Blinking several times, the first thing that came into focus were heavy chains that hung from the ceiling overhead. Attached to a thick shackle, a hook stained with crimson swung above me, only making the nausea I woke with worse.

Turning my head to empty the bile from my throat, I was met with resistance. A firm pressure encapsulated my head. Not just my head I quickly came to realise, but my entire body was strapped down and I was unable to feel a stitch of clothing on my bare flesh, only the uncomfortable pressure of leather restraints.

Choking on my stomach contents or lack of, I spluttered as I tried to expel the liquid. The acidic bile burnt painfully at the back of my throat and nose as it forced its way free. Unable to find oxygen as I drowned, I began to panic, attempting feebly to thrash free under my restraints that dug in painfully the more I attempted to break free.

Where was Trent? Had he done this to me?

Deep laughter echoed around me, only increasing my panic and causing me to inhale the bile so it filled my lungs making my chest burn.

"Welcome back to the land of the living, precious," the deep voice taunted. "You will regret it soon enough. It won't be long lasting though," he promised with an unnerving chuckle. "Just long enough for us to have a little fun."

My vision began darkening with those final words as my oxygen depleted, and I drowned in my vomit. As my eyelids fluttered closed, whatever I was strapped to began moving under me, with a mechanical clicking, then my entire body was thrown face down, leaving me suspended by the restraints that were holding me immobile, as they bit into my flesh under my weight.

The position allowed a small amount of liquid to be expelled from my mouth freely, but I could already feel my consciousness slipping away again.

Suddenly my eyes flew open as a heavy fist met my stomach radiating pain throughout, expelling some of the bile that was drowning me with the force of the hit. I was caught between choking, gasping for air and retching as my body's natural instincts took over.

Snot and saliva strung down from my face, meeting a pool of vomit I had released on the floor. I wanted to wipe it free from my face; I wanted water to alleviate the burn in my throat. I wanted to curl up on my side to ease the discomfort in my stomach.

"I will leave you hanging until you stop trying to die on me prematurely."

I made a small whimpering sound unintentionally; this only seemed to please my captor as he chuckled deeply.

Rolling my eyes to the side, I could just make him out in my peripherals as he squatted down beside me. His sinister smile spread wide; it was the only thing visible under the hood he wore disguising his other features from me. It didn't matter though, I remembered his face distinctly.

Had Trent passed me along to his friends to use for their own nefarious kinks after he had gotten what he wanted from me?

What had I gotten myself into?

Opening his mouth, he poked out his tongue, licking back and forth along his bottom lip before sinking his teeth in firmly.

"The sweet sounds you will make for me, precious," he groaned. "Your cries will be the sweetest symphony to my ears. I want you begging my name sweetness."

He pressed his lips to mine ignoring the fact that they were covered in my own vomit. "Kyden, remember that name."

Kira

27

I was bound with coarse rope tight at my wrists and ankles, splaying my limbs out wide.

Kyden stood over me, his dark gaze raking over my body in a carnivorous manner, a blade rubbing against his stubbled cheek. He was just as devastatingly handsome as I remembered. That didn't make him any less dangerous. Even the devil was an angel once.

Positioning the tip of the blade at my chest, he pressed down firmly, cutting through the fabric and into my flesh. The sharp sting caused me to cry out, my voice muffled behind the gag.

His eyes widening, a malice grin formed on his lips when my tears spilled over as the blade travelled lower down my abdomen towards my navel.

"You bleed so pretty," he voiced lyrically. "It will be beautiful to watch you bathed in scarlet after you take the aspirin I give you. Your blood will flow like a river, your life coursing from your body before my very eyes." His face dipped down to lick a line through the cut in my flesh, making his way up my body to stop between my breasts.

He lifted his head to meet my terrified eyes, red smearing his face.

"But I want to bleed you slowly, take my time. I want to see your pain, soak in your screams."

His head leaned back, eyes closed, and a euphoric look passed over his features. When he looked back at me, it was anything but peaceful—it was terrifying.

"I want to take you apart, piece by piece. Have you balanced on the precipice of death from blood loss, only to allow you to recover enough to start all over again."

He pushed his blade against my jugular. I could feel warmth as a trickle of blood ran across my neck, fear rising inside of me as I waited for my life to be stolen.

Kyden closed the distance between our faces, his nose brushing against mine so I could smell the scent of coffee on his breath.

"I want to consume you, eat up your torment, drink your pained tears, inhale your breathy whimpers. I want to feast on you until your dying breaths, and even then I think I would be famished, never getting my fill of you. You are the most delicious, delectable thing I have ever tasted."

He licked my gagged mouth, his free hand gripping my jaw

in a painful hold, digging his fingers into my cheeks. His eyes flicked back and forth between mine, trying to get a read on me while I did everything I could to train my expression neutral. I would not bow and give him what he wanted. I would not show him the fear he was craving to see.

He licked the spilled blood on my neck with a slow motion.

"What is this hold you have over me? You are an addiction. A drug that soothes my insatiable hunger, but the moment I'm done, I will crave more from you."

He was staring as if he were waiting for me to answer, as if he could find the answers in my eyes the harder he looked.

He dropped his forehead to mine, closing his eyes. He released the hand on my jaw, yanking down the gag at the same time, but the blade at my throat remained. His hot breath now smelt of my blood.

Slowly he lifted back from me, taking with him the weapon at my throat. His eyes never once left my face as he rocked back on his heels, tapping the blade against his cheek with a deep frown settling on his face, seemingly lost in deep thought. His head kicked to the side suddenly as if an enticing thought had crossed his mind, and his menacing grin returned.

I held back my whimpers, not wanting to encourage any

more of his erratic and unhinged behaviour.

"I know, let's … spark this up a bit."

He disappeared through the door hurriedly, with an excited bounce to his step, leaving an uneasy feeling settling in my stomach.

When Kyden returned, he was joined by another male I had seen accompanying him and Trent outside the cafe. I tried to look to where they had arrived, hoping to see Trent appear, waiting for him to rescue me. I knew deep down that it was an illogical expectation. I was clearly here because his fun with me had run its course. Meaning that, once these two have had their fun, if I was correct, then I would be subject to one more male to unleash his depravity upon me.

Providing I survived Kyden's plans for me with his knife.

The accompanying male with Kyden looked questioningly at me, then cocked his head to Kyden with an expression that said, *really?*

Kyden laughed and shrugged. "She's a tough one. Wanna see just how much she can handle?"

The other man's face lit up at those words. Slowly, a devilish gleam twinkled in his eyes—his grin, all teeth. Running a thumb and index finger across his stubbled chin, I could see him contemplate the best method of torture.

I squeezed my eyes closed, not wanting to know what he

was planning. Perhaps if I ignored them and concentrated on something else, whatever they were about to impart upon me wouldn't be so bad.

"Open your eyes or I'll sew your eyelids open, precious," Kyden said, pulling the gag down from my mouth.

My eyes snapped open with a gasp. "No, no, don't," I said more forcefully than I expected.

The other man leaned over me frowning, with a look of disappointment.

"I don't know what to do with that."

He licked across his upper teeth before sucking his tongue against the back of his teeth.

"If she isn't going to beg, then I have another idea. Get the needle and thread."

What? "No, I'm not going to beg. It won't change your minds no matter what I say." I said determinedly, trying a different tactic from what they were probably used to. "I'm asking you not to do this. I don't want you to sew my eyes open. I will keep them open, I assure you."

"Oh, don't worry, we aren't going to sew your eyes open," he told me with a sly grin, reaching to take the items from Kyden.

I sighed with relief.

But then, why did he want a needle and thread? He saw the

realisation on my face. He and Kyden both chuckled darkly.

"I'm going to sew your pretty mouth closed, because you refuse to respond in the way we are used to."

What? I went to open my mouth to scream in protest, but fingers had already pinched my lips together before I could open my mouth.

Grady

28

Oh, the sound of her struggling screams behind Kyden's fingers were an aphrodisiac. The melodic screams of fear sent blood rushing to my cock. But they weren't screams of fear, they were frustration because she couldn't fight back. This was new and exhilarating. Finally, we had scored ourselves a fighter.

I wasn't quite getting the same kick that I had been from our past few subjects. It had become too repetitive with the same response each time when their life was balanced in our hands. The same lines were always repeated, "No, please don't hurt me. I'll do whatever you say. I won't tell anyone; just let me go. You don't have to do this." Yadda, yadda, yadda....

I loved this next part of what we do, the torture. I hadn't actually planned on sewing her perfect pouty lips closed. She had a raspy voice that in itself was sexy as fuck, but when she whimpered, that was pure ambrosia for my soul.

"Oh, Chocolate drop, keep making those sounds and I'll

cum in my pants."

She cut deep into me with her glare. A tingling shudder coursed through my body, giving me all kinds of jubilant feelings from that one look. I wanted to live in that sensation for a while longer, while she tickled all my happy places. Oh, hello, even the big guy wanted to say hi.

Biting my lower lip to fight the groan that wanted to escape, I kept eye contact with our little nettle as I pressed the curved needle through her upper lip, watching as she clenched her jaw so tight she almost shattered her teeth. Her face quivered as she fought back a scream.

Hmm, that is disappointing.

Adjusting the needle in her lip, I pushed it slowly inside her lower lip, feeling the resistance of her flesh, adding a slight amount of pressure until it pushed through the first few layers. Her eyes welled. When she blinked, her tears rained down the sides of her face, overflowing into her hair, but she still didn't scream.

What does a sadist have to do to earn a little appreciation for the work I am doing? At least give me a whimper, for heaven's sake.

I pushed the needle through with a forced thrust so its curve sat from the top to her bottom lip, looking like a fish caught on a hook. Then, I grabbed both sides of it and gave it a firm tug, finally earning a grunted sound from her. A minute amount of satisfaction brushed across my damned soul, feeding my hunger.

"Someone's a bit of a masochist, Ky. Should we feed her pleasure?"

Ky pressed his knife into her neck. Her eyes widened, and she gulped thickly, causing the blade to nip her skin ever so slightly. Kyden sucked in a hissed breath at the sight of the fresh blood.

"No, keep going, Gray. This is for our pleasure. I'm hoping she flinches and I slip."

She tensed, her wide eyes lingering on Kyden, with her chest heaving heavily. But not a single sound of protest fell from her throat. Oh yeah, this chicky was as fucked up as we were. We were going to have to up the ante on her if we wanted a real reaction.

I continued stitching her lips slowly while I switched between humming and whistling. Kyden's focus was held by the small holes around her mouth, where tiny drops of blood welled around the line forcing her lips together. When I was done, I gave the line a tug and tied it off, then held the excess up for Kyden to cut it with the knife he was playing with.

I stepped back, admiring my work. "What do you think? Would I make a good surgeon?"

Kyden scoffed and gave me a disbelieving look. His hand waved off my seamstress skills.

"You are delusional if you want credit for that."

Only he could get away with speaking to me that way. Probably because he lets me fuck him up in return. I pressed my hand to his chest, running my fingers down his abdomen until they reached his raging erection. He sucked in a breath when I rubbed my palm against him.

"I do love it when you talk dirty to me, Peaches."

Kyden chuckled darkly. With a heated look, he lunged for my face, ravaging my mouth with his tongue before pulling back when our little plaything let out a little whimpered moan. We both looked at her, surprised by the intrigued look in her eyes at seeing us kiss. Fuck, if she lives through the next hour, I was going to make use of that knowledge. Who knew that this prize that fell into our lives was into male on male action. I wonder how she would feel about being subjected to a bit of voyeurism while I took Ky. Then, when she was wetter than a slip and slide from watching, we could double penetrate her pussy. I always wanted to try that. Plus, any excuse to have Kyden's cock gripped tightly against mine always puts a smile on my face.

I heaved an annoyed breath when Kyden pulled away from me to approach the table. "Ready to make her scream? Let's see if we can make her tear her stitches."

I fanned myself with one hand, making a show of adjusting my hard cock with the other. "You need to stop flirting, or we won't get that far." I gave him a wink, then picked up the thick nails I found in one of the sheds outside and a hammer. I made a point of waving them in front of her eyes, waiting for a sign of fear. This girl gave me only a look that promised my death if she got free. Something about that stirred a new emotion in me, one I couldn't quite put a finger on.

"Do you know what he plans to do with these?" Kyden spoke quietly in her ear. "No? Allow me to indulge your curiosity then. Grady is going to take one of these nails and hold it against your forehead. Then, he is going to hit it with a hammer hard enough that it cracks through your skull. With a little luck, he won't go too far and hit your brain, but I can't make any promises."

The look of anger in her eyes swelled once the shock wore off, then I got what I had been waiting for. Her screams forced through her stitched lips made my body humm. I lined the nail up on her forehead, watching the fierce determination in her eyes that we weren't going to break her.

Poking my tongue out the side of my mouth to aid in concentration, I lifted the hammer. With one firm tap on the head of the nail, it embedded in her skull. Pained tears poured from her wide eyes, sparkling like diamonds as she screamed through her stitched lips.

Finally!

"When we are done, I'm plucking those beautiful eyes from your skull and keeping them in a jar," I told her.

Kyden leaned forward and licked her tears. "Maybe we should bottle her salty tears to keep her eyes in."

"Now there's an idea," I mulled. Not bad at all.

He sat back grinning like the psychopath he was, watching as blood began dribbling from the new accessory adorning Kira's smooth skin.

"One more," I told her, watching her strain under the restraints binding her in place. She could do nothing more than blink and clench her fists.

"Gray, I want to do the next one," Kyden pleaded.

My face fell. "I don't know …"

The last time we did this to a girl, he hit the hammer too hard, hitting it directly into her brain, killing her instantly. I was all too aware of the fact that he should have known better, being a genius with a medical degree or two, and all that, which made me wonder if it was intentional.

I watched him as his tongue lapped at invisible blood he was eyeing as it flowed from her wound. "…not too hard, okay?"

Kyden's gaze swung to me with an eager nod, his grabby hands stretched out, coaxing me to pass over the hammer and nail.

Reluctantly, I handed them over, hovering close as he lined them up.

Kira's screams from her sewn lips grew louder, knowing what to expect this time.

"Go for it," I said, wanting him to enjoy this just as much as I was. Look at me being a good boyfriend. Shit! Is that what I was? We hadn't actually discussed that. Too late now, I had just decided it was what we are.

"Scream for us," Kyden purred a second before he brought the hammer down onto the head of the nail. I gasped in suspense, waiting to see if he had gone too deep. Undulated relief soared through me when she cried out with pain, then tried to yell from behind her stitched lips, no doubt cursing us with every foul word in existence. I almost wanted to cut the stitches free just so I could hear how creative her vocabulary could be.

Kyden tilted his chin up to the corner of the room where the next part of our torture was set to unfold. I threw him the blindfold from my pocket to cover her eyes so she wouldn't see what was coming next. I needed her fear, and so far she wasn't delivering.

I paused once the blindfold was on. The sight of it suddenly gave me creative inspiration.

"What are you doing?" Kyden asked, confused when I turned in the wrong direction.

"I need to capture this moment," I said excitedly, running over to a narrow bench by the far wall and picking up a sketchbook and pencil I saw there.

Kyden gave me an exasperated look with a slight shake of his head, but didn't make a motion to stop me as I jumped up on top of the girl, straddling her waist. She grunted slightly, her lips straining against her stitches as my weight settled on her stomach, making her discomfort intensify.

I smiled happily as I opened the sketchbook to the first page and began sketching out her face, not including the strap that sat on her forehead above the nails. Meanwhile, I hummed happily, rocking my shoulders and wiggling my hips against her slightly. I made sure I captured the cute little freckles that peppered across her nose and the pretty bruising on her jaw, with her eyes hidden behind the blindfold and the nails embedded into her forehead with a trickle of blood. I bit down on my lower lip as I drew lines across her lips where they were stitched closed. I sketched the contours of her shoulders and her clavicles, then moved down to the beginning of the cut Kyden sliced between her breasts, where the skin parted slightly.

"I'm going to frame this so I never forget how perfectly you take our savagery. It really is a shame that you won't be around long enough for us to enjoy you more." I sighed, staring down at the artwork. "I'm a little out of practice, but what do you think, Ky? Did I capture her torment?" I spun the sketchbook around to face him.

Kyden's glower remained; however, I caught the edge of his lip ticking up as he fought back a smile, giving me the satisfaction I needed.

"You really need to stop looking at me like that, or I'll bend you over the table and have my way with you before we are finished here."

Maybe I should sketch him next. I had been wanting to draw his scowl for sometime and right now, he was the perfect specimen. I flicked the page over, but before I began my drawing, he ripped it from my hands and threw it to the ground.

"Enough fucking around. We need to do this before Chris or Trent comes down."

I ground my teeth, unfortunately, he was right. I glanced up the door at the top of the stairs. We have been lucky so far.

"Righto." I jumped down off the table and fetched the cords. Passing the first clamp to Kyden, he attached it to the nail. I grinned when she finally bristled with the first flicker of fear. Kyden and I shared a moment—both of us soaking it up before I passed him the other clamp and adjusted the surrounding cords. Hooking the second clamp to the nail, Kyden stepped back, admiring our work. This was going to be an energising experience. Let's see if we charge up this little bunny, we can have her hopping around the table.

The door at the top of the stairs smashed open suddenly.

"What the fuck is going on?" Chris bellowed, storming down and taking in the situation.

His furious eyes flicked from Kira, taking in the cuts and marks on her body, then settling on her face, where her perfect pouty mouth was held closed with stitches. His nostrils flared, barely containing his rage. Then, when he followed the nails in her head to the set up I had, where I was about to make her body convulse from the volts of electricity…

Uhoh!

"You fucking idiot," he snarled.

Walking over to Kira, he unclasped the clamps at her head and threw them to the ground like they were live snakes. Well, the live part was right. A small zapping sound passed between the clamps when they landed too close together.

"Trent had his fun, now it's our turn," I snapped back, subtly kicking one of the clamps away before they caught fire to the sketchbook they sat on. Damnit! That was my art.

"It's not like this isn't what we were planning anyway," Kyden added. "He had his fill of her pussy and arse, you could at least let us get in our turn."

"This isn't how we usually play this out, and you both know that." Chris snapped back.

Fuck. I threw a fist into the wall.

"This is bullshit. I expect this sort of shit from Grady, but not you, Ky. She wasn't supposed to be touched until we had a discussion first. I figured you would both still be on board for our previous plans anyway, not go off-kilter and try to fry her brain."

Chris

29

"What the fuck is going on?" Trent stormed in, having woken up, repeating my words from moments ago.

I fisted his shirt, holding him back before he went for Grady or Kyden, because I wasn't sure how he would fare while they were in the mood to *play,* not to mention there was still the unresolved issue in motion from before I knocked him out.

This shit just keeps getting better. Fuck my life.

"What the fuck have you two done?" he yelled, looming over Kira, taking in the abuse on her body.

This was the first time I had ever seen him react this way towards the methods of depravity they had unleashed. It made me wonder just how much this girl meant to him.

"Nothing we wouldn't normally do," Grady snapped back. "And if you have a problem with it, then leave. No one invited you here."

Kira's whimper brought his attention to her mouth. "You sewed her mouth shut?" he snapped his head to Kyden. "You fucking sewed it shut?" Trent's face turned a deep scarlet as he struggled to contain his rage.

Kyden smirked. "That was Gray's handiwork. I wanted to sew her eyes open." He spoke as if it were as normal as choosing a shirt for the day. Fucking sociopath.

"This…." Trent waved his hand over Kira, then carefully lifted her blindfold up slightly so she could only catch sight of me. "This wasn't ever meant to happen. I told you all, she was off limits."

"Since when do you get the final say in who we do and don't take as a sub, Trent?" Kyden asked in challenge. "Well?"

Trent's chest was heaving as he struggled for restraint. He looked at me for backup.

"They have a point," I said. "It is a joint decision, and we all took an equal interest in her."

Clenching his teeth, Trent turned, knowing he was outvoted. Throwing his fist through the closest wall, he cursed repeatedly as he continued to punch through the wall until his knuckles were torn open and a gaping hole bared the framework beneath.

Approaching Kira while Trent's back was turned, Grady attempted to reattach the clamps on her forehead. I placed a hand on his, shaking my head to stop him. Grady gripped the clamps tightly in his fists, baring his teeth at me, then threw them to the ground frustratedly.

"We need to discuss this. What are we going to do about this…situation?" I said to the room.

Kira's whimpers made me pause. I looked down at her sewn lips, curling my own up in disgust at what had been done to her. I don't know why the idea of it repulsed me. Nor did I know why I felt the urge to protect her.

"Knife?" I held my hand to Kyden without looking at him, knowing he always had one on his body or nearby at all times.

"I'll do it," he said with a disappointed sigh, leaning over ready to slice her entire mouth open, no doubt from cheek-to-cheek.

"No," I added sternly, grabbing his wrist before he could press the tip of the blade into her cheek. "No more until we have a discussion."

He growled, sheathing the knife he held in his hand and walked over to a bench with tools laid out, returning with a smaller knife, handing it to me begrudgingly.

"Trent. Grab the pliers," I instructed, giving him something to assist with.

"Don't move, I won't cut you," I told Kira, my voice coming out gentler than I expected. "I'm going to remove the stitches on your mouth, then Trent will remove the nails. It will hurt more if you react. Do you understand?"

She made a small noise in response, maintaining eye contact, and, to her credit, slowed her breathing—inhaling deep through her nose, holding it, then releasing it with control.

I lowered the blindfold again, so she didn't flinch when she saw me lower the blade to her mouth. Holding the excess line at the side of her mouth, I ran the tip of the blade through the knot. She sucked in a deep breath through her nose at the feeling of the stitches pulling, but to her credit remained perfectly still as I carefully cut the stitches free from her mouth. When they were free, I ran my thumb across her bottom lip, unable to help myself.

"Good girl. Now this next part *will* hurt," I warned her and nodded for Trent to remove the nails.

I glanced up to see Grady standing with his jaw tight and arms crossed, glaring daggers at us for ruining his masterpiece. But he made no attempt to stop what we were doing or object any further.

Kyden watched with unbridled fascination as Trent placed a hand on Kira's forehead, the other around the handle of the pliers and pulled the nail free. Kyden moaned, biting down on his lower lip as blood trailed from the open wound.

Grady just rolled his eyes and stared at the roof with a disgruntled sigh.

Other than a small gasp, Kira didn't make a sound, a single tear rolled out from under the edge of the blindfold. Trent saw it too, leaning forward he kissed over the tear and I heard a faint, "sorry," whispered, before he removed the second nail.

"I'm cleaning and covering her wounds, then we can convene upstairs for a *discussion*," Trent told us, pointing to Grady and Kyden in warning. "After all, we wouldn't want her to die before we can discuss what we are doing with her."

Grady exasperatedly threw his hands in the air. "Fine, whatever, fucker. While you play nursemaid, I'll go take a shit in your bed."

"I'm getting food," Kyden mumbled, following Grady with one final wistful glance over his shoulder to the girl.

"You know he wasn't joking about that, right?" I shuddered. "Shitting in your bed."

"I'm aware," Trent shrugged, then smiled. "I already left a surprise in his and Kyden's rooms as payback before I came down here and found …all this."

He looked over Kira, and his smile dropped to a look of sadness and anger. Lifting the blindfold from her face, his expression softened, watching as her tear-filled eyes blinked at the light. When her eyes came into focus and she saw Trent's and my faces, her mouth pulled down into a firm line. Oh yeah, she was pissed. Not the usual reaction from our subs.

"I'm not going to ask if you're okay. That would be insensitive, as I can see the evidence of what *those two* have done. I need to tend to your abrasions and cuts to avoid infection," Trent said firmly, with a don't argue with me tone. "I will also cover you with a blanket so you don't feel so exposed. Unfortunately, I have to leave you on this table for the moment. We have things to …*take care of* before we can fix this *situation.*"

"Or you can return me to my home and I keep my mouth shut." Her voice came out hoarse and scratchy, but there was a fire there.

I raised my brows in surprise that despite being told not to argue and having been through half of what Kyden and Grady had planned; she hadn't folded. Other subs had never held their fight this long. Trent didn't seem affected by her brattiness, if anything, it fired him up more. Lighting something in his face I hadn't seen in a long time. There was excitement in his eyes.

Interesting.

"Now, now. Where would be the fun in that? I think we

both know that the inconsequential life you had was nothing compared to what I have already shown you it could be."

"Oh, you mean trying to wear me like a puppet?" she snapped. "No thanks, I'll pass."

I snorted, unable to fully hold back my laughter at her response. I hadn't even thought of it that way before, and now I couldn't get the image out of my head.

"Your orgasm would beg to differ," Trent said, ignoring my amusement. "Now, if you would like a reminder, I would be more than receptive to offering a repeat performance."

She scoffed, directing her eyes away from his face.

"You have such a greedy cunt, I bet you are already drenched. Admit that the idea of being used and abused, held against your will, and having the combination of pleasure and pain being used to manipulate you turns you on. You secretly desire it– crave it. There is a part of you that is just as sick and twisted as us, I have seen it in your eyes, Kira."

I tilted my head, examining the girl restrained before us, pinching my lower lip in thought.

"That has given me an idea."

Trent was taping gauze across Kira's abdomen when I spoke. Lifting his head to look at me, he pressed firmly down on the tape holding the gauze against her wound. She let out a sharp hiss at the pain, raising her hips slightly in response before relaxing into the pain. Trent smiled at me, knowing where my mind was running. Redirecting his attention back to Kira, his fingers drifted lower on her abdomen. Kira's breathing hitched when he hit her pubic bone. Pulling his hand away, a small whimpered mewl fell from her throat at the loss of contact.

"So responsive," he crooned, flicking his sight to me. "And I haven't even done anything yet."

I grinned at him, then looked down at Kira. "Be a good little girl and wait here quietly. We will return shortly."

Turning away from them, I hastily made my way up the stairs to try to get my arousal under control. I stumbled on the top step, hearing Trent kiss her forcefully. It was the moan that fell from her lips that almost made me want to turn back down the stairs, it also let me know I was on the right track with what I was thinking. Now to convince the other two.

Trent

30

Ascending the staircase slowly, I braced myself for the verbal and physical sparring that was about to unfold. I attempted to get my head straight, considering the precarious balance of Kira's life. Chris and I had discussed the idea of a hunt with our last sub before her untimely, premature death, and the look he gave me a moment ago suggested he was on board with continuing with the plan—only this time, it would be met with different circumstances.

I didn't have a shadow of a doubt in my mind that Kira would fight back if cornered by one of us. Fuck, I hoped she would.

The damage she had withstood at the hands of Grady and Kyden made my blood boil. How dare they touch her when I had already laid claim. Yet, despite everything they had done, she was still yearning for a release. Our sweet little flower was brimming with hostility rather than fear. She was actually a dark little masochist—only she didn't know it yet.

That was why we were all inexplicably drawn to her. She

could counter our urges, survive and bloom while we indulged in our depravity. Blossom where our other subs wilted.

The silent exchange Chris and I shared was going to tip the scales on our previous hunts; this time, we were going to see what it was like to be both predator and prey.

The door sat open at the top of the stairs. As I walked through the doorway, I halted, as the barrel of a gun was pressed into my temple making me clench my jaw.

"Give me one reason why I shouldn't blow your fucking head off right now."

I unclenched my jaw. "Grady, I should have known you would be waiting to ambush me."

He pressed it harder, forcing my head to tilt to the side.

"Before you pull the trigger, maybe you should consider how much you need me."

Grady made a buzzing sound. "Wrong answer, dickface." He released the safety.

"Without me, who will stalk our future subs?"

"That's piss easy, I can do it."

I took a risk and turned to face him so the gun was trained between my eyes.

"Remind me what happened to the last one you tracked."

Grady's face fell. He faltered, with the gun lowering

slightly. "I got too excited and scared her away, then when she ran I …ah, accidentally snapped her neck."

With the gun hand he scratched the back of his neck.

"And why can't Kyden do it?"

Grady looked up at the ceiling, dropping both arms to his side, mouthing the word fuck. "Because…" he dropped his head back to me and muttered, "when he becomes overwhelmed, he passes out."

"And Chris?"

Grady chuckled and gave me trigger fingers with one hand and pointed the gun with the other, accidentally firing a shot. His eyes widened at the mishap.

I patted down my torso, my heart in my throat, trying to find a wound.

"Grady!" Chris bellowed before storming up behind me and snatching the gun from Grady's limp hand. In his other hand was the handle and rim of a mug. "The next time you fire a gun, check who is in the firing line. My coffee does not need to suffer because you have a jumpy finger." Chris directed the gun at me, which sat loosely in his hand. "You, table. Grady, move your arse too, preferably without any attempts to kill anyone."

"But you're not saying that I can't…" Grady hedged.

"No killing anyone," Chris and I snapped at the same time,

walking to the kitchen with Grady in tow, muttering under his breath.

Chris and I took our seats at the table with Kyden, who was already waiting for us. In front of him were various pills lined up, where he was taking his daily doses of whatever he self-medicated with to treat his …issues.

Grady stomped in, dropping down to lie on the two-seater couch dramatically, with an arm resting over his eyes. Chris rolled his eyes and sighed, shaking his head at his twin's theatrics.

"How is our precious little subject?" Kyden asked before throwing back a handful of pills, swallowing them down with a bourbon chaser.

I went to open my mouth to question the effectiveness of the concoction mixed with alcohol, but thought better of it. Now, knowing he was actually a doctor, I assumed he knew what he was doing, or maybe he didn't give a shit. Either way, it wasn't my place to judge or point out the obvious.

Chris nudged my knee with his. "Oh, uh. She has spirit," I answered. "I still can't believe what the two of you were about to do. You're damn lucky Chris put a stop to it before you fried her brain."

"So what if we did?" Grady scathed. "You had your fun, the way I see it, it was our turn."

I ground my teeth, turning to the gun beside Chris, debating if he would have a problem if I took a shot at his brother. Chris gave me a raised brow, seeing where my mind was focused, and gave his head a small shake.

"That isn't how we do this," Chris interjected. "The three of you all made a mistake. Own up to it, then maybe we can turn this around and actually have some fun."

"Fuck. You." Grady spat, flipping off the room with both hands.

"What kind of fun are you thinking?" Kyden asked, seeming interested as he began screwing the lids back on the medication, stacking them to the side, then propped his head on his fist with his elbow bent on the table, waiting for Chris to elaborate.

"A hunt."

Grady sat bolt upright on the couch. "Please tell me you aren't pulling my leg? Unless it's my third leg… Scratch that, only Kyden gets to do that, and incest isn't my thing. You know, I'm still pretty pissed that the last one carked it before we got to chase her." His hands pressed together in front of him as if he were saying a prayer. "Please, please, please tell me you're serious. I don't want to get all excited only to discover it's a lie, just like Santa."

As pissed as I was at Grady, I couldn't help chuckling. His

behaviour was split between a bipolar psychopath and an overgrown man-child with tantrums and all. "

I don't think I have ever seen you beg, Gray. If you are a good boy, maybe you can have a lolly pop when we are done."

Grady grabbed his crotch. "I'll give you a lolly pop if you want something to suck on, T-man."

Kyden let out a strangled noise. Chewing on his bottom lip, he focused his sight on where Grady groped himself. Now that we knew about what went on between the two of them, it made it hard to miss their blatantly obvious responses to one another. I have no idea how I missed it for so long, they weren't even subtle about it. Ignorance is bliss, I suppose.

I scoffed, "Haven't you heard? It's a choking hazard to put small objects in your mouth?"

"That is why my mouth will never be on your cock," he retorted, looking down to where I was sporting an erection from being in Kira's presence. For fuck's sake.

"No one's mouths are going on anyone's cocks," Chris interjected, making Grady cross his arms and pout. "Now, back to the point. I say we up the ante in this hunt and make it more interesting. Let's give Kira the opportunity to earn her freedom."

"Are you insane, Chriso? No fuckucking way," Grady

yelled, jumping up to his feet.

Kyden reclined back in his chair, tucking his hands behind his head, not entirely shooting down the idea. "Explain."

"No," Grady repeated. "We aren't…"

Kyden reached one arm out and snagged Grady's wrist, pulling him to his side. "Let's see what he has to say before you shoot him down, okay?"

Grady stared down at Kyden for a moment. Whatever he saw in Kyden's face made him let out a deep breath, and he dropped his shoulders. "Fine."

Well, hallelujah for small miracles. Maybe them fucking wasn't such a bad thing after all. Provided we could get Kyden on our side. It was a shame I hadn't picked up on their interactions sooner, I could have used Kyden's sway over Grady to have made life with him more manageable.

Chris turned his attention to me. "Do you have any objections?"

"I don't want a hunt to kill." I couldn't bear the idea of these assholes killing her, stealing her from me. It tore me up enough to see what they had already done.

Chris nodded. "Okay, here's what I propose, we hunt to capture only. We also give her the opportunity to capture each of us in return. If we win, she is ours to do with as we please, but if she wins, she can earn her freedom or choose to stay."

"I'm not letting her leave," Kyden spoke first, with firm authority. "She belongs to us."

Grady nodded in agreement. "We couldn't even get her to beg. I'm not even done breaking her. She belongs here."

"She is getting the chance to earn her freedom." I insisted through gritted teeth. Shit, this isn't going how I thought it would. I need to turn the tables. "Unless you are afraid she might catch you before you capture her?" I goaded.

Grady burst into laughter. "You don't really believe she has a chance, do you? Her trying to catch us would be like a one-legged man in an arse-kicking contest. There's no chance in hell."

"You have nothing to worry about then." I shrugged, hoping he would take the bait. Chris wiped his mouth to hide his smirk, knowing full well what I was doing.

"Righto," Grady relented, annoyed, but disbelieving that she was a true threat. "We will let Chocolate drop *try* to catch us in return. But when the hunt is over, five minutes after I catch her, I'm putting those nails back in her head and welding a chain to them so she can't escape."

I clenched my hands into fists under the table, biting my tongue. Over my dead body would he be doing anything of the sort to her again, not if I had my way.

"As it's four against one, what if we offer her a head start?" Kyden suggested. "Make it more challenging? I think she might surprise us all."

"Yes, that's not a bad idea," Chris mused, stroking a finger over his bottom lip, with his fist at his jaw. "Even without the incentive of her freedom, I believe you are right, especially after what you both put her through," Chris glared at Grady and Kyden. "She would have slit your throats in retaliation if given the opportunity. She has an iron will, and she has a personal vendetta against us."

Grady grinned. "You really think so?" he asked hopefully, as if we had promised him a trip to the lolly shop with no limit as to what he could get.

"Oh yeah," I nodded. She definitely had it in her to commit murder. That only drew me to her even more.

Trent

31

"Well, well, well, if it isn't the infected splinter that has embedded itself under our nails," Grady sing-songed, as he descended the staircase in front of me, coming to a stop just out of sight from where Kira's head remained strapped to the table, leaving her unable to look at him.

Her hands balled into tight fists at the sound of his voice, and I couldn't help the small amount of satisfaction that she was probably going to try to fight him when she was freed.

"Do you know the best treatment for an infection, Chocolate drop?"

Her lips remained closed tight, her eyes searching for the face that belonged to the voice. When she caught sight of me as I stepped to the side of Grady, she did a double take. Her hands relaxed in my presence, uncurling her fists, so her hands opened loosely.

"No? Let me tell you then… or maybe I should get Ky, after all, he is the medical expert," Grady continued when Kira refused to answer. Her eyes moved frantically around to try to catch sight of Grady as he moved around erratically.

"Grady," I warned.

He bared his teeth at me with a sneer. "Fine."

Stomping over to Kira's side, allowing her to lay eyes on him, I warmed seeing the venomous glare she shot him. Grady was immune to reading facial expressions—or so I assumed—he had never reacted to our expressions directed at him. Perhaps it was more ignorance, which was a strong possibility.

He patted the top of her hair, then ran his finger down the centre of her forehead, over her nose, her lips, her chin. His finger dipped to the hollow of her throat, only stopping where the blanket covered her chest.

"The best course of action is naturally to take preventative measures. But as you very well know…" Grady looked at me. "T-man fucked up and inserted you here under our skin, so now we have to remove the splinter so we can treat the infection."

"Why does it sound like you're telling me that you're about to *off* Trent and myself?" Kira asked.

Grady pulled his head back in surprise, then gave an approving nod. "Perceptive."

"Tell her, or I will. Quit fucking with her," I growled in warning, sick of this game.

Kira's eyes rolled to me. "Why don't you just tell me instead, but without the theatrics."

She had Grady pegged.

"Okay, you are being given a choice," I told her.

"At least one of us was," Grady muttered under his breath, which I chose to ignore.

"Participate in a game of cat and mouse, and if you win, then you go free."

Her eyes flicked back and forth between Grady and me. "What's the catch?"

"You don't miss much," Grady noted while studying her intently. "Why aren't you afraid?"

Kira blinked. "Of you? Please! You may hide behind your sadist mask, but you're nothing but an insecure, broken boy. I'm not afraid of death. I have nothing to lose anyway, and the pain you put me through made me feel more… more alive than I have in years."

Grady's jaw hit the floor. "You were right," he said to me, running a hand over his face and storming from the basement, but not before stopping halfway up the stairs to glance back and shake his head, conflicted.

"I don't understand what's going on," Kira said after Grady departed, slamming the door at the top of the stairs closed behind him.

"Look, you must understand, we have never had a sub cause so much conflict between us before." I began undoing the straps on her body, starting with the one on her head. "You do not respond like our usual victims, nor do you realise just how much of a reaction you have forced from each of us since we first laid eyes on you." I moved to undo the restraints at her ankles and thighs next. "Usually, under normal circumstances, none of us would think twice about killing you just for defiantly refusing to bend to our whims, but there is something about you…"

"That's comforting," she muttered snidely. Letting out a huff, she raised her voice. "Tell me more about this game of cat and mouse."

With only her hips and arms left restrained, I sat at the bottom of the table beside her knees so she had to move her legs over slightly to make room.

Lifting her head from the table to look at me, she waited for me to speak. I rested a hand on her thigh. The muscles tensed under my hand, but she didn't make any attempt to move away.

"We used to make a game out of killing our subs. We would find a secluded area and set traps around the perimeter, then tell them to run. If they got away, they were free. If not… they would be ours to do with as we pleased. It heightened the experience — the adrenaline, the rush of hunting our prey made the finale so much sweeter a reward because they never got away. In their panic, they always became turned around and would surrender in defeat when we closed in."

Kira's brows pinched. "So, you're saying you want to hunt me down to kill me and want me to just… give up?"

"No. Yes, but no," I ran a hand down my face. "I said you were different, so this time the rules are different."

"How so?"

"First, it's a fairer playing field. We are hunting to capture and not kill… Well, two of us are trying not to kill." I muttered the last part.

"Thanks for the reassurance," she said dryly.

"You are also allowed to hunt us, in return. In other words, if you capture …or *kill* us, then you win and are free."

"What's the catch?"

I shook my head. "No catch."

Her eyes narrowed. "Call me sceptical, but I won't take you at your word. What's stopping any of you from changing your mind?"

"Nothing more than our word."

I moved the hand that I had been trailing absentmindedly along her thigh under the sheet, to the buckle at her hip. Her gasp when I made contact with her bare skin formed a grin on my lips. Slowly, I brushed my fingers lightly across her skin under the restraint until it bloomed with goosebumps. Fuck, she was responsive to my touch. Kira's rapid breathing told me just how much of an effect I was having on her, boosting my already inflated ego. Pulling the sheet from her body, exposing every inch of her flesh to me, I held her eye contact, watching her lips part in anticipation of whatever I was going to do.

"What if I don't want to leave?" A soft whisper came out.

At first, I wasn't sure I had heard her correctly. Did she really want to stay?

"If you win, you can choose to stay or leave. If I win, or Chris wins, we want to keep you," I told her as I slowly unclipped the restraint on her hips.

"Like a pet?" She scoffed, seeming unimpressed. Oh yeah, I had to admit a collar would look fitting around her throat.

"Like an equal," I corrected, not wanting to scare her off.

With the final restraint undone, I offered Kira my hand to help her sit up. She looked at my hand as if it were a snake ready to strike.

"Let me get you cleaned up properly."

"Only to die in some messed up game of depravity?"

Not giving her the option, I clasped her arm in my hand and pulled her up. She winced under the motion, but didn't pull away.

I left her on the table, giving her my back. I walked to the sink, ran a cloth under the water, when it warmed, then walked back to where she still sat, watching me cautiously.

I carefully wiped across her skin, cleaning it of the dried blood and stale sweat.

"Why did you take me?" her voice was almost a whisper.

I continued cleaning her skin, not answering, rinsing out the cloth when the dried blood began to streak, then returning with it rinsed clean to continue.

"Why me?" She pressed, determined to get an answer.

"Because behind your sad eyes something more was begging to be set free. I saw it the moment you ran into me. You want this. I can see it plain as day, no matter how much you try to hide."

"You're wrong," Kira said after several minutes when I could see her skin back to its beautiful brown.

"I'm not. You are just afraid of accepting who you truly are."

"You don't know me. Just because you think you saw something in me, it doesn't mean I am anything like you. I'm just an innocent victim who caught the attention of the wrong men."

"You are wrong. You didn't catch the attention of the wrong

men; you ignited a foreign emotion in four serial killers."

She scoffed. "You know nothing about me. If you did, then you would know that there are no similarities between us. I don't belong in the messed-up delusion you have, where I join your little band of psychopaths, sociopaths and sadists. I am a normal, innocent girl, who has been caught in the clutches of four unhinged men because of a small incident. I was in the wrong place at the wrong time."

"I don't believe that for a second." I told her truthfully.

Kira

32

Whatever. I rolled my eyes. I didn't feel like arguing. My face was swollen and painful. There wasn't a single spot on my body that was free from discomfort. I was hungry, thirsty and tired.

I hugged my arms around myself tightly, wanting to return to a few days ago, before I had met these men. They may have changed something inside of me, unleashed a hidden, caged desire, but that did not mean I wanted to accept them as the ones who would be free to share this side of me.

"Come play with us, let your darkness out. Your demons are exquisite and have been caged for too long. I want to see you bare your soul and unleash your true potential." Trent ran his fingers through my hair, tucking it behind my ear, then cupped my cheek, breaking me from my thoughts. "Don't fear what you crave, embrace the monster inside and dance under the moon with us. Defy death and make us bleed in return, so you can realise that we are what you need when you try to return to the meek existence of life you were living. No not living, you were dying every day. With every breath and each second that passed. That mundane existence was killing your true self, dampening your soul and weighing it down." He pressed his forehead against mine, closing his eyes, he sighed sadly. "You were drowning and suffering without even knowing." Pulling his head back, he ran his thumb back and forth along my cheek, his eyes flickered back and forth between my eyes. "Release the burdens and constraints of morality and expectation set upon you by those who deem themselves the hierarchy of what is good and evil. There is no one on this earth with the power to judge you for choices, there's only yourself. Never forget that. Now, agree to our proposal and join us in the shadows."

I stared back, opening and closing my mouth twice. How could he speak as if he saw into my soul? Did he truly know how difficult it was to be me?

I swallowed before I found my voice, and it came out breathless. "My shadows are fractured, but I'm still standing in filtered light, leaving me broken. I don't know how."

A smirk hinted at the corner of his lips. "Yes, you do. You're just afraid. Break away from your insecurities and embrace those fractured shadows, climb inside of them and wear them like a cloak instead of avoiding them. You can be the light in the darkness, drawing me to you like a beacon.

237

Together we can thrive."

I gulped, my hands shaking. "I… I can't," I protested, looking away. "I don't have it in me. I don't know what you all see, but I'm not like you."

"You're right, you're not like any of us," he said, clasping my shaky hands in his. "You are uniquely *you*. Only you can figure out who that is."

When he pulled his hands away from mine, there in his place he left a knife, its blade no longer than my hand, a beautiful Damascus pattern of folded steel. The handle grip fit perfectly in my hand, as though it were made for my grasp. The silver pommel was adorned with intricate spun silver and delicate flowers. My eyes rose to meet his. "I don't know if I can use this."

He shrugged. "Then don't. No one will force your hand. It's your choice to decide how badly you want to be free and live a life of your own choosing, but when the time comes, you *will* have to choose. I only hope that you have enough fight left in you, and enough will to choose to thrive."

"What about you?"

He winked. "Don't worry about me, little shadow, I can take care of myself. I have the very reason before me to choose to live."

My stomach did a weird little backflip flutter at his

declaration, leaving my mouth dry, unable to form words.

"Just don't tell anyone you have this. It's our little secret."

I turned it over in my hand, feeling the weight and balance in my grip. It was comfortable and moved like an extension of my arm when I flicked my wrist. A smile bloomed across my lips at the thought of using it, defensively of course.

"You like it then?"

"I do. Only…" I glanced down at my body. "Where am I supposed to hide it?"

Trent opened his mouth and then snapped it closed, coming to the same realisation. "You're naked."

"Well spotted, Captain Obvious. Unless you have clothes on you for me to wear, I don't have anywhere to hide it… I don't have anywhere I am willing to hide it," I corrected.

Trent's eyes crinkled with amusement. "I'm sure you wouldn't mind too much if I helped you. In fact, I think you might enjoy the thrill of danger it posed to walk upstairs, naked, clutching a knife in your pussy. Unless that turns you on so much that you're worried it'll make you so wet that it slides out."

I scoffed and crossed my arms, flinching from the sting of the movement. Trent didn't miss the reaction.

"I'll look after the knife and slip it to you on the morning of the hunt. Follow me upstairs and I'll have Kyden take a look at your injuries while I find you some clothes. Until then, you can wear my shirt."

Trent swiftly pulled his shirt from his body, bearing the tanned, muscled flesh hidden beneath it to me.

"No," I said quickly, raising my eyes from his torso before my mind lost the ability to function. "I don't want to give him another opportunity to try to kill me if we are alone."

Trent handed me his shirt with an empathetic nod. "I can understand where you are coming from. You have every right to be afraid of him and Grady, but he won't harm you. Not anymore."

"What do you mean anymore? What changed between the time you stopped them from trying to fry my brain to now?" I asked as I pulled on his shirt. His rich scent clinging to the fabric, I couldn't help but inhale it deeply as it slid over my face. It stopped at the top of my thighs, barely leaving me unexposed, no matter how much I tugged on the hem.

Trent scratched along his brow and grimaced. "He is kind of in love with you now."

"What?" A man who tied me down, almost let me drown in my own vomit, then cut me, and put a nail into my skull, is in love with me? Call me naïve, but that just sounds all kinds of messed up.

Trent let out a strangled laugh and looked up at the ceiling with a curse. "Look." He dropped his head back down to face me. "Kyden is a … unique individual. I give you my word that he won't do anything to you that you don't want. If it eases your mind, I will remain present whilst he attends to you."

I didn't like the idea of having Kyden touch me again, but if Trent said he wouldn't harm me, I suppose I could accept that, as long as he remained present while Kyden tended to the very wounds he inflicted.

"Yes, please."

Trent smiled at me, then let his eyes lower down my body, languidly taking me in. A blush tinted my cheeks. Suddenly, I felt more exposed wearing nothing but his shirt than I did naked.

"I like you in my clothes," he said.

A fucked-up part of me enjoyed hearing that. Stockholm syndrome at its finest, right here. I felt conflicted by the emotions I did feel for Trent and this whole situation, versus the fear and hate that I should feel.

Grasping the front hem of the shirt in my hands, I pulled it lower on my legs, squirming.

Trent let out a throaty chuckle. "You're cute." Tilting his head to the side, he gestured to the staircase. "Follow me, beautiful. We can collect Kyden on the way if he hasn't passed out yet, then get you cleaned up and rested in your own room."

I simply nodded in response and followed slowly, wincing with every movement from the injuries in my body. I would wait until I had been checked over—play the innocent card, the willing victim—then when the coast was clear, I would escape.

Kyden

33

I was staring towards the doorway that led to the basement. Ever since Grady had emerged in an odd manner before dismissing himself outside, I was curious as to what was spoken. More than that, I wanted to lay eyes on our new little sub. But she was more than that, hell, I was fairly certain we had each already nicknamed her.

Every so often Chris would look up in the general direction of where my attention was focused. He would flick his eyes to me with a smirk playing on his mouth, then return to whatever it was that he did on his laptop. I bit my tongue, not initiating small talk with Chris just in case I missed the exact moment Trent and Kira emerged.

I was also battling my hypersomnia, fighting my body's natural defence to force me into sleep. It was taking every ounce of willpower to force myself to remain conscious at this point, not wanting to miss seeing her and how she fared after our session.

Would she glare at me with those big beautiful eyes narrowed into vertical slits? Oh, how I hope she did. The venom in that one look was enough to incapacitate even the most dominant man. Chris was a prime example, and he hadn't even found himself at the brunt of her ire. When he had been caught in the trap of her gaze, he lost the ability of rational thought. He assumed no one had noticed his fumbled movements and the slight softening of his tone, but it did not pass me by. He was as much a victim of her presence as the rest of us.

Trent's voice carried up the stairs, increasing in volume with his steady footfalls on the stairs. I straightened in my seat with anticipation when I heard her melodic voice and slow steps follow.

My heart began racing, my knee bouncing of its own accord. What was happening to me? I ran a hand down my face, not appreciating this reaction I was exhibiting without any control.

The door opened out, and my breath caught when Trent came into view shirtless, then reached out grasping a small brown hand in his and pulled her into view cautiously. She stood unsteady on her own two feet, shoulders hunched forward slightly, and a hand pressed against her sternum. She was dressed in Trent's top. I hissed between clenched teeth seeing that, some fucked up part in my brain was telling me she should be in my shirt instead.

"Are you okay?" he asked with concern when a small whimper left her lips.

"Yes," she answered through gritted teeth, showing just how resilient she was.

I noted the slight quiver in her limbs, the stiffness of her movements and tense muscles.

"You're in pain," I noted.

Her eyes widened when they found me, and just as I hoped they would, they narrowed, promising me a thousand painful deaths with just one look. My stomach did a backflip, and I had to fight the urge to run over and take her from Trent.

"Gee, I wonder why." Her snide comment only antagonised the beast inside of me.

I smiled darkly. "Come back for seconds?" Come back forever.

She scoffed loudly. "What, not happy that I didn't react the way you wanted and now you've been left with an inferiority complex?"

Chris hid a laugh behind a cough, very poorly I might add.

"Kira," Trent warned, carefully taking her upper arm in his hand. She shrugged him off, trying to hide a grimace at the action.

"Allow me to look at your inflictions," I offered, sounding bored, so she didn't catch on to just how badly I wanted to take care of her. She glanced up at Trent, who gave her a look insinuating that they had already discussed my tending to her. I crossed my arms, feigning impatience, waiting for her response.

"Fine," she gritted out. "But I want a shower first."

"Demanding little thing, aren't you precious?" I taunted.

"A psychopathic haemophiliac, aren't you?" she countered, crossing her arms delicately across her tender chest.

"Hematomaniac is the correct term," Chris interjected before I was able to, without even raising his eyes from his screen.

"Great, now that you know one another more personally, I am taking Kira to the spare room to shower. Are you up to treating the injuries you gave her?" Trent eyeballed me with a warning not to fuck with him for a second time. I didn't give two shits about his sensitive feelings; my focus was solely directed on the pretty girl who was promising my death with her glare.

"I'll wash up and grab my medical bag. Be with you directly to tend to your needs." I told her, enjoying the way she stiffened. She was afraid of me. Even if she wouldn't admit it to herself, her body language gave her away.

Trent's blatant ignorance meant that he missed her subtle response as he placed a protective arm across her shoulder to direct her through the hall.

"I'll see what clothes I can find her to wear while she showers," Trent spoke over his shoulder to me when he reached the room he had taken as his own. Yes, ever the gentleman and ladies' man.

"Take her to the spare room, not your own," Chris growled, sounding frustrated.

I glanced back, noting that Chris wouldn't have been able to see where Trent was leading Kira, and chuckled when Trent cursed under his breath, turning Kira across the hall to the spare room.

Chris

34

I watched the girl from over my laptop sitting on the couch with a deep scowl on her face and arms crossed. The shock collar on her neck was a necessary evil after she tried to escape through the bathroom window. It was placed on her while she slept so she wouldn't fight us on securing it. Perhaps the term slept was a slight exaggeration; after she was drugged would be the better term. Now, if she steps outside of a set boundary within the house, then she is hit with bouts of electricity coursing through her. Grady was particularly fond of encouraging her to test its effectiveness, which she vehemently refused.

We should have known better than to trust her with the privacy to tend to her own wounds with the first-aid kit. It was only allowed after she realised she would have to be bare in front of Kyden in order for him to treat the wounds caused by his own hands. She naturally refused.

The swelling around her mouth and forehead had gone

down considerably overnight after she *passed out* with ice packs covering her face. Despite the swelling and bruising, she was still breathtaking. A unique beauty that was unlike any I had encountered. Being in such close proximity, I found it difficult to keep my eyes from straying to her and focusing on my work instead. I had just moved half a million from an account in the Cayman Islands belonging to a corrupt government official who had been laundering the party's funds under the pretence of administration costs. After a few misguided trails, moving the money around through several accounts and organisations, if anyone looked into it further it would only lead them to an anonymous donation being made to a conservation sanctuary for the Western Gobbleguts. With volunteers providing a protected area of the ocean in the south of Western Australia. Of course, the organisation doesn't actually exist. It is merely a front we have used on various occasions to hide the money we diverted from those with shady dealings on more than one occasion. Mainly to be sure not to link anything back to us. In reality, the money had been used to buy stocks, gaining a high dividend return, allowing us a comfortable and stress-free lifestyle without monetary concerns.

I found myself staring yet again at Kira, noting the slight pallid tone her skin had taken. "You should eat," I suggested.

"You will need your energy if you have any hopes of making it more than ten feet before you're caught tomorrow."

Kyden has been sitting there staring at her creepily for the last forty minutes, twirling his favourite knife between his fingers, pricking each fingertip and sucking the blood until it slows, then moving on to the next. I don't think he had even blinked the entire time. The girl's eyes flicked from Kyden's, where she was having a stare down, to mine with annoyance.

"And how do I know you haven't poisoned the food?"

I harrumphed. "You don't, but where would be the fun in killing you when the hunt was my idea to begin with."

Her eyes widened. "You.. yours?"

Kyden's chuckle brought her attention back to him.

"You didn't think it was his idea, did you?" I asked.

"His or Grady's." She frowned, then muttered quietly, "Both are pretty fucked in the head."

I bit back a laugh at her assessment. She had no idea just how dead-on she actually was.

"Everyone is a little fucked in the head, some just choose to wear it like a badge of honour, while others cower behind masks, denying themselves their inner crazy." Kyden had his head tilted, unblinking at her. "What's yours?"

"Mine?"

Still unblinking, he twisted the knife in his hand and

nodded. "Yeah… what's your crazy?"

Kira drew a blank face, "conversing with psychopathic, bloodthirsty murderers who are planning on hunting me like a wild animal, like it's a normal Wednesday morning."

"All of that is true, other than the fact that it is actually *Thursday*," I said in a bored tone, distracted by finding precisely what I was after on my laptop and zooming in. You beauty. This was exactly what I was after.

"Thursday?" she squealed. "How is it Thursday? How did I lose a day?"

"Probably because I drugged you?" Kyden told her, sounding proud of the fact. I don't know if she was even aware of the method he had used to bring her here. As far as I was aware, it hadn't been brought up, nor had the finer details of Trent's one-on-one time with her been discussed.

I glanced up between the two of them when I heard Kira's seat crunch under her movement. She was standing, looming over a very amused Kyden, her fists balled tight at her side and her jaw locked.

"You drugged me?" She snarled.

"Yes, yes, very scary," Kyden drawled. "You're like a cute little bunny stepping up to face off against a savage rottweiler."

"Trust me, *Kyden,* even a bunny has teeth and claws."

I don't think that I had ever seen Kyden grin so wide before, his eyes sparkling with the challenge. Dipping his tongue out, he ran it across his lower lip and then sunk his teeth into it with a moan. "I have something you can sink your teeth into."

"Is it your jugular?" Kira retorted, not missing a beat.

I had to give her credit, few would dare to antagonise the masochist.

Kyden whimpered, baring his neck to her. What was going on? Was he… submitting to her?

"Glad you have fight in you, girl. You will need that tomorrow. Now eat." I ordered, needing to call an end to whatever the fuck was going on before blood was spilled and we lost another subject… or Kyden.

Kira swung her head towards me, with clenched teeth. "Yes, sir," she snapped, her tone dripping with sarcasm. She then sank back down into her chair, wincing in pain briefly from the abrupt movement, before shooting daggers at Kyden—the source behind her discomfort.

Kyden whistled and then tutted. "Brave, brave, words, Precious. Chris doesn't like mouthy little brats. He punishes them harshly. His singular tastes are preferable to good little girls who allow him to order them around and bow down before him submissively."

Now it was my turn to chuckle, walking over to slap Kyden on the shoulder. "Something tells me she isn't exactly the submissive type, Ky."

Scratching his blade across his cheek, he studied her with narrowed eyes. "Anyone can be if you break them first. She just needs the right motivation. It would have been fun seeing how much she could take."

Yeah, it would have been. It had been a while since I had broken a sub in. I had a habit of killing them by accident, of course, before I could mould them into the perfect pet. When I was in the moment, I tended to forget they needed to breathe–breath play was my specialty after voyeurism. We all had a thing for choking, but I took it to the next level, keeping them balanced on the precipice for extended periods. Adding to the clamps and suction…fuck, she would look so pretty tied up at my mercy.

Despite the defiant look in her eye, something about her made me wonder if she would be a good girl and submit if presented with a situation. She seemed to respond well to praise… an idea began formulating in my mind. Could we potentially keep her?

"*She is* sitting right here and can hear every word you are saying, you obnoxious assholes."

I snickered, picking up the plate of food from the small

table and passing it to Kira. She clenched her jaw, taking it without a word. I stood there, waiting until she muttered curses under her breath, aimed at both Kyden and me. With a frustrated grunt, she shoved the food into her mouth, chewing it forcefully. Once I was satisfied she'd continue eating, I returned to my seat, focusing on the information I'd just found about a potential hunting ground.

Kyden began yawning loudly, signalling his hypersomnia was playing into effect. Without excusing himself, he walked towards the hall that housed the bedrooms, but not before glancing back over his shoulder one last time at Kira with fascination. Tomorrow would be interesting to see how it played out.

After several minutes of blissful silence, Kira placed her plate down and spoke quietly. "You don't come across as intimidating as the others."

I lifted my eyes from over the laptop questioningly, looking at the girl who was staring at me with interest. "And what makes you say that?" I asked.

She shrugged. "Grady seems rather proud of being a psychotic sadist and happily announces his fucked-up fantasies. And Kyden…" she touched her chest with a wince where he had sliced her. "Trent, well, he screams dominant and possessive. But you…"

I leaned back in my chair, crossing my arms. "I believe Kyden did in fact warn you of my preferences. Besides, haven't you ever heard the term, *you should watch out for the quiet ones?* The most unassuming are the most dangerous, because they aren't predictable."

She squinted, chewing on her lip thoughtfully as she examined me slowly, then with a slow shake of her head. "I still don't see it."

I stood and walked over to her slowly, methodically, leaning down so she was forced to tilt her head back. She didn't cower. There was a flicker of surprise in her eyes, but she quickly masked it, straightening her shoulders in defiance. She tilted her head further and batted her bloodied lashes.

"Are you failing to also recall that Kyden mentioned not too long ago that the *hunt* was my idea?"

"No, I have not. But that only means you like to plan." She held my stare in challenge, not intimidated in the slightest.

"Control," I corrected her. "I thrive on control." And more than anything, I wanted her on her bare knees before me, accepting that I was in charge of this situation.

"You can't control me, and that bothers you." It wasn't a question, she saw right through me, right through the shields.

"I could have you at my mercy in a heartbeat, little girl."

She arched her brow incredulously. "I highly doubt that, and don't call me little girl."

I smirked, enjoying knowing that name got under her skin. "Would you like to bet on it?"

Her gaze narrowed, not taking the bait. Instead she asked, "And exactly how do you think you could bring me to my knees so easily?"

Oh, the image that painted in my mind had me all kinds of fucked up for this little minx. I could understand Trent's desire to hold her captive away from us, wanting to unravel her for himself. What I would have given for that opportunity myself!

"Pressure points, little girl. They are a remarkable form of persuasion."

She threw her head back, laughing. "Hilarious, big guy. I know exactly how good it feels manipulating pressure points to relieve tension or pain, neither will drop me to my knees."

Oh, the nerve of this girl! Perhaps she required a firsthand demonstration. There were no rules set between us stating that I couldn't use my particular skill set on her. The only agreement was that Kyden didn't draw blood, Grady didn't harm her, and Trent didn't fuck or fist her.

I crossed my arms over my chest, considering it. "I use pressure points as my form of torture."

A devious smile spread across her face. She leaned back in the chair and trailed a hand from her neck, slowly to between her breasts, over the wound from Kyden.

"Me too. With one finger on my clit for extended periods…" her voice dropped low and seductive, her hand slowly gliding lower down her abdomen. "Not letting myself get off." She closed her eyes, leaning her head fully back with a deep inhale, then opened her eyes half mast with her hand gripping her thigh tightly, her nails digging in making me wish there weren't a barrier of clothing, so I could see the indentations on her skin. "Edging myself—denying myself release. It's the best kind of torture." A small moan slipped from her lips.

My cock sprang to life, forcing me to gulp back a groan. My mind littered with images of her splayed out before me bare, enacting the very words she was knowingly taunting me with. She was dangerous.

"Because," she smiled, biting down on her bottom lip, knowing full fucking well what kind of game she was playing. She was fucking with me. "When I finally come, there is no better feeling than knowing just how much the pain and torment was worth it."

Unable to help myself, I reached out, yanking her by her hair, tilting her head back. "You have no idea who you are playing with, little girl. I know full well that little trick of yours is nothing compared to what I could do."

"I don't believe you. All you have proven is that you're all talk. Nothing but big fancy words. You like to think you're in control, but who really has the upper hand here."

Fuck!

"I could bring you immense pleasure or indescribable pain with just the touch of a single finger."

"Oh yeah? I bet I could do the same," she challenged.

I smirked. "Oh yeah? Other than your clit, how exactly?"

"As for pleasure… there is this endogenous zone in your prostate…"

"And…" I cleared my throat, "the pain?"

"The eyeballs," she stated plainly, widening her own. "One finger hooked in the eye socket and they will pop right out." She hooked her index finger inside of her cheek, flicking it out with a popping noise.

Fuck, she was as twisted as we were. She would get along well with Kyden, no wonder he stared at her like she was his next meal. I brushed away that thought. No, I wanted her. I just had to win this hunt to claim her.

"You're not like our other subjects," I noted aloud, taking a deep breath trying to calm my increased pulse.

She glanced up. "You all keep saying that. I don't know if

that's a good or bad thing."

"You're still breathing, aren't you?"

"For now.." she left the sentence hanging.

We both knew tomorrow would change everything. And after this conversation, I wasn't sure how I felt about it anymore.

TRIP DOWN MEMORY LANE.

35

♦

"Consider this trip a chance for us to bond," Chris said.

"This ain't some chick flick, Chriso. We're not gonna walk outta here holding hands suddenly getting along just 'cause we went on a camping trip and found out we have shit in common. Next thing I know you will suggest one of us was switched at birth and we aren't even twins, then you will profess your undying love for me," Grady scoffed.

"For fucksake Gray, I never suggested holding hands, and don't make it creepy."

Grady shrugged, hiking the carton of beer from the tub of the ute up to his shoulder. "Just saying."

"Just forget it, okay," Chris sighed, walking off.

Something in his tone made Grady pause. "Hey wait up! Does it really mean that much to you?" He placed his hand on Chris's shoulder, stopping him.

"I said don't worry about it," Chris snapped, shrugging off Grady. Grady wasn't letting it go and clasped his hand back

down on Chris's shoulder, spinning him around to face him. "Chill bro. I'm asking. Does it mean that much to you?"

Chris nodded, then shook his head and shrugged. "I dunno. I guess I just …. I need to get away." Chris looked at the shithole their deceased parents had left them a month ago after a drug deal went bad. Orphaned at eighteen wouldn't have been so bad if it weren't for the fact they were left to pay back the debt their parents had left them. They were forced to put the house on the market to cover the debt, not that it would be enough. The property was being sold for its land value only, with a demolition order put against it. The house itself was a beaten old small weatherboard place with peeling eucalyptus green paint and a rusted tin roof full of holes. The window panes were cracked, the frame rotted and warped, letting in the elements. The front verandah leaned to one side where the support had rotted away, now being held up by a stack of precariously balanced mismatched bricks. It looked one gust of wind away from collapsing. The interior fared no better with mould stealing the white ceiling, the threadbare carpet worn down to the floor underneath. The shower leaked in the bathroom that once had tiled walls; now, it was nothing more than old grout on the walls. The oven in the kitchen did not work. Chris and Grady couldn't remember a time when it was ever used for anything more than a place for them to store their heroine. Despite it being the only place they lived, it was never home.

Between the current predicament and the even more depressing job doing data entry Chris picked up after graduating high school, his stagnant and mediocre life was nothing more than a depressing routine that would continue until the day he died. "Figured we could camp, hunt down some wild pigs, snags over a campfire, booze ...."

Grady stared at Chris. "You've sold me."

"What?" Chris snapped his head up, "really?" He asked suspiciously.

"Yeah," Grady grinned. "'Specially the hunting part."

Chris beamed, looking back at the house and then to the beer on Grady's shoulder. "Chuck that back in the tub then. Let's go."

♦

Working as a private investigator wasn't a bad career, but it was time consuming especially for the considerably mediocre amount of money actually earned for the hours sacrificed. It wasn't a profitable job; that wasn't why Trent did it. Trent enjoyed the investigative and stalking aspect of the job though, knowing the person or people he was watching were none the wiser of his presence while he discovered their innermost darkest secrets provided him with a small amount of satisfaction.

The only issue with a career dependent on others' needs or desires to find out information otherwise unattainable to them was that there would be long stints between requests hiring his talents. People were often deterred by his age, not confident that a twenty-one-year-old would be proficient in handling their needs. It didn't matter about the reviews from satisfied clients or the discounted prices Trent would offer as an incentive; people chose to be biased and judge him by lack of life experience in their eyes. Little did they know that he had been doing this type of work for most of his life, spying for his father to keep a close eye on their allies and enemies. His father never trusted anyone close to him. Besides, who would question the motives of a young boy? Unassuming and innocent, he was the ideal undercover spy.

After such a period of no work, Trent had been approached to assist the local police force and council in finding the culprit behind the mass of slaughtered bodies of wildlife that had been discarded throughout the local community. It wasn't his usual investigation, but he was becoming desperate, his income running dry. Upon further investigation, Trent discovered it wasn't the first case of this

263

being reported. Over the past eighteen months, there had been over sixty accounts of similar circumstances being recorded within a two hundred K' radius. Though it would seem that the perpetrator had escalated their crimes as of late, increasing the number of kills and the depravity in which they were slaughtered and bled. The other noticeable concern was the size of the animal being killed having grown considerably larger in size over time. It was only a matter of time before the assailant would move to human victims, no longer satisfied with the taking of animals' lives.

He had targeted a person of interest so unassuming he almost didn't acknowledge them when being called to examine the last body. A wild boar had been strung up. Meticulous cuts had been strewn across his flesh, each tooth pulled and its eyes plucked. The entrails braided together, decorating a nearby tree along with other organs that were strung up.

"Fucking hell, this is like some kind of horror Christmas movie," the parks and wildlife assistant gagged, eyeing the decorated tree.

"Hmm," Trent responded. His eyes watched the collective group of witnesses, who were watching as evidence was being bagged. No one stood out as a potential culprit. Trent assumed he or she would want to be present as their last

victim was discovered. His eyes passed over a male with vacant eyes who looked like he had zoned out, not surprising considering the gore. It would be difficult for most to stomach. As his eyes continued to search through the crowd, Trent noted something about the male that he had missed at first glance. Not only was the male entirely unbothered by the messy autopsy, his entire stance relaxed almost at ease amongst the brutality. But he was no stranger to using a blade. At his hip, a sheath with a large hunting knife was visible beneath his coat. At his right ankle, where his jeans bulged slightly around his boot, there was a distinct additional shape of an additional sheath with a smaller knife. That was when he saw those unfocused eyes were actually trained on the ground below the carcass. Following the male's line of sight, he pinpointed it to the puddle of blood that had mostly soaked into the soil, creating a dark muddy area. Watching in his periphery for a reaction, Trent bent down, examining the ground. Then, dipping his gloved finger into the small amount of blood that still sat at the surface, he lifted his hand, examining the crimson liquid, which was a stark contrast to the white of his glove. The male's breath hitched and lips parted before his tongue came out, swiping across the lower lip. Then, as if shaking off the thought, he turned on his heel and left without a glance over his shoulder.

"Got you," Trent whispered to himself.

♦

Kyden's first kill had been accidental. He was whittling a totem in memory of his sister, who had succumbed to a rare form of cancer at only four years old. His parents had devoted the past two years to her fight, all their attention solely focused on her recovery, ignoring Kyden's presence. At twelve, he didn't need their hovering regardless, his intelligence surmised most adults having already graduated high school and been offered a full scholarship to university for a bachelor of medical studies. Kyden decided that when his sister fell ill, he wanted to do what he could to help find a cure. Unfortunately, she didn't live long enough for him to fulfil the dream.

As Kyden sliced the blade along the wood, rounding one edge, it caught on a small knot in the wood, careening his hand out at an angle directly into the path of his approaching puppy, who had come to offer companionship. Kyden didn't move or react as the puppy flinched back with a small yelp, tearing the blade from its throat. Kyden watched with fascination as the blood flowed freely from the small incision in its fur, unlocking a morbid curiosity inside of him. Frozen in place, Ky watched until the life left his pet's eyes, surrounded by a crimson pool. Then, and only then, did Kyden blink and move towards the puppy. Bending down, he dipped his fingers in the pooling blood, bringing his fingers up and rubbing them together, feeling the silky warmth. His eyes locked on the small knife and then back to the tiny wound, taking it all in. Unconsciously, he lifted the bloodied fingers to his lips, tasting the essence of life.

Over the years that followed that first eventful day, Kyden managed to resist the urge to replicate the incident, instead finding solace in his studies of human anatomy and the practice on cadavers. It wasn't until he encountered an injured dog by the side of the road one evening on his return home from a shift at the hospital where he had been given clear instructions that unless he got his pernicious anaemia under control, then he would be dismissed from his residency. It had caused a B12 deficiency, triggering hypersomnia. It had affected his work schedules and ability to maintain focus and remain alert for his allocated shifts, which had already been significantly shortened to compensate for his declining ailments.

Kyden did not take lightly to the threat highlighting his incompetencies. He felt as though he were being singled out, inferior to his colleagues because of his underlying conditions and age. Judged and treated unfairly for something beyond his control.

Emptying his locker, he threw his badge at the consultant in charge of his rotation and then threw a fist at his face. Blood sprayed from the man's face, and for the first time in a long time, Kyden felt a wave of peace wash over him. Before security could close in, Kyden exited the building, not looking back at the interns who crowded to assist their favourite medical personnel, who he had just assaulted. Kyden smirked to himself, feeling a sense of satisfaction at ruining the man's face. A face that was used to woo his way into the med of every female he encountered.

When he happened across the injured dog at the side of the road, a new urge had been rekindled. Between the blood on his hands from the assault and the memory flashing through his mind of his first kill, he could not control the incessant need to recreate that day. Running back to the car, he rifled around in the glove box until he found his box cutter. Glancing up and down the street, he walked over the where the injured dog lay, its heavy panting evident of how much pain it was suffering.

"I'm doing you and me both a service," he told the dog and then stabbed the blade into the carotid artery, watching its

life bleed out. Again, that feeling of utter peace washed over him, drowning out the unnecessary noise and tension plaguing him.

♦

Grady and Chris had just finished setting up their swags and gathered wood to start the fire when they were approached by Trent, who was scrutinising them as if they had an ulterior motive for being there

"Oi, you got a problem, fucker?" Grady stood facing off against Trent, ready to smack him the fuck out. Chris didn't interject, instead letting his brother go, choosing to recline back in the camping chair watching the drama unfold with keen interest.

Trent, not backing down, stepped up to Grady in challenge so they stood nose to nose. "If I were you, I would tread carefully."

"Oh yeah, and who are you and what are you gonna do about it if I don't?"

Trent's mouth hitched up at the corner a split second before he had Grady on the ground, one hand pinned behind his back. Grady wasn't going down easily without a fight and threw his body and Trent's to the side, rolling free and leaping to Trent ready to throw a fist.

Trent, however, was experienced in dealing with scrappy fighters and evaded Grady's punches with well-practised moves.

"The fuck?" Chris's startled voice snapped both men from their squabble, turning to see Kyden casually stroll into their campsite. His black clothes damp, and from the red smeared on his bare hands it didn't take two guesses to tell what it was.

"You," Trent said, pointing a finger at Kyden as Grady caught him in the chin, seizing the opportunity of Kyden's distraction.

Kyden looked over his shoulder and then pointed to himself questioningly. "What about me?"

Trent pushed Grady off, finding his feet and approached Kyden. "I am detaining you until the authorities can arrive to take you in for questioning regarding the slaughter of local wildlife."

"You're a cop?" Chris baulked.

Kyden crossed his arms over his chest and narrowed his eyes at Trent. "Rent a cop. You have no proof and no authority. Go back to playing pretend elsewhere."

Grady barked out a laugh. "Rent a cop? I like you, man." Grady met Kyden's side, slinging an arm over his shoulder.

Kyden glanced at the hand resting on his shoulder, then at the male on the other side with a raised brow but made no attempt to dissuade him.

Trent unclipped his holster, grabbing his gun. "Hands in the air, on your knees. I am placing you under citizen's arrest."

"Do you suppose there're bullets in the gun, or do you think it's fake?" Grady whisper-shouted to Chris.

"Move," Trent barked at Grady, who stayed beside Kyden. Both remained unmoving. Grady seemed amused by the turn of events, and if anything, Kyden looked bored. To prove the point, he yawned loudly, slapping a bloodied hand across his mouth, to which Grady laughed and gave his shoulder a small shake.

"The kid has balls," Chris remarked, hitching his chin to Kyden and walking cautiously towards Trent. "How about lowering the weapon so we can discuss what the fuck is actually going on here, yeah?"

"How about you go back to sitting on your stump like a good little boy and let me do my fucking job?" Trent rebutted.

Grady whistled and shook his head quietly, muttering, "You shouldn't have said that."

Before Trent could process Grady's comment, he found

himself on his back with his own gun trained between his eyes and Chris looming over him. "Do not dare respond to me in such a demanding manner again or you will find out first-hand what it's like to be on the receiving end of this barrel. Do. You. Understand?"

"Got it," Trent gritted out.

Chris stared down at him, reading him for a moment before stepping back but holding on to the gun. "Now, I say we all sit and discuss what the fuck is actually happening here before an unfortunate accident happens and one or two of you find yourselves as mulch."

Kyden grinned at that comment. Trent clenched his jaw. "Did you threaten me, boy?"

"First, I did not threaten you, I warned you. Second, if you value your mediocre life as a rent a cop then I would refrain from using the term boy to me again."

After a tense standoff, Trent finally relented. "Fine. But once we have this 'discussion'." Trent made inverted comma motion with his fingers. "I expect my weapon returned, and the assailant relinquished into my care."

"We will see," Chris responded.

Grady pulled Kyden towards a fallen log, directing him to sit while he fetched four beers from the esky. Trent took the offered beverage but made no attempt to crack it, watching his potential payday sit metres away from him.

"Tell me why you're so intent on having the kid arrested," Chris asked.

Trent explained that he had been following a trail of slaughtered wildlife, leading him to pinpoint Kyden as the perpetrator. During Trent's explanation, Kyden did not react in any way other than settling back comfortably in a relaxed manner as though he was listening to a campfire story.

"That's sick," Grady commented when Trent was finished. "So did you do it?" he asked Kyden.

Kyden shrugged.

"Come on, man, give me something."

Chris watched Kyden with interest. "Why kill the animals?"

Kyden smirked at Chris, cocking his head slightly. "Would you rather I bleed a human?"

"You admit it then?" Trent sneered.

Kyden gave nothing away. Slowly moving his sight onto Trent, he stared emotionlessly. "You are one to cast stones when your past is dirtier than my own."

"I don't know what you are talking about."

"Really?" Kyden stretched and yawned again. "Then I'm guessing that it is entirely normal for a natural cause of death to be obtained from a seven-inch blade with a

0.025-millimeter thickness being thrust into a jugular, then isn't it, Mr. Lerost?"

Trent paled. His throat bobbed as he swallowed the lump. "How...?"

"I am an expert in my field and make it my business to investigate particularly suspicious causes of deaths especially from high-profile people such as heads of notorious criminal gangs. It also struck me as unusual when I was offered a substantial amount of hush money to write the report stating that your father died from a heart attack."

"That monster was not my father," Trent ground out. "He was an abusive tyrant and a child molester." A gasp came from Chris.

"No? And I suppose your fingerprints weren't found on the murder weapon I found in the bins at your work premises either? Very sloppy for a professional investigator."

"Fuck!"

"This camping trip is the best idea you've ever had," Grady beamed at Chris, loving the unfolding drama

"He has you over a barrel, man." Chris didn't try to hide his amusement as he addressed Trent. Cracking the beer, Trent skulled it back then stretched his hand out with the empty bottle to Grady for another.

After two cartons of beer were emptied between the four of them, they found there was a camaraderie they never expected. All victims of pasts they couldn't escape, each with their own unsated urges forged from trauma.

At some point around two am, the rough idling of a cut engine dragged them all from their place around the small fire. They approached quietly as a young woman stepped out from a Kombi, her features lit up by the dull interior light, casting the attention of the four men on her.

Trent approached her first, offering his unwavering charm that never failed to attract the attention of the opposite sex. "Hi, there. Name's Will. I heard you pull up near my campsite and thought I'd come and introduce myself."

The woman caught by surprise turned around unsure until she saw his face and melted. "Hi, Will, it's nice to meet you. I'm Shiloh," she squeaked, tucking her hair behind her ear. "Sorry if I disturbed you. I know it's late. I've been travelling and needed somewhere to pull up for the night to rest."

"You're all alone?" Trent made it sound as though he was concerned about the fact.

She nodded, humming in answer.

"Such a shame," he drawled with a small shake of his head. "Perhaps I can fix that."

Chris, Grady and Kyden stepped into the light surrounding the woman.

"What's going on?" she asked, taking a step back, making contact with her vehicle. Her hands came out beside her, patting across the side of it blindly, trying to locate a door handle.

"Well, you see, you have provided us with an opportunity," Trent stated, steepling his fingers in front of him.

"Please don't hurt me," she whimpered in fear. Her hand making purchase with the door handle, she yanked on it desperately, turning to make an escape. Grady's hand shot out, holding the door closed. Shiloh screamed, taking a step back into Trent's chest. He spun her, pressing her back against the door of her Kombi so she faced them all again. Her shuddering breaths caused her chest to heave rapidly, catching the attention of the men on her breasts as they moved. Shiloh moved her hands to cover her chest, noting the attention as tears began flooding her face.

"Don't hurt me," she repeated. "Let me go, and I'll never mention I saw you. Please?"

Chris stepped forward, grasping her chin and directing her attention to him. "Unfortunately, we cannot promise that. We discovered something tonight." He looked to the others and then back to Shiloh. "We all have an unsated desire we are unable to fill, and you, my dear, could be the solution we have been looking for."

Shiloh's bottom lip trembled. Her eyes widened as she took in her predicament.

Chris stepped back, allowing Grady to approach with a piece of nylon rope in his hands that he was pulling taught in his grip. "I hope you're a screamer because out here, no one can hear you."

It was the beginning of a partnership where, between the four of them, they found peace and a feeling of acceptance and family no longer forcing them to hide who or what they were.

The only prerequisite made between them after that fateful night was that no matter what, at the end of the day, they would not allow one of their victims to ever come between them. They would all play an equal role in taking what they needed.

Grady

36

"So what do you say, our willing victim? Do you want to play? Want to be consumed by your fear and dopamine? Want to understand the high from hunting and being hunted?" I asked, watching a slight tremor ripple through her.

She gulped and then narrowed her eyes, her lips tightening into a firm line. I saw the determination and desire in her expression. Yeah, she wanted me. She wanted me bad! She wanted to catch me before I caught her, and I'd wager that she wanted an up-close and personal introduction to my big fella. And why wouldn't she? It was magnificent after all. I knew she didn't stand a chance of catching me. Still, the thrill in knowing she would fight with her dying breath. Fuck, I wanted to bury myself deep inside of her, watching as the dying light left her body. My cock thrummed in my pants, wanting to be personally acquainted.

Down, big fella!

Kyden surveyed her eagerly from beside me, watching her forced silence refusing to give us an answer.

"I am going to catch you, bind your hands and feet and bleed you out slowly, my pretty little cherry-filled dessert. I want to hear you beg for me to end you. Then, when I've drunk my fill, I will slice you open from your tight little cunt all the way up to your jaw, scoop you out and wear you like a cloak."

I chuckled deeply, slapping Ky on his shoulder. Trent calls me fucked up, but Kyden takes it to a whole other level. I can only hope to aspire to his level of unhinged one day. His depravity outmatches my own. The only difference is that I'm the only one who gets to hear just how deep his urges go. Whereas I share mine willingly, whether or not anyone wants to listen. I get off on knowing they fear me. That control over them helps me sleep like a baby at night. After I fuck Kyden's arse raw, of course.

"You won't catch me," Kira snarled with confidence, managing to keep her voice steady.

I had to give her credit, if I were in her position, I would be close to shitting my pants. Nah, I wouldn't, who am I kidding.? I'd laugh like the fucked up maniac I am and embrace the thrill of the challenge with a smile on my face.

"You have underestimated me since you caught me," she

jutted her chin out defiantly. I respected her bravado.

"True," I admitted. "If the circumstances were different, we may have even kept you as our pet. Have our fun between kills with you."

I stepped in close, my mouth brushing against her jaw, relishing the sharp intake of breath from her pouty lips.

"And something tells me you would have loved it, just as much, if not more than us."

Kira turned her head nose to nose with me. "I would have slit your throat in your sleep, then cut off your limp dick and shoved it down your esophagus."

Kyden groaned, his hand gripping his erection through his pants. "Fuck Gray, are you sure we can't keep her?"

Damnit, what was the spell this little witch had cast over us?

"No," I snapped. Grabbing her by the back of her hair and yanking her head back. "Trent fucked that up claiming her as his. She will be our best hunt yet, though."

I licked down the side of her cheek, holding her head steady and yanking her hair harder when she tried to pull away.

"You would never have had a chance with me anyway. You probably have to blow pepper on your cock and wait for it to sneeze so you can grab it with tweezers just to find it." She snarled between clenched teeth.

I slapped her face hard, ripping hair from her scalp in the process. Part of me instantly regretted it, wanting to soothe her and run my fingers through her hair. This had to be some voodoo shit. There was no way I could be catching …

feelings. I almost gagged at the thought. "Watch your mouth, Chocolate drop, or I will sew it shut again."

Her jaw tightened, seething with anger. I could still see the indentations where the stitches had been in around her mouth, the area scabbing perfectly. I bit down on my lower lip, wishing it were her lips between my teeth. I wonder if she would like that? Chocolate drop spat on my face, relishing in the surprise of my expression from her action. Fuck, she was intoxicating.

"Tsk, tsk, pretty girl. You're walking a dangerous line," Kyden warned.

"Indeed. For that, I'm going to punish you."

"What's worse than your presence?" she snarled.

I shared a look with Kyden. Maybe I was beginning to think the same thing. We wanted to keep this girl. I wonder if I could trick the others into believing the mannequin I used for target practice was our little victim? I could dress it up and make a frame so it sat on a remote control car or something. Make it look like it was running away, then when no one was looking, dispose of the evidence and act surprised when she *escaped.*

Oh no!

Then, when they were distracted looking for her, I could come back here with Ky and have some fun with our guest. When we weren't playing with her, she could live in a cage at the foot of my bed. I would even put a blanket and pillow in there because I'm not a complete asshole. Then what? When we moved on, I had no way of explaining a human-sized cage, even if I dressed her in an animal costume. I don't think they would buy it.

Fucking Trent. All of this is his fault.

"What's worse?" I chuckled darkly. "How about when we hunt you, we tip the playing field in our favour?"

"I'm not sure if you're aware of this, but four against one is already in your favour. Unless you can't count…?"

Oh, she was playing a dangerous game. Kyden stepped up behind her, wrapping a hand around her throat. I didn't miss her breath hitch or her lips parting slightly. Nor did I miss the way she relaxed into his hold and the way her eyes rolled back before she corrected her composure, pretending that she wasn't turned on. There was probably a whole slip and slide in her knickers.

"That wasn't very nice," Kyden whispered in her ear, tightening his grip on her throat.

"Well, you would know all about that," she rasped venomously.

"Snarky! Let's see how long that lasts when Gray tells you just how much of a disadvantage you are about to find yourself in." Kyden released his grasp slightly when her face began to redden, letting her suck in air.

Her eyes narrowed. "As opposed to being held against my will by four men who outpower me and want to kill me?"

"Hunt you. *Possibly* kill you. Undecided as of yet," I told her.

"Yeah, well, I don't see how anything you say will make the entire situation worse."

Kyden's chuckles matched my own. I had already discussed my plans with him beforehand, knowing full well she would do or say something to trigger the disadvantage.

"Now, that is where you are mistaken. You see, when we come for you, we will be strapped with as many weapons and traps that we can carry."

I walked around her slowly, watching as Ky's hand traced circles on her abdomen. I knew he was thinking about how her intestines would feel wrapped around his hands. I frowned at the thought, the idea of it not sitting as well in my stomach as it usually would. Maybe it was the dodgy curry takeout from last night? I thought it tasted a little strange at the time. No anal for me, just in case I end up with an uncontrolled mudslide.

Stopping back in front of Chocolate drop—no, Kira. I didn't want to be thinking of brown if my stomach was off. I leaned down, so I was eye to eye with her.

"You, however, will be hunting us in return, with nothing but your wits and bare hands."

Kyden tightened his hold on her for a split second before she began thrashing. "You motherfucking piece of shit. How is that fair?"

"It isn't supposed to be. This is our game. Had you kept that smart mouth of yours closed, then you wouldn't have been punished."

"I'm going to kill you first," she rasped under Kyden's fingers at her throat, which were tightening every second. When her lids began to close, losing consciousness, I gave her one final crumb. "Thirty minutes headstart. That's your only advantage." Her head lulled after that, and Kyden dropped her unconscious body unceremoniously to the ground.

"Do you think you'll actually be able to kill her?"

My eyes flicked from Kira up to Kyden, who was studying her with interest. He was conflicted too.

"I guess we will have to wait and see."

His face looked troubled. Nudging her with his foot, he squatted down beside her, brushing the hair from her face tenderly. I was about to ask what he was doing, but then he pinched her nose, cutting off her air. When her face flushed, he released his hold, watching with fascination as she sucked in deep breaths, oblivious to what he had done.

"She's special," he muttered to himself, tilting his head.

"Yeah, she is. Maybe we should get rid of Trent and keep her in his place," I joked.

But in the back of my mind, the idea didn't seem quite so absurd. We could use her to lure females to us easier, maybe convince her to partake in a little girl on girl action. Kyden would enjoy it if it were during shark week. Oh, the nefarious plans I had in mind for this little treasure we have uncovered. Clearly, Kyden thought the same. His brows hit his hairline, and he looked at me, intrigued by the thought.

I laughed it off, offering my hand for him to stand.

"Come on, let's go find you something to eat before you pass out. You'll need all your energy tomorrow."

Ky nodded, already looking seconds away from sleep. "Yeah righto. You coming in later?"

"Mm," I pressed up against him, nipping his bottom lip. "Do you want me to? Do you want me to come in while you are out cold and fuck your tight little arse so hard it hurts to walk tomorrow?"

"Fuck yes," he breathed, gripping the back of my head and kissing my mouth deeply. "Do what you promised. Pierce my cock and use me to get yourself off. I can't stop thinking about it since I watched the video."

"You like that? I wonder what else I can pierce? Maybe your nipples?" I pinched one between my fingers, making him groan. "Maybe your tongue?" I kissed him again, this time biting down on his fleshy tongue until I tasted blood. He shoved his erection-clad jeans against mine; the sensation was almost too much. "Perhaps…" I pulled back from his mouth. "Perhaps, I will see just how many barbels I can fit along your shaft, then ride your cock while it's tender and bleeding, finding my own pleasure, leaving you in agony when you wake, swollen and too sore to touch, unable to get off until you heal."

Now that my stomach seemed to have settled, I passed it off as a moment of gas. A good fart can do wonders for an off gut.

Unleashing the beast, Kyden shoved me hard on my chest, hooking his foot behind my ankle, he sent me splayed out on my back, hitting the floor with an *oomf*. He didn't give me the chance to recover before he was on me, sliding my pants down my legs and freeing himself from his own pants. Yeah, he wanted me bad.

"You said that deliberately," he growled, lifting my shirt to expose my chest so he could cut me.

"Make me bleed, Peaches, mark me as yours."

I don't know if he realised just how much I enjoyed seeing the scars he left on my skin, marking me up like a well-used chopping board. Instead, to my disappointment, he cut through the fabric, half tearing it from my body and tossing it aside.

"You knew I wouldn't be able to resist you."

Duh, I'm irresistible, of course I know. My sexual appeal knows no bounds. I'm ravishing.

Kyden's blade met my flesh, carving a deep line across my pectoral. I hissed at the sting, which morphed into the rush I was craving. Leaning forward, he attacked my mouth with his again desperately, his cock rocking back and forth through the blood pooling from my gut. I moaned from the sharp sting of the combined friction and arousal from him assaulting mouth.

"Fuck me," I pleaded. Needing him like I needed air. "Make me hurt."

Kyden's deep growl was the only response I received before he moved back, kneeling between my legs. He lifted my hips. With one hand wrapped around his blood-covered cock, he lined himself up to my arse, his other hand tracing through the blood smeared across my stomach, painting me scarlet. He pushed in with one hard thrust, crushing my balls with a painful force between our bodies, causing me to gasp from the infliction. I choked on vomit, swallowing it back down behind pained tears. My poor scrotum was just pancaked.

"Suck. it. up. Bitch. Tits." He jackhammered in and out, his fingers digging into my wound, making the blood flow faster.

The combined pain and pleasure was an experience I had only ever known with Ky. It was our dirty little secret until recently. Reaching down to grasp my cock, unable to resist any longer, I needed to cum.

Kyden slapped my hand away. "No!"

"Fuckuck Ky, I need …"

"You will fucking wait, Gray."

Reaching down, he cupped my tender balls, squeezing them with a bruising grip. I dug my fingers into the sides of my upper thighs to restrain myself from batting his hands away instinctively. The high-pitched squeal leaving my lips would have been embarrassing in front of anyone else—giving every girl a run for their money—but Ky loved to stretch my vocal chords, seeing what noises he could expel from my body when I was at his mercy, and he was in control. Pain was a mindset, and he knew just how much I enjoyed swimming in the deep end of that pool, whether it be inflicting it or being on the receiving end.

Kyden bellowed out his release in a guttural groan, throwing his head back in a purely animalistic manoeuvre. My man was more animal than human at times, and I didn't want to tame him. My wild, feral beast. Did that make me Belle? I was totally the Beauty to his Beast, and he could destroy my rosebud arse anytime.

Before he had even finished filling me, Kyden's eyes rolled back, and he collapsed forward, his entire weight falling on top of me. Already anticipating him passing out when he hit his high, I braced my hands on his chest so he didn't crush me. When his cock had finished twitching, I wiggled my hips, freeing him from inside of me, then rolled him on his side, pressing a chaste kiss on his forehead. He hadn't eaten, so I was going to have to insert a nasogastric tube while he was out so he wouldn't wain tomorrow during the hunt. He had run me through this yesterday after acknowledging how much weight he had lost so I could keep him filled with more than my cum when he was out. Fuck, I should set up a full I.V. and fill him with as much of the good shit as I could so he was in prime condition.

Kira would have had a pretty hot soundtrack while she dreamed. The noises that came from Kyden's throat in the throes of ecstasy were enough to get a woman pregnant and turn a straight man gay. It had given me the idea of recording him and selling that shit on more than one occasion.

First things first. I needed to clean up both Ky and myself and tend to my wound. Fingering the cut, I hissed, noting the depth. Well shit. This needed stitches. I guess I deserved it considering how I played him.

"So worth it," I muttered to myself, using my destroyed shirt to staunch the bleeding. Chris would be returning soon with Trent, so I needed to get a wriggle on. Walking to the kitchen, I fumbled around in one of the go bags until I found a thick roll of duct tape. Cutting off a strip, I roughly pressed it against where I held the t-shirt and then cut off more strips, binding Kira's hands and feet, with another strip across her mouth in case she woke. Bending down in the pool of blood on the floor beside Kyden, I grabbed his arm, yanking him upright. I tucked my head in under his arm and lifted him up onto my shoulders. It was a difficult task considering his size, but with a few wobbly motions, after falling and dropping him twice, I stood and walked him to the bedroom with his dick still swinging free from his pants slapping my cheek with drying blood and the scent of shit. Ahh, the aroma of a good time.

After a quick sponge bath, which naturally I recorded on my phone for Kyden to watch later, allowing him to enjoy where I took extra good care of my little sex doll, cleaning his cock meticulously and sucking him off. I then tucked Kyden in bed with the promise to return after I had superglued my wound closed. It was easier than stitching it, despite getting off on the sting of the needle piercing my flesh, probably because now I was also feeling all kinds of faint, likely from blood loss. Not to mention I had other things on my mind. Like finding a local stockist for needles, tubes and barbells. Hmm, perhaps I should hit up the tattoo parlour and see about purchasing a gun too. I smiled to myself imagining Kyden's reaction to waking with my name tattooed on his cock.

"Fuck yeah, I'm doing it." I decided excitedly.

Kissing him on his dick and then his lips, I raced out of his room in search of my keys and wallet. The anticipation of what was to come was better than what a kid experiences on Christmas Eve. The difference being when I come, or cum rather, and my sack gets emptied, Kyden isn't disappointed because he didn't get the present he was expecting. I'm the gift that keeps on giving with endless fuckery, because I'm generous like that.

Kira

37

Despite the uncertainty of the day ahead, my nerves were not playing havoc. Perhaps it was the change of atmosphere the storm brought the night before, offering a brief reprieve to the unbearable heat—even if it meant spending the day trudging through mud for however long I survived.

I tilted my head back, staring up at the cloud-covered sky, embracing this fleeting moment of peace that was encompassing me. The silence before the storm, or acceptance before death. However you want to paint it, I was having that moment.

"Unless you can fly, there's no escape up there," Kyden said from over my shoulder. "You will have to be quick and cunning if you plan on walking away." He walked with a slight limp, his movements cautious, and he walked with discomfort. I wondered how it would affect his chances of catching me today. I bit back a smirk.

"Maybe you should tell yourself that," I shot back, not looking at him, my focus remaining on the sky for several more heartbeats. He chuckled, moving to Grady's side.

Dropping my chin, I focused my thoughts on what lay ahead of me. I wanted to run, but knowing these men, I would be dead before I made it three steps. Winning this little game was my only option. I steeled myself as a low whirring sound filtered through the air. Before me, thick steel bared gates vibrated slightly, then slid open.

Chris stepped beside me on one side with Kyden and Grady on the other side. I had been given a thirty-minute head start. Supposedly the edge of the thick forest was surrounded by a tall chain-link, electric fence. I had no idea if it was true or not, but I wasn't really wanting to find out first-hand.

"You know the rules?" Chris asked, looking down at me. If I wasn't mistaken, there was a slight hesitation in his demeanour.

I nodded, clenching my hands into fists at my side to hide the shake. It wasn't nerves or fear; I think it was adrenaline. A small part of me was excited by this.

"Kill or be killed." I was proud when my voice came out strong, not wavering.

"Incapacitated," Chris corrected, looking at me side-eyed.

"Tell them that," I muttered, flicking my head to the side, glaring in Grady and Kyden's direction.

Chris's arms crossed over his chest, which was covered in a

camo patterned vest, adorned with buckles and pockets for the countless weapons he had on him.

"We only need to capture you, or vice versa. But if you're out for blood …?" He looked me in the eyes and wiggled his eyebrows, then nodded his head towards Kyden, who was stifling a yawn.

"I have no intention of leaving any of you alive," I spat sardonically.

Grady pouted, looking offended. "And here I thought we had something special between us, Chocolate drop."

Kyden laughed, grabbing Grady by the shoulders and giving him a slight shake with excitement.

I rolled my eyes, directing my attention back to the enclosure I was about to walk into. I should say arena, because I had a distinctive feeling this battle was going to be bloody.

"Ready?" Chris asked.

No, I was at a disadvantage with only one hidden weapon compared to the countless varied weapons they each carried. Not to mention the ones they would grab when they began their hunt.

"Yes." Where was Trent?

"Tic tock Kira. I'll be seeing you *real* soon," Grady whispered to me, making me tense with his unpredictability.

It didn't slip his attention either. His low chuckle forced my feet forward through the gates and into the unknown, with the steel bars closing behind me once I was clear. I spun on my heel when I heard them moving. Grady was smiling, waving his fingers at me. Kyden watched me with a knife spinning effortlessly between his fingers. Chris tapped the face of his watch in warning.

Turning right, out of their field of view, I darted between a row of trees so I could take stock of my surroundings briefly before the light began fading. Near the entrance was a large clearing with high grass and wildflowers covering the space. Surrounding it, sparsely planted trees and native shrubs grew, before thickening further back into the distance, creating a foreboding entrance of midnight under the thick canopy of tall dense foliage.

"I wish I could help you escape." Trent's voice broke me from my observation. Somehow, despite the predicament of being one another's prey, he comforted the unease within me.

I launched myself into his arms, inhaling his scent. "You're breaking the rules," I told him. "You are supposed to give me a head start."

The corner of his mouth kicked up. "And you aren't supposed to be fraternising with the enemy" "

"Trying to get a head start on the competition?"

"On the contrary. I've come to offer advice and a warning. There are things out there just as, if not more dangerous than the four of us who will be hunting you."

I scoffed. "I've had my fill, thanks. I'll take my chances with whatever kangaroo or wombat tries to take me on."

"Oh? And what about the elusive drop bear?" he smirked, teasing me.

I rolled my eyes.

"In all seriousness, keep a sharp eye. There are over five hundred hectares with undiscovered trip wires, claw traps and pressure bombs. This area was once a training facility. The scrub is filled with ticks, spiders and bugs. The waterway is croc infested, so no swimming, and brown snakes will strike if they feel threatened."

"I'm no threat. I'll keep an eye out."

Trent shook his head exasperatedly. He glanced out over the expanse of the thick bush that was the hunting grounds, then turned his head in the direction of the gate—despite it being hidden from view.

"Everything in this world is considered a threat if you pose enough danger to it. Self-preservation is a natural instinct in the order of life, the kill or be killed scenario. Therefore, there is not a living being I would trust with your life." Trent stated, returning his sights on me.

"Not even yours?" I asked.

"Especially mine," Trent said matter-of-factly as he studied me. "You're not afraid," he observed. Words that had been used before.

Not of you. I shrugged, feigning indifference, while my fingers toyed with the front of my shirt, rubbing it between my fingers.

"Why should I be? Did you not just tell me that everything in this world should be considered a threat? Perhaps it is you who should be afraid of me."

A sly smile spread across his face. "Then, my little predator, I will enjoy being your willing prey in the hunt."

"When I capture you, will that make me the villain?" I asked, picturing him tied up before me, our previous roles reversed.

He took a step closer. "That…" he reached out, pinching my chin to lift it higher, so I met his nose with my own, "makes you a force to be reckoned with. One that the others should never underestimate and not dare cross." Trent rubbed his nose against the side of mine, brushing his lips softly against mine. "I cannot wait to see you come undone and unleash your wrath against us. You will no doubt be magnificent."

I squeezed my eyes closed, shuddering at his words, feeling my chin released. I inhaled deeply before opening my eyes again. But in that brief moment, he had vanished out of existence, leaving my chest heaving and goosebumps trailing across every inch of my skin. I rubbed my arms, glancing around, then began my trek, staying in the light line of trees while I navigated deeper into the enclosure. Trent's words played back to me, reminding me to keep an eye out for anything slithering and moving through the grass.

A loud grinding noise echoed through the air. Pressing up against a nearby tree, I waited until it halted, then slowly peered around the thick trunk. In the distance, four male figures walked through the entrance. They spoke briefly as the gate closed. When did Trent go back through? And how hadn't I heard the gate open when he did? I rubbed my temple, hiding back behind the tree when I saw them all gaze across the expanse in front of them. When I peered back around, they were gone.

Shit! I don't know which way they went.

Mindfully treading through the thick scrub, I remained conscious of my surroundings so as not to disrupt the leaf litter and branches underfoot with too heavy a foot. I couldn't afford to alert them to my presence, or leave a trail of flattened grass, essentially leaving a trail of breadcrumbs for them to follow to my location. I had to be smart about how I was going to survive and win this hunt.

There were no clues as to the direction in which any of the men had travelled or Trent had disappeared to, and I couldn't help but wonder if the moment between us was in itself a test. A wave of frustration washed over me for having allowed him to get the best of me.

I paused, holding my breath to listen more intently to my surroundings, waiting for a noise to indicate the direction in which I should travel. There was nothing but an eerie stillness and silence surrounding me. Not even the low hum of insects, or rustling of the trees under a gentle breeze. It was as though time itself stood frozen, waiting and watching.

I let out a slow breath, my eyes scanning the shadowed sections where the light of the late day didn't filter through the dense foliage—hoping for a glimpse of movement or anything really, to let me know I wasn't alone. I knew I wasn't, not really.

I swear I could feel eyes on me, stalking my every step, watching to see what I would do. Waiting for me to find them before they found me.

The hairs on the back of my neck stood up in response to the unknown while my mind ran rampant. Gulping, I spun, half expecting to see someone standing at my back with a weapon in hand. I was only greeted with my own fears, not irrational, just cautious.

"This is stupid," I whispered to myself, debating if I should turn on my heel to retreat back the way I had begun.

I didn't want to, though.

I liked a challenge.

Crouching down, I picked up a thick stick at my feet as long as my arm. Deciding that if the need arose before I could at least arm myself with a weapon of some form to hold them back before surprising them by brandishing the knife tucked into my waistband. As far as I knew, Trent was the only one aware of it because he gifted it to me. Who knew what lay hidden in the scrub other than the four men who were playing this game with me?

I ran with purpose, dissolving myself into the dark. I braced against a tree for a moment, allowing myself a moment for my heart to slow and my eyes to adjust to the darkness surrounding me.

It had been stupid of me to have remained under the light of day. Surely they had watched as I slunk away to where my position was. A quick glance around in the low light my eyes were adjusting to that surrounded me told me that if I was being watched, then my silhouette was still very visible.

Backing around the tree in the shrouded vegetation, I began

formulating a plan. A descending branch overhead and to the side brushed against my forehead, the tip branching out to a fork. Turning my head and leaning forward, the front of my hoodie snagged on the branch. Perfect.

I carefully dropped the branch down so it leaned against my leg, then slipped an arm from one sleeve and then the other, sliding them inside inconspicuously. I slowly wiggled free from the warmth, moving the fabric as minimal as possible while it hung from the branch at the top of the hood. Sliding my hand above my head from inside the jumper, I adjusted the position of how it hung as I began bending at my knees to slide out.

A steadying breath later and I was adjusting the branch that I had planned to use as a weapon inside the hoodie and across the shoulders, giving it somewhat of a shape. It held too flat, but I hoped that the bushes surrounding it would disguise the fact.

In a squat entirely camouflaged, I moved forward so I was surrounded by the low vegetation. I noticed what looked like a hollowed tree within sight. It was difficult to be certain because it was enveloped entirely in blackness.

A peculiar sound tore through the air, sending my heartbeat galloping wildly in my chest. Before I gained the opportunity to lay eyes on the cause of the sound, it ended with a *thud,* followed by the sound of splintering wood.

Violent uncontrolled shuddering rocked my limbs as my gaze caught a refraction of light off the tail of a metal arrow that was now embedded in the centre of where my face would have been, if I still wore the hoodie.

Crippling fear and shock held me paralyzed for several moments as I took in what had happened. The sound of a branch snapping to my left froze my tremors. Eyes widening, I slowly twisted my head to the sound with a gulp, swallowing my stomach before it emptied, giving away my position.

The thick underbrush was disturbed by rapid footfalls that came to a stumbling halt.

"Fuck," Grady cursed.

"Fucking bitch," Kyden added with a machete held firmly in his right hand, poised to strike. "She's good."
Was that admiration in his tone?

I felt a small triumph in outsmarting them momentarily.

Grady spun on the spot, furious, his hands clenched at his sides, one gripping a bow with a white-knuckled grasp. Even in the low light, the contrast in the colouring was evident. I held my breath, hoping that he couldn't hear the rapid beating of my heart in my chest. In my own ears, it was deafening.

Kyden's head whipped back and forth rapidly scanning his surroundings, then turned back to where the hoodie was impaled and yanked the arrow free, sending my hoodie falling to the ground. Grady was examining the ground closely, trying to track the disturbed ground.

Grady took the arrow from Kyden, grasping it in the same hand as the bow. He reached into his pocket and withdrew a phone. Lighting up the flashlight, he directed the light to the ground. He searched it meticulously, looking for footprints or any evidence of which direction I had travelled. Lifting the light, he moved it slowly around him, lighting up the underbrush and heavy foliage. I knew the moment the light hit me I would be visible. The light drifted closer. I had mere seconds to decide if I should flee now and risk an arrow in my flesh, or wait to be seen and then attempt to flee, or attack my predators knowing my chances of overpowering them when I was unarmed were nonexistent. All options are guaranteed to end in my demise.

Grady swept the light up and down beside me. With one more motion of his hand I would be seen.

A whistle cut the air. The light flashed straight past me, lighting up my face for a millisecond before it was directed to where Chris had silently approached.

I could briefly make out several hand gestures between the

trio as they silently communicated between one another. I remained rooted in my spot only allowing myself short, shallow, slow breaths, which made my chest burn painfully.

With the phone in one hand, the light directed to his feet and out again, Grady continued to search for any evidence of my retreat. He wasn't happy that I had evaded him; it was obvious by the tightened grip of the bow, his tight jaw and flared nostrils. When he eventually finds me, I know it will not be pleasant.

Eventually, he let out a guttural groan after circling several times in a frustrated motion. Clicking his fingers to the other men, he turned off the light on his phone, pocketing it and retreating back the way he had come. Releasing a bated breath, I sighed in relief when the others gestured to one another silently before they stealthily separated in opposite directions, all with bows drawn and loaded as they continued to hunt for their prey. Me.

The only way to escape them, to escape victorious and still breathing, was to do just as they do. I had to become the killer. I decided I would take out the most dangerous first, but was that Grady or Kyden?

Kyden seemed to suffer from some form of narcolepsy, so I could only hope I would find him already incapacitated and take him down easily.

Taking the odds against Grady, I began making my way in the direction he disappeared, hugging the trees and remaining as hidden as possible by the foliage while hunting. The predator becomes the prey.

I wrapped my hand around the pommel of the blade in preparation. Grady's unpredictability held me on edge. He claimed to want to drag out my torture, but he did also just try to shoot me in the head with an arrow.

It also wasn't about hunting; it was about avoiding being captured. Trent didn't appear with the other three. But then again, he wasn't exactly in their good books for deciding not to share.

Would they hunt him too?

Why am I worried about him? My life is in peril because of him to begin with.

I clenched my free hand into a tight fist, fighting the urge to punch a tree or something. With my anger bubbling inside, what was wrong with me? I must be suffering from Stockholm syndrome, falling for my abductor.

A noise directly behind me broke my train of thought. I spun on the spot, my hand snapped out in front of me defensively, the tip of the blade meeting friction as it sunk into flesh. I gasped, almost dropping it and letting go of the handle.

Then I saw teeth smiling wide at me.

The masochist and sadist, Kyden, had found me.

"Pretty girl," he purred. "You do know how to flirt."

I screamed, yanking my hand back with the knife, and plunged it in again and again without conscious thought. Kyden grunted and grabbed my wrist.

I slapped his face, catching him by surprise. He released my wrist. Taking advantage, I ran. I had already given myself away when I screamed; it was stupid on my part. My footfalls were heavy and frantic in desperation to put distance between myself and the man who wanted to wear my body like a skin suit.

Maybe I had been trying to chase the wrong person down first and should have let his condition take him out instead. A whistle sounded beside my ear, followed by a sharp sting and the sound of wood splitting.

Fuck, arrows. Meaning Grady was close behind. Zigzagging between trees, I avoided the blow as several arrows whizzed past, barely missing me.

My chest was burning from exertion, my body fueled into fight or flight by pure adrenaline as I powered forward, through the thick underbrush, somehow managing to remain steady without tripping over my own feet.

"You can run, but you can't hide," Grady sing-songed.

"You fucked up by not killing Ky when you had the chance, Chocolate drop. Now you have only enticed the beast inside of him, and now he's going to be out for blood."

Oh, fuck. A whimper escaped my mouth. I darted to the left through a heavy cluster of tree trunks. Squeezing my body through the narrow gap in the limbs, I slapped my hand over my mouth to silence any noise, pushing myself further into the small space. My heartbeat was careening out of my chest as my body shook violently, despite being covered in a thick layer of sweat.

Kyden came crashing loudly into view through the shrubs, his frantic movements erratic, and I could distinguish a noticeable blackened area across the front of his light grey shirt where he held his hand, attempting to stem the bleeding.

He growled, the sound purely animalistic.

Lifting his hand to his mouth, sucking his own blood from his fingers, he groaned deeply, then took off again in the opposite direction to where I hid.

I couldn't stay here long, just long enough to catch my breath. Or until Kyden hopefully bled out, leaving me three men to take down.

Another arrow broke the air. I didn't see where this one hit, but the sound of impact sounded close.

Grady appeared a split-second later, yanking the arrow free with three pulls from a tree further away than I estimated. Then he turned to face where I stood, cloaked in darkness, and I swore for a heartbeat he stared straight into my soul. He smiled broadly, walking towards me, one hand clutching the bow, the other the arrow he had freed from the tree.

I attempted to back up further between the gaps of the trunks behind me, but was met with a solid tree wider than the others. Not a tree, I quickly realised when a hand came around my mouth and nose, cutting off all oxygen.

"Shh," Trent breathed into my ear in a barely audible tone when my hands came up to fight him off. "He can't see you."

Trent uncurled the fingers around my nose so I could breathe, but kept his hand firmly against my mouth. I was grateful when Grady stopped directly in front of the tree cluster and yanked an arrow free from a tree at eye level, directly in front of me. He inspected the other arrow clasped in the same hand, then turned his back to me and stalked in the same direction Kyden had taken off.

I attempted to shrug Trent free when the coast was clear, but he tightened his grip, pulling me even closer, if that was even possible.

"Chris will be close," he warned. "I don't know where his loyalty lies yet."

Oh, I did. He was working firsthand with the other two psychopaths.

"You aren't supposed to be helping me," I whisper-shouted.

"Oh?" His hot breath tickled my ear. "Must have missed that memo."

I elbowed him in the stomach, or at least tried to, but the only thing I managed was to crack my funny bone on a tree limb. Gulping back a cry of pain, I tensed, gritting my teeth with a hiss.

I felt Trent's silent chuckle behind me. Bringing my foot down, I stomped on his foot, feeling the sole of my shoe flex over his steel-capped boots. Of course. I rolled my eyes, huffing with annoyance at his increased silent amusement.

Trent

38

She pretended to be angry, but I knew otherwise; I could practically smell her arousal. She loved to fight me. I could see it in her eyes when they crinkled at the corners, smiling when her mouth was set in a firm scowl. Her continued need to inflict pain on me was her way of accepting the uncontrolled urge to touch me. She craved me as much as I craved her. The only difference was that she was in denial.

Admittedly, I enjoyed riling her up, encouraging her rage and watching her come undone. It was more beautiful and radiant than any sunset to ever grace the sky. I could feast on her anger and never hunger again, drink in her fury and never thirst. She sated the uncontrollable urges that plagued me in a way I never knew to be possible.

"You do know a mosquito bite is more painful than what you're attempting to do." I somehow managed to keep the smirk off my face, even when her nostrils flared as her teeth gritted. Her eyes narrowed into little slits with her fists balled at her side. She wore her fury magnificently.

That's it, my dark shadow, hit me, show me what you've got. Own your darkness and allow it to consume you. I raised a challenging brow. Crossing my arms over my chest, I crossed one ankle over the other and leant against a tree trunk.

She stomped towards me, practically vibrating with rage. Her shoulder pulled back, and I expected her arm to pull back. Instead, I found myself dropping to my knees. Blinding pain sending my stomach into my throat, tears rolling down my face from her foot connecting with precision against my testicles, where they now retracted inside of my body, either from the unwarranted attack they just received or as a way to protect themselves from being harmed again.

"What's that?" She loomed over me mockingly, her hand curled around her ear. "Anything I do would hurt less than a mozzie? I don't know about you, but I would personally hate to see what kind of mozzie can leave you writhing on the ground."

She had the nerve to condescendingly pat my cheek. "Bye, bye Trent. I'll give you a head start to hide before I catch you, because I'm winning this hunt. You have, oh…" She checked an invisible watch on her wrist, tapping there. "Maybe five minutes. Better get moving."

She left me on the ground, my hands caressing my crotch through pained whimpers.

Oh, it was on.

Kyden

39

Despite the lingering pain in my cock from waking up with a series of heavy gauged barbels penetrating through the underside of my dick—along with Grady's name tattooed in gothic script—I had managed to push aside the discomfort for today's hunt. I had spent enough time this morning admiring the new accessories and replaying the video of Grady marking me and riding my cock after he pierced it. If I hadn't been sitting there with a bag of ice on my crotch to relieve some of the swelling and preventing an erection, I probably would have foregone today's activities in favour of burying myself in Grady when it was time to depart this morning. Then again, I more than likely would have requested a delayed start, because there was no way I was missing out on the opportunity to claim Kira as my trophy.

Riding a high like I had never experienced before, adrenaline coursing through my veins, I crashed over shrubs and ran with purpose through the forest that was brimming with energy. Everything lit up before my eyes, highlighted in a kaleidoscope of fluorescent colour. The sharp sting where I bled fueled my urgency to find my pretty girl. I had to taste her essence, bathe her in my blood and fuck her raw.

I wasn't going to kill her, just scare her. If I caught her, I was going to keep her. Even if it meant she spent the rest of her life chained to my bed.

Hmm, I wonder if it would be more efficient to drill directly into her bone and attach a length of chain? It ran the risk of infection unless I could keep the point of entry clean until it healed around the point of the incision. She wasn't going to escape me again, no matter what.

The idea sparing a million other scenarios in my head.

Fuck, I saw red when Grady released that arrow from a distance. I truly thought he had killed her. I don't know if I was more angry with her creative deception or the fact he was out for blood. She would pay for that little trickery.

Raising a hand to my mouth, I sucked the blood running down my arm dripping from my fingertips. Not as sweet as my pretty girl's blood, but it was the hit I needed to keep searching before the others claimed the prize. My prize.

Under the light of the moon, I caught sight of Chris skulking behind a hollowed tree, observing my hurried steps as I tore past him. He gave a brief nod in the other direction, informing me he was moving that way. I paid him no attention. I didn't give a shit which way he went; his position was of no interest to me. The only other person I was concerned about was Trent, the fucker. He had evaded us after stepping foot in the enclosure at our side, and I had no doubt he was somehow assisting my girl in avoiding capture.

With his cunning nature and desperate need to lay claim to her, I wouldn't put it past him to take each of us out so he would be left the victor. Plus, he was kind of salty about being knocked out and locked in the boot naked. He should be grateful that's all I did to him after his little act of betrayal.

As I continued running, my eyes darting around, taking in my surroundings, I felt a rush of exhilaration catching sight of my prey.

Gotcha!

She was frantically jumping around over fallen tree limbs, trying to keep on higher ground, sticking to the thicker trunks. Her eyes moved so quickly across the ground it gave me whiplash watching.

I strode towards her, making no attempt to hide my approach when she heard me move.

"No, stay back," she urged, returning her eyes to the ground, with an edge of panic.

Was this a ploy to trick me into thinking there was something attacking her, so she could catch me off guard? I wouldn't put it past her. She was smarter than I had originally anticipated.

"Nice try, pretty girl."

"Oh my God, don't be daft, I'm serious."

My step faltered, looking to where her attention was caught. She jumped to a corresponding fragment of a fallen tree, squealing high-pitched as a snake lunged at her, missing her by a breath.

I shuddered. Of all the things that could freak me out, snakes were at the top of the list. The rest of the list was barren, except for snails. Don't ask me why, but the mere thought of them makes me gag. On queue, my chest heaved at the thought. I was quickly snapped from my own moment of detest when the snake whipped up, preparing to strike again. Without hesitation, I withdrew a throwing knife and sent it soaring through the air just as it sprung. My feet were already taking me to her before the knife made contact. Without time to move from the impending strike of the snake or my knife, my pretty girl flinched, her foot hooking on a raised branch, and she fell back with a scream, landing heavily on her back. The snake landed across her legs, still moving despite the tip of my knife making precise contact. I was hovering over her before she had registered what had happened. Her face morphed from fear to a combination of uncertainty and relief as she was faced with her own morality by two predators. One being a natural-born killer, the other attacking because it was threatened.

Grasping my throwing knife by the handle. I lifted it with the spiked head of the snake still twitching slightly. The blade met the back of its head with the exit at its open mouth, between its fangs. It hung limp as I lifted it into the air to examine it more closely, feigning bravado to appear the hero before my damsel in distress.

Kira pulled her knees to her chest, moving herself away from the dangling tail which had been hanging above her feet, swallowing thickly. Her eyes caught on the snake, no doubt thinking of all the ways she would worship me now, knowing that I not only saved her life, but won the hunt.

Whipping its tail with a sudden second burst of life, the not-dead-snake curled its tail around my arm, coiling tight. I shook it free and threw it down, knife and all, with a manly squeal of my own. I danced on the spot, shuddering with repulsion and brushing my arm where it had made contact with my skin.

Nervous, scared laughter diverted my attention back to my prey. Her amused body vibrated with a mix of shock and adrenaline. Ahh, the high.

I cleared my throat, glaring at the snake, which had stopped twitching and lay belly up looking entirely innocent, then looked over at Kira. Her focus had followed mine when I glared at the now-dead reptile. She was chewing on her lower lip with an edge of sadness softening her eyes.

Squatting down beside her, I lifted the hem of her shirt to check her over and see if she had been struck by the snake.

"Stop! What are you doing?" She swatted my hand away. Or at least tried to.

"You're being difficult," I snapped, forcing her shirt higher, inspecting her flesh, despite her reservations.

She pulled her shirt from my grasp and pressed a hand to my chest. Her mouth parted when she felt my pectoral under her fingers. She ran her hand lower before snapping from the distraction, yanking her hand back with a scowl.

"Stupid me, and here I thought the idea of the game was to try and not let you catch me."

I tilted my head, looking at her blandly. "And here I am saving your life, with no thanks," I said dryly, wishing she would return her hand to my chest.

"Good, because I wasn't going to offer it," she snapped back, forcing her top back down from where she had still been holding in her grasp after she had pulled it from my hand.

I continued attempting to do a visual check over her clothing, looking for any signs that the snake had caught her with its fangs.

"Did it bite you?"

"Why? Worried I'll die before you can bleed me out?"

"Oh, look at that, you know me so well," I smiled, unable to help myself at her snark.

She rolled her eyes with a huff. "Go on then, get it over with. Restrain me, stab me, fuck me—whatever it is you were going to do. I'm kind of getting bored waiting for one of you to show me just how much of a big bad serial killer you are."

Oh, you have no idea, pretty, just how tempting everything you suggested is.

"Sounds like a proposition." I smiled, my eyes widening with anticipation.

Kira leaned forward on her knees with her hands on my thighs, so her face was centimetres from my own. A low rumble of approval rolled through my chest while she held eye contact, all while her hands explored, slowly, up and down the sides of my bent legs.

"Oh, yeah?" she rasped, sounding like she wasn't opposed to her own suggestion.

"Mmm," I hummed. Cupping her cheek, she tilted her head into my hand with half-lidded eyes.

Her hands ceased roaming, then there was a sharp sting in my leg followed by grogginess that swam through my veins seconds later… Wait! That isn't right.

I looked down to see her hand wrapped around a syringe—one that she must have lifted from my leg pocket during our interaction. My sweet little psychopath had pulled one over on me.

"You…." My words became lost as I slumped forward, already in love with the pretty little devil, who not only just captured me but warmed my stone-cold heart, breathing life into it —giving it a reason to beat.

Kira

40

The look of surprise and pride on Kyden's face when he realised I had drugged him left me confused. Not only had he sprung into action to save my life, but he was genuinely concerned for my well-being, ascertaining that I hadn't been bitten by the snake.

Naturally, I couldn't help being a snarky bitch—especially after everything he had done to me. Trapping him with the pretence that I was letting him think he'd captured me, that I'd let him do as he pleased, may have been deceitful. But it was enough to keep him distracted while I pickpocketed one of the syringes poking from the thigh pocket of his cargo pants. I had no idea what the liquid inside was, but I assumed it was some kind of drug or sedative, like the one Trent had used on me before. My relief was granted when he curled over, out like a light, seconds after I pricked him.

Patting him down, I emptied him of the other syringes and a few smaller weapons that I could carry on myself.

He had a pair of cuffs in his back pocket and a few plaited

nylon ropes, but I couldn't find a key anywhere on his person.

Blowing out an exasperated breath, I cuffed his hands behind his back, then fully disarmed him, throwing his weapons—that I wouldn't be claiming—some distance away. When he was clear of weapons, I untangled the ropes and began wrapping them around his ankles and lower legs, tying them off clumsily. Then, with difficulty, I tied his arms against his sides, keeping his hands tied behind him. I then made sure the knot was at the front so he couldn't find a way to manoeuvre his hands and undo it behind. When I was satisfied with my work, I rolled his body away from the fallen tree and thick branches, ensuring he wouldn't be able to cut himself free on them. I mean, nothing was stopping him from rolling back and doing just that, anyway. Perhaps I had seen too many movies.

I felt slightly guilty leaving him there, especially knowing there were snakes slithering around. Where there was one, there were bound to be more. There wasn't much I could do about that. Besides, I had probably already alerted the others to my location with my scream, so time wasn't on my side. I had to retreat.

As if my thoughts were being broadcast, the sound of hurried footsteps whipping through tall grass, and broken twigs underfoot, drew closer, encouraging me to make haste.

I gave Kyden one last glance before taking off through the trees, making my escape.

I could feel my body beginning to come down from the adrenaline high. The crash was inevitable, especially since I hadn't had a chance to rest. I hadn't eaten or drunk anything either, and my body's survival mode was in overdrive under the stress. I didn't know how much more I could endure before it gave out on me. I pushed on, finding a second wind.

Darting through a narrow gap of thick trunks, I glanced over my shoulder to make sure no one was following.

My foot snagged on a tree branch, sending me sprawling forward. Blinding pain shot through me as my hands hit the ground, taking the impact, ricocheting up my limbs like fire. My body curled in on itself, tucking my arms into my stomach in a futile attempt to alleviate pain, as I rocked back and forth on my knees, silently screaming.

Chris

41

"Falling for me already? I do love my subs willingly on their knees waiting for directions."

Kira's sharp intake of breath followed by her wide eyes snapping up to me almost undid me on the spot. In the dishevelled state she was in—her hair was slick against her scalp with sweat, dirt clinging to every inch of her skin and clothes, her flesh was covered in nicks and scrapes — she looked wild, and untamed. Yet, she was clearly not someone to be underestimated; she had managed to avoid being captured for this long.

For a fleeting moment, I saw fear flash in her eyes, and it stirred something protective in me. But when she quickly replaced it with a scornful expression that promised retribution, I was filled with pride.

She bared her teeth, hissing in my direction as she slowly rose to her feet while cradling her arms. I could see the force at which she hit the ground, I wouldn't be surprised if she had at the very least broken a wrist from the impact.

"You can call an end to all this, you know?"

"Ready to surrender already?" she rebutted.

I bit back a grin. The snark on this brat. She was going to be fun to break. I couldn't wait to see her on her knees, begging to swallow my cum.

"Oh, little girl, I don't know the meaning of the word." I closed the distance between us, showing her that my hands were empty when she retreated a step.

"Don't call me little girl," she gritted out between clenched teeth. "I am a fully grown woman."

I grazed my eyes down along her languidly, taking note of every curve and committing it to memory. In her current state — sweaty, dirty, fueled by fear and adrenaline she was a sight to behold.

"I am fully aware."

She scoffed with disgust at my leering, but I saw the telltale sign of her arousal when she squeezed her thighs and squirmed slightly.

I grabbed for the arm she cradled. Pulling her shoulder back, she attempted to pull out of my reach.

"Don't," I warned, clamping my hand down around her elbow, forcing a hiss of pain from her lips.

She attempted to hold her arm locked tight, but was no match for my strength. I overpowered her, easily pulling the injured hand free from its confinement. I clasped my fingers around her hand, examining it carefully with my other hand holding her elbow steady.

"I don't think it's broken. Likely just sprained."

"Thank you for that clean bill of health. Now you can kill me with a clean conscience knowing the only injuries I'll die from are by your own hands," she snarked.

Releasing her elbow, I wrapped my hand around her throat, then with my index finger dug into the pressure point on the back of her hand between the thumb and index finger. This one was not considered painful, more a cautious warning, but as she had landed on this part of her hand, it was already tender and highly receptive to stimulus.

"Do not tempt me, little girl. I had other plans for your brattiness. But since you clearly lack any sense of self-preservation, I'll take your disregard for my compassion as a sign—it would be a waste to use my desire watching the life leave your eyes."

I had to give her credit. Despite suffering an immense amount of pain, she didn't make a sound. If it weren't for her racing pulse, sharp, shallow respiratory patterns, and dilated pupils, I would not have known otherwise. She was a mystery.

Too distracted by studying her heightened responses, I missed the subtle movement of her free arm. Brandishing a knife that I was intimately familiar with—having gifted to Trent–she swung it up. The tip of the blade connected with my inner wrist, opening my artery.

"Fuck." I clasped my hand over the wound with enough pressure to stem the bleeding.

Kira stood defensively, with the knife in front of her ready to strike again.

"Maybe I should end your life before you have the chance," she threatened.

This wasn't how I had planned for this to go. "Fuck, stop. Look, I wasn't going to kill you, okay?"

"You're only saying that because you're at a disadvantage and about to bleed out."

Fumbling in the side pocket on the leg of my cargo pants with my injured wrist, while keeping the pressure on the wound, I retrieved a small basic first aid kit. It wasn't fatal—providing I could tend to it — but would seriously impact my next decision.

"Truce?" I asked.

"And why should I trust you?"

Smart girl. "You shouldn't," I admitted. "But you're right, I am at a disadvantage and in need of immediate medical assistance. How about a deal?"

She didn't bite, but also didn't run or attempt to cut me again, so I continued. "Take the gun from my holster, the knife from my hip sheath, and the throwing knives on my belt, they're yours."

She eyes me cautiously, looking over my weapons but not making a move. From her expression, I could tell that she was considering it.

"In return, help me stop the bleeding and I'll willingly allow you to capture me."

I failed to mention that I had two knives in my boots and another gun strapped to my calf, so I was still able to use them to threaten her when the moment arose.

"Keep your hands raised above your head."

She approached once my hands were raised. Keeping the knife trained against my throat, she began disarming me, tucking the weapons into herself.

Then she stood on tiptoes and took the medical kit from my hands, but I purposefully fumbled it, dropping it to her feet. When I began lowering my arms, she pressed the knife into my throat, breaking the skin.

"Uh, uh. I'm not done."

I frowned. "You took my weapons. I need…"

She let out a small laugh. "Do you really believe I'm stupid enough to believe those are the only weapons you're carrying?"

Well, I had hoped…

"Honestly, I don't know how you four have gotten away with so many murders if you underestimate people so much."

She began slowly patting my body down, taking my phone, and pocket knife I had forgotten about, then the paracord keychain. Lowering the knife from my throat, she moved it to my kidney.

I was skilled enough to overpower her at any point, but I was intrigued by her method. With her eyes studying my face closely, she lowered herself down my body, keeping enough distance so if I lunged suddenly she could move back out of reach.

Finding the gun at my calf, she threw it a distance behind her, then ran her fingers around my ankles, catching the handle of the first blade between her fingers. She levered it out cautiously, so as not to cut me, dropping it behind her. She then did the same to the other boot. When she was satisfied that she had found all of my weapons, she stood with the medical kit in her hand.

"Hold it," she instructed, thrusting it back into my hands,

then retrieved the paracord. With her teeth, she unknotted it, pulling loose the length.

"Colour me impressed," I praised, when she skillfully wrapped the cord around my wrist above the wound to stem the bleeding. "I promise I won't attack, you can lower the knife."

She shook her head. "Not happening. Open the kit and take out what you need to stop the bleeding."

Fumbling, I pulled out wads of gauze and a bandage. "Can you hold the gauze?"

Hesitantly, she applied pressure over the gauze, releasing the length of the paracord. It was wrapped around enough times that it still served its purpose.

Using my teeth, I pulled the tape off the bandage and adjusted the end above where Kira's fingers rested, trying to wrap it around my arm. When she saw me fumble with one hand, trying to wrap the bandage, she did as expected and moved the knife from my kidney, tucking it into the waist of her pants. Then she grabbed the end of the bandage from my hand, helping me to wrap it around my arm. As I reached the gauze area, she moved her other hand to hold it in place.

Staying close as I finished bandaging my arm, I watched her movements without making it obvious. She still held her hands as if in pain but made no attempt to go for the weapons she had disarmed me of.

"Can you grab the tape from the bag?" I asked when I came to the end of the bandage.

As she moved a few items around in the small kit I was holding in my injured arm, I tucked the end of the bandage into where it was wrapped, and then, I lunged for the gun at her hip. She was faster, spinning on her heel she pushed her hips back out of reach. She grabbed the dangling paracord and somehow wrapped it around my throat with my wrist bound tight, effectively limiting my oxygen. With my free hand, I grabbed for the hand at my neck. Next thing I knew, she pulled me back, so we fell onto the ground with her under me. Rolling onto my side, I freed one of my throwing knives from a side pocket on her pants, noticing the area bloomed red. She must have fallen on the tip in the scuffle.

Before I could react, she had thrown me off of her, her knee connecting with my balls. I crumpled forward, tucking myself into a ball, momentarily stunned from the pain.

But Kira wasn't letting me off the hook that easily. After a tousle, she wound up on top, straddling my waist—both of my hands expertly restrained, with the paracord wrapped tightly around them—without my realising.

I swear my heart just about leapt from my chest. I did not submit. I never allowed anyone to restrain me, or have me bend to their will, yet here sat this tiny female who dominated and captured me, and I willingly accepted it.

I allowed her to tie it off, effectively capturing me, distracted by her breasts being pushed into my face as she leant over me.

Sitting back with a satisfied smile, she patted my cheek.

I snarled, allowing her to think I wasn't happy by this turn of events, despite my erection that pressed up against her.

"Don't move, and I'll stop the bleeding."

I didn't take orders–ever. But for some reason, I wanted to listen and obey her. What was happening?

She wrapped a bandage firmly around my wrist. I could have outmanoeuvred her easily, and I think she knew this too, but I was letting her have this. She had earned it.

"Two down, two to go."

Two? Who else had she captured? Seeing my unasked question, she patted my cheek again, this time harder.

"Guess you will have to wait and see when it's all over."

With that, she climbed off of me and grabbed my tied hands.

"Up," she commanded, waving a knife at me.

I had to bite back my instincts to fight her and take back control. Disgruntledly, I sat up while she held my hands above my head, then instructed me to shuffle against a tree on my knees. Before I could turn around, I felt a prick in the side of my neck.

"Clever…" My words lost to the sedative.

Kira

42

The sky began lightening, signalling dawn. It had been a long night so far, but there were still two more prey to hunt down.

After I caught Chris, I found a sturdy tree and climbed up high enough so that I was camouflaged by the foliage. Securing myself on a stable branch, I had meant to stay there long enough to catch my breath and rest, but I must have fallen asleep. My body protested as I forced my stiff muscles to move, the sounds of cracking joints accompanying each movement as I finally found my feet back on solid ground.

I stretched, trying to relieve some of the tension in my limbs, before glancing around, checking it was safe. Then, dropping my pants, I relieved my bladder, silently thankful that I didn't have to deal with the added inconvenience of having poop without toilet paper.

Taking advantage of the brief moment of peace, I took in my surroundings. Sunlight dappled through the branches, casting an ethereal ambiance over the slow-running riverbed.

The surface of the water glinted where it caught the light, reflecting back like stars. Quiet hums of activity from insects and birds filled the space around me, filling me with serenity and peace. It allowed me to momentarily forget that this was a dangerous game of life and death.

Kneeling in the moist earth on the bank, I dipped my hand into the cool water, cupping my hand, I brought it to my mouth, quenching my parched throat. The water tasted stagnant and dirty, but it beat dehydration. I forced myself to drink as much as I could, fighting the urge to spit it back out.

Exhaustion was taking its toll after such a long and eventful night, even with the small amount of sleep I stole, it still wasn't enough.

I leaned against a tree, forcing my eyelids to remain open. I should have asked if there was a time limit on this hunt. After it proceeded for a specific time frame, was the offer of freedom considered null and void? Or do we call it a truce with no victors?

My stomach rolled with hunger, with the water I consumed sloshing heavily in my stomach. Searching for food, I managed to find a quandong tree and some prickly pear—which earned me several spines in my fingers. It wasn't much, but it gave me a small amount of energy to continue on with this hunt.

Mesmerised by the beauty of the water as I picked spikes from my fingers, I forgot Trent's warning until I saw a log float towards me against the current. Wait, that isn't right.

It moved closer, adjusting its direction towards me. A knot of bark moved, revealing a green eye with a slit that widened its focus on me.

"Shit, a croc," I gasped, stepping back from the edge of the bank.

Giving the predator my back, I ran in the opposite direction. I knew crocs were slow on land, but that didn't deter me from putting as much distance as I could between me and the steel jaw, lined with teeth.

I glanced back over my shoulder knowing the croc wouldn't be there, but I had to check to make sure. Sure enough, there was no croc, just half a kilometre of thick shrub, concealing the river and its deadly inhabitants from me.

I came to a stop to catch my breath when a hand wrapped around my bicep, yanking me to the side. Instinctively, I swung my hand and leg out, a surprised squeal escaping my lips. My hand was caught before I made contact, but my foot connected with a shin, causing Trent to grunt in pain.

I quit struggling when I realised who it was, annoyed that I had yet again found myself in his grasp.

"Shh it's okay. Who's chasing you?" he asked in a concerned whisper, peering around me as he pulled me behind a tree, effectively hiding us.

Technically, he could have already claimed victory twice now in this hunt, yet he surprised me by continuing to aid me, working against his friends.

"A croc," I gasped.

"Oh?" Trent licked his lower lip, focusing on my mouth. "Do you have something personal against teeth being sunk into your flesh?"

"I don't want to be eaten."

His face morphed into a devilish grin. Leaning in close so we stood nose to nose, he brushed his lips across mine.

"That is exactly what I want to do," he whispered.

My heart palpitated in my chest. "And what if I don't want you to?"

"I would say you're lying." Trent placed his hand on my chest, over my heart.

"In fact, I think you want it. You want me to tear your clothes from your body and lay you down on the ground, with your legs spread wide."

His lips brushed across the pulse in my neck, causing a small whimper to escape my lips.

"You want my mouth on every inch of flesh, to have you

coming on my tongue, lapping at your release."

His hand pressed against my pussy, and I mewled when he rubbed me through the fabric. He moved his mouth to the other side of my neck, peppering it with light kisses, then sunk his teeth in.

"I'm marking your body as mine, so when this is over, I will mark you more permanently."

I pushed him back. "What? You are not marking anything permanently on me. When I win this little game, I am walking away from you. All of you.

Trent chuckled, pulling me back in close to him again. "Quit lying to yourself. The idea appeals to you. I can taste your desire, there is no denying it. Now try to tell me you aren't dripping wet right now."

"Oh, Chocolate drop," Grady sang through the dark, cutting off whatever retort I was about to make.

"Shit!" Trent muttered, pulling me into a tight space between a thicket of trees.

"I can practically smell your fear. It's fragrant and addictive. Surrender, and maybe, just maybe, we won't end your life. Would you like to live? Be our good little pet? At night you can warm our beds like the whore you know you are. And during the day, be on your knees. We promise to keep you well fed. You will be so full of cum, it will leak from your pores so you know who owns you."

I silently gagged. Yeah right. Like that would convince me.

Trent silently chuckled behind me. Well, it was supposed to be silent. The rumble of his amusement sent shivers through me, making me shudder in response.

Trent mistook my reaction and ran soothing hands down the sides of my arms. Leaning back into him, I soaked up the brief moment of comfort while we waited for Grady to move on. I couldn't believe I was in the same situation so soon after already evading him under a similar circumstance, not long ago.

He stood with an arrow nocked, ready to release, training it in front of him as he spun slowly, taking measured steps, waiting for me to reveal myself.

My breath caught in my throat when I felt the arrow trained on me once more, taking with it my last hope of walking out of here alive. He pulled back the string and released the arrow.

Trent

43

My little shadow stiffened as Grady inched closer, catching sight of something in the dark where we hid that had caught his attention.

I had to believe he couldn't see either of us or he would have already released the arrow, in turn killing one or both of us with a single blow.

I continued running soothing hands down Kira's arms, which did little to soothe her anxiety. Perhaps it was more for my benefit than her own craving the feeling of her under my hands. I longed for her touch. The moment the connection was lost, I spent every moment she was away from me desperate for that bond again.

She continued to try to press further into me. The only way she could have been any closer was if I was buried with my cock inside of her. It was something I couldn't live without doing again, repeatedly, for the rest of my life.

Her breath hitched as Grady pulled back the bow of the string, his eyes trained in our direction, but … not on us.

At the very edge of the tree level with Kira's eyes, I caught movement just as Grady released the arrow.

My hand clamped down over Kira's mouth before she could expel the scream from her throat, cutting it off.

The arrow thudded with a sickening crunch, spraying a small splatter of blood back into the darkened crevice where we hid. I felt droplets flick across my arm, in front of Kira's face, and on my forehead.

Grady smiled, "gotcha fucker."

With two steps, he reached forward, yanking the arrow free with a couple of heaves. The body of a possum fell to the ground at his feet.

Grady wiped the arrow on the leg of his pants. Kicking the dead marsupial, he walked off in the opposite direction, whistling a made-up tune—with the arrow cocked back in the bow ready to strike.

I tentatively lowered my hand from Kira's mouth, letting her sag against me. I was equally relieved that neither of us was at the pointy end of the projectile.

"It's okay, he didn't see you," I reassured her when she released a stuttering breath on her exhale.

Spinning around, she wrapped her arms around me, pressing her face into my chest. I embraced her, running a hand through the back of her hair with soothing hushing sounds, in an attempt to ease her rampant heartbeat that I could feel beating against me.

I couldn't help but continually acknowledge how perfectly her body moulded against mine. As though she were carved from the most precious elements on earth, made just for me. I don't think she realised just how much I would fight her if she ever tried to escape me. I would never let her go, even if she hated me, because it meant keeping her permanently shackled. She was mine.

Grady

44

My Chocolate drop thought she was concealed in the shadows, pressed against the traitorous T-man. But there was nothing in this world that would disguise the signature scent of her fear. I had tracked her, savouring the endorphin rush as her body beaded with sweat from the hunt. Her natural scent was sweet, and as unique as she was.

I had been conflicted as fuck whether I was actually going to just kill her for the rift her presence caused the moment she ran into our lives, or as payback to Trent.

Then I began to see how she ticked—I was intrigued by her. She was a master manipulator and resilient as fuck. I watched her intimately at the beginning of the hunt as she tried to find her footing. I almost gave up on sparing her when she made no real attempts to begin with at camouflaging, or making any fucking effort to fight back. Then she surprised me with the little hoodie decoy. I saw real potential and decided to drag out this little game, always staying within range. Watching and waiting.

This has been the most fun I've had in my entire life. It was truly amazing watching people when they thought no one could see them. The brief moments when they let down their walls without hiding behind the persona that was worn like a mask.

Kira's true self was a lot more corrupt than she would ever allow anyone to know. Our girl was a keeper; she sealed her fate when she refused to bow down to us.

Our girl, yeah, I liked the sound of that.

The images my mind conjured of having her take all four of our cocks at once, covered in our cum, did strange things to me. I needed to see for myself just how well she would take us all. I bet she was a kinky little nympho under those scowls—even with those scowls.

She would be hot in a pair of horns and a butt plug, with a little demon tail. Yeah, that fantasy tickled my happy spot.

Kyden sealed the decision to leave her alive for me when he saved her, *without* spilling blood. He protected her. Then, he checked to make sure she wasn't injured.

For him to want her badly enough not to let his urges overtake him in that moment was phenomenal progress. He has never had the control in the years I've known him not to draw blood when faced with such a circumstance.

Now I just needed to work on my own urges—maybe. Then

again…. I liked that I left everyone guessing what I would do next.

She was clever. I'll give her that. She not only subdued and restrained Kyden, but Chris as well. She used her smaller frame and somehow grappled him to the ground, gaining the upper hand. Then she had used the same method she used on Ky, catching him off guard by using a sedative, then tied him to a tree.

Fuck, I nearly came in my pants like a hormonal teenager seeing tits for the first time, watching her.

I chuckled to myself at seeing my twin—who doesn't like not to be in control — bend down to this girl. He was completely enraptured by her and conceded defeat at the hands of our intended target.

She had somehow not caved when we showed her who and what we were. She dug her claws into us, tearing us down one by one. If anything, I'd wager that her viciousness matched or even outweighed our own.

She was like a stonefish, unassuming and dangerous; you wouldn't look twice at it before stepping into its trap. Then, you were impaled on its venomous spines, incapacitating you before you realised what happened.

Now I just had to get rid of Trent so she was mine to do with as I pleased. I wanted to see just how far I could push her until she broke. I wanted to see genuine fear. Because those few moments that Kyden and I had her down in the basement were not enough. She did not once beg for us to stop, or to let her go. That was new and exciting. No one had ever not pleaded when faced with their own mortality. This girl, she accepted whatever we were doing, and now—she is facing us and targeting us, without fear. Even when I had the arrow trained on her from within the shadows, she looked at me with bitterness, despite coming face to face with the Grim Reaper. I would have given anything to have seen that determination on her face under full light, where she stared death in the eyes without bowing down. I bet she would smile in the final seconds as her life faded, making the reaper her bitch.

Fuck! I think… *I'm in love.*

Kira

45

I could feel eyes on me, watching from the shadows. It unnerved me, and I was afraid to step out into the light.

As if Trent was able to read my thoughts, he ran soothing fingers up and down my arms, and pressed a gentle kiss to the side of my cheek. "He's gone for now."

For now being the operative phrase.

"I'm going to need your help."

"And what exactly is it that I can assist you with?" his voice dropped to a seductive purr, his fingers brushing across my breast down to my stomach, where they continued to follow the path down.

"Stop." I grabbed Trent's wrists, halting him from going any further south. "Don't distract me."

"I thought you liked my distractions. You most definitely weren't complaining the last time…"

I spun and slapped my hand across his mouth, feeling his lips turn up to a smile below my palm. He pushed his tongue between his lips and began licking my palm with small moaning sounds.

"Stop," I giggled, removing my hand and wiping my palm on his shirt. "We can stuff around after, but I need your expertise with something first."

He waggled his eyebrows. "Promise?"

"Yes, now will you help me?"

"Always, sweetheart."

I rolled my eyes, attempting to be annoyed by the comment. In reality, I wanted to drop to my knees before him. The worst thing was the bastard knew it too. His quiet laughter was poorly hidden behind his own fist.

"Okay, okay, how may I service you?"

"Don't you mean, *be of service*?" I corrected.

"I stand by what I said, but if it makes you feel better, then sure."

I shook my head. "You're impossible," I muttered.

He leaned down to my ear and whispered, "Impossible to resist. Now quit distracting me and tell me what it is that you require."

"I'm distracting you?"

"Glad you can admit it," he taunted.

Why the asshole! I was seconds away from punching him in his beautiful smug face. Ignoring the unease I felt, I stepped away into the light, putting distance between Trent and myself. Well, I actually stomped away heavily and dramatically, but I wasn't going to dwell on the fact that I no doubt looked utterly ridiculous. Naturally, my soured mood only seemed to fuel Trent's amusement, and he made no effort to hide his deep laughter as he followed me.

"Piss off, I'll figure it out on my own," I snapped when I heard him at my back.

Hands came around my waist, lifting me off the ground. I threw an elbow back, causing Trent to let out a small grunt, but he didn't lessen his grip.

"We can fight dirty later, baby. Let me know how I can help now."

I quit squirming in his arms. "Fine." When he didn't release me, I tried again to squirm free.

"I won't let you go until you tell me."

"You are really annoying, you know that, right?"

"I prefer the term endearing." I could hear the smile in his words. He was baiting me, and I was falling straight into his trap. Asshole.

With Trent's assistance, I set the snare ready to trap my next victim and then set the bait—me.

Kneeling down and grasping my ankle with a pained cry, I kept my line of sight diverted to the ground. In my periphery, I saw the unmistakable silhouette of Grady as he crept closer, with his bow raised in front of him. I locked my limbs, fighting the norepinephrine coursing through me, so I didn't run and hide. Right now, I was vulnerable to his potential attack, and my mind was trying to kick into fight-or-flight mode.

His weapon wasn't pointed directly at me; however, it waved back and forth through the air as he searched his surroundings, inching forward cautiously—untrusting of the convenience and ease of the situation in which he found me.

For a split second I thought he had caught on to my deception when he halted and retreated a step. I wiped my face on the back of my hand and adjusted my position so I sat on the ground and cradled my ankle in my hands, rubbing it gently while I sniffled a sob—acting the distressed damsel, in need of saving.

Come on, come on, take the bait.

Seemingly convinced by my act, Grady lowered the bow and arrow, keeping his hands trained on them, ready to fire, as he approached me slowly. He stepped onto a branch. The sound of it cracking under his foot forced my head to raise towards him instinctively.

"Fuckucking hell," he muttered when I made eye contact.

I let out a surprised gasp, then looked around fearfully and inched backwards on my butt, looking as though I was trying to find an escape. Then, forcing myself to stand on one foot, raising the other to limp, I slowly retreated, glancing back to see if Grady was following. He grinned hungrily, like the predator he was. Licking his lower lip, he took two fateful steps forward in my direction.

I turned to face him, putting my weight back onto my foot. I crossed my arms in front of my chest and waited as he lifted his foot. Grady's face fell as the pieces fell into place. The snare caught his left ankle, tightening and catapulted him into the air, dangling him from a tree upside down, causing him to drop his bow in the motion.

He bellowed loudly, his free limbs waving around desperately, trying to find purchase on something. His mouth was bloodied, having connected with something when he was snared.

Trent stepped out of the shadows that were concealing him, casting him in fractured morning light. The moment Grady caught sight of him, he stopped struggling, allowing the line he hung from to spin him; a smirk playing on the edge of his own lips matching my own.

"Oh look at that, I caught a drop bear," I taunted. "You're not so scary now that you've been snared."

He sneered and reached to his hip for the knife strapped into a sheath at his belt. I raised a brow at him, waiting for him to wonder why I wasn't stopping him when he moved to cut himself free. He was too arrogant to even consider I had another plan. The sound of breaking branches from behind redirected his attention from where he was folding himself up to cut the line free.

"What the fu –" was all Grady managed to say before Trent swung the large branch he had found, smacking it across his head and knocking him out cold.

Relief washed over me with him swinging unconscious. I only hoped Trent hadn't actually hit him too hard and done damage. What was I thinking? He probably deserved it. Besides, his skull was so thick the most he would probably suffer was a light headache and a deep sleep.

"Who's up for a game of human pinata?" I laughed.

Trent looked at me with an aghast expression, dropping the thick branch at his feet in surprise.

"My, my, my," he clucked. "You embraced your shadows," he smiled, meeting me in four large strides, stealing the air from my lungs with his mouth.

I melted into the kiss, frantically attacking him back with my tongue, my hands grappling at his hair and back desperately.

Trent pulled back, sucking on my lower lip. "It turns you on, doesn't it? Embracing your desires."

I hummed, leaning forward trying to capture his mouth again.

Trent tsked, bending down he gave my rear a firm slap, then stepped out of reach despite me desperately trying to cling on.

"We aren't finished here yet," he reminded me, and I pouted, crossing my arms.

"I know," I mumbled. "But in my defense, you started it."

"And I plan on finishing it later. But first…" His gaze landed behind me. "You have to decide whether you want them left alive or not."

I was exhausted, sleep-deprived and hungry. This decision was too important to make in my current emotional state.

"I say we chain them up to deal with later. I need food, sleep and a fuck." I looked up to Trent, "and not in that order."

His smile was predatory, hungry, promising. "In that case." He grabbed the back of my head, tilting my face up, brushing his lips briefly against mine.

"How do you feel about voyeurism?"

My eyes flicked over to Grady, then back to Trent. With a smile to match his own, I said, "Let's tape their eyes open so they have no choice but to watch. Gag them and tie them up naked, so we can see just how turned on they are."

Trent growled in approval, then smashed his mouth against mine hungrily, stealing my breath with the onslaught of his tongue. Pulling back, he gave my lower lip a bite. "You were made for me."

"Is that so?" I taunted.

"You walk amongst your shadows so beautifully, you have made the darkness inside of you, your servant. I knew it was where you belonged."

"Fractured means I can still stand in the light to remain unassuming. I love knowing that I'm underestimated, and I plan to use it to my full advantage too." I ran a finger along Trent's chest and then stepped back from his embrace.

"I don't underestimate you, Kira," he said. "I never have once."

I had to turn my face away and bite down on my lips to hide my laughter. Clearing my throat to compose myself, I turned back to face him. Reaching out for the hand that had just been behind my head, I quickly snapped the other side of the cuff onto his wrist , the one I had attached when he'd been distracted by kissing me.

"You just did," I told him matter-of-factly. "I won." Looking down to where I captured him.

He glanced down at his hands with a frown, then burst out laughing.

"My dear, I am your willing captive. You can have me gagged, restrained and my undivided attention any time you want. You need only say the words, now let me go."

I raised a single brow, then lifted three fingers one at a time. "The rules of the hunt were to incapacitate, kill or capture."

I took a step back from him, then began to circle around him slowly, his head tracking my every move.

"I have captured and incapacitated three of you, with no kill… yet. But then again, this all began because of you."

In truth, Trent had won by a technicality, so he would be joining me when I claimed my reward. I stopped in front of him, watching the smug expression waiver on his face when he took stock of what I held in my hand. Holding the gun in front of me, I aimed at his chest.

"What do you say, Trent? Are you going to beg for mercy?"

I clicked off the safety.

His face fell, his eyes flicking from the barrel of the gun to me. I watched as he swallowed a lump in his throat, the colour leaching from his face.

"Kira…" he said softly.

I made a buzzer sound, "wrong answer."

I pulled the trigger.

Kira

46

Watching Trent fall to the ground with an expression of utter shock when I tranquilised him was the highlight of the hunt. I had admittedly used him on a few occasions to gain the upper hand. I think that realisation came to pass when I pulled the trigger on the tranquiliser gun; the dart sinking into his thigh. I was sure he would forgive me when he woke and would help me carry out the next part of my plan.

The most difficult part of the entire exercise was now that they were captured, what was next? It was never specified. Creating my own narrative, based on the generosity they showed me when I was initially abducted, I began setting the wheels into motion for the ideas that had been hatching in my head. First, I needed their vehicle and hoped they all remained unconscious until I returned.

Eventually, I found my way to the entrance of the enclosure. With my energy levels waning after fighting through so many adrenaline rushes, it was only a matter of time until I blacked out entirely. I didn't know how long the effects of the tranquiliser or sedatives would last, and I was acutely aware of just how resourceful these men were. There was no shadow of a doubt in my mind that they would try to escape my pathetic attempts to apprehend each of them and continue the hunt, so I needed to be quick.

Once I met the gate, I was pleasantly surprised to see it wasn't fully closed, with the mechanism jamming.

With the car keys in hand—which I had pocketed from Trent—I pushed on the gate, triggering it to grind open, and walked slowly to the car.

I opened the boot, having prior seen it loaded with bottles of water and packaged food for after the hunt, for when my captives presumed themselves to be victorious.

I basked in a moment of triumph, knowing I had outsmarted them. Grabbing an armful of both water and snacks, I climbed into the driver's seat, relishing the brief moment of recovery while I stuffed my face with food and emptied bottle after bottle of water.

When the hunger pains no longer controlled me, I turned on the engine and drove through the scrub as close as I could to where my closest victim was left.

Driving through the dense shrub, I cringed as the car rocked back and forth over the rough terrain, hoping I didn't fuck up the car in my off-roading adventure, causing us all to be stranded.

When Trent came into view, exactly where I had left him—his unconscious body still slumped on the ground with his hands bound—I jumped out and raced over to check his pulse. Feeling the steady rhythm, I released a deep breath, then sprinted back to the car. Grateful that the four-wheeler was equipped with recovery gear, I grabbed the tarp I'd found in the back, along with the ratchet straps. I then extended the winch as far as it would go, pulling it toward Trent.

Once Trent's body was strapped to the tarp and the winch was attached, I had to drag his enormous form four meters across the uneven ground before winching him toward the vehicle. When he was under the bullbar, I unhooked the tarp and stood there, momentarily at a loss. I hadn't planned beyond getting him to the car—my mind had skipped over the part where I actually had to get him inside. *Dammit!*

I let out a soft whimper, slumping forward with my head bowed and arms hanging limply in front of me. The sooner I got this over with, the sooner I could sleep. I jumped back in the car, made room for a quick U-turn, and reversed, deciding I'd pile all four bodies in through the rear.

The car hit something with a thud. Heart in my throat, I slammed on the brakes and ran to the back, expecting to see

Trent crushed under the rear wheel. Relief washed over me when I found a dazed kangaroo lying on the ground, which quickly bounced to its feet and bounded off.

Shame the rear panel didn't fare as well, now sporting a generous dent. At least the roo had done me a favour, and I was close enough to drag Trent into the back. Any closer, and it might've been his body that caused me to slam on the brakes.

After lifting, dragging, dropping and falling on Trent—many times, I finally shoved him into the back of the car. I was glad he wasn't conscious to bear witness to some of the methods I used, or the fact I had manhandled his body, groping his arse and, erm, accidentally fell with my face landing in his crotch with one of my awkward manoeuvres.

Lying down beside him in the back, I gave myself five minutes to catch my breath before dragging myself away to sit back in the driver's seat.

That's one down.

My limbs were sluggish and slow to respond. I didn't know how I was supposed to do this three more times.

I came across Chris next, who stood patiently as if waiting for my arrival. His hands and feet were still bound, but he was free of the tree I had tied him to.

How the hell had he managed that? I was going to have to

watch him closely.

Muttering a string of expletives, I opened the back door.

"Get in," I told him, gesturing for Chris to climb in beside Trent.

Chris raised a brow at me and then twisted slightly, holding his bound hands in my direction, silently asking me to untie him.

"Not happening, big boy. I won this game." He smirked at the nickname, but remained tight-lipped. "I say jump, you say how high? Now show me your skills and get in the back."

Chris ducked his head. "Just so you know, for future reference, I'm partial to rope being used on me. If you really want me to enjoy it, use cuffs next time… just make sure they're tight enough to hurt."

I rolled my eyes. "Get in and stop trying to chat me up. I'm hungry, tired and grumpy."

Chris expertly jumped up into the back, rolling onto his side. Before I closed the rear door, I ducked my head in.

"Oh, by the way, I almost forgot."

Pulling out one of the syringes I had found on Trent, I stabbed it into Chris's thigh.

"I wouldn't want you waking up before I get you to my next destination."

"Fuck!" Chris managed before his eyes dropped, the sedative taking hold.

Patting his cheek, I chuckled to myself. "Two down, two to go."

This was so much harder than I thought.

Just like Chris, Kyden was standing there waiting for me. The only difference was, he was completely untied, reclining back against a tree with his massive arms crossed over his blood-stained chest.

"Fuck."

He smirked at my annoyance, slowly prowling towards the car.

Winding down the window, I poked my head out. "Go on then, get in. As long as you keep your hands to yourself, though."

He shook his head and smiled, pointing at me with one of the knives I had disarmed him of, and tossed aside. He had gathered up all the weapons I had discarded, strapping them back onto himself.

"Not possible, pretty girl."

I threw my head back against the headrest, cursing myself for leaving them behind.

"At least until we get out of here?"

He narrowed his eyes, poking his tongue in his cheek,

considering it. "Fine."

I watched as he climbed into the passenger seat, taking in every strong muscle that flexed under his movements. Why were the hot ones all insane?

I waited until he closed the door before reaching down the side of my door. Grabbing the tranq gun, I fired a shot into his leg.

"Oops, I slipped," I smiled innocently, batting my lashes as he fell forward, smacking his head on the dash. In hindsight, I probably should have made sure his seatbelt was on first.

When Kyden was belted in, with my hands having an up-close and personal moment with Kyden's abs, I navigated and backtracked my way through the heavy scrub, towards my final captive.

Squeezing between narrow gaps in trees, and driving over fallen logs, I finally found Grady, who was still hanging by his ankle in the tree. He wasn't moving, and part of me hoped Trent hadn't actually killed the psychopath when he hit him, or that he had died from being left upside down for too long. I hadn't considered the latter at the time.

As I slowly approached Grady to check for a pulse, he suddenly sprung up, his hands outstretched and a crazy smile on his face. The sight scared the living shit out of me. I screamed loudly, and unfortunately for Grady, my natural reaction was to swing. That meant the tranquilliser gun I still held in my hand met his face, knocking him out again, but not before my finger came down on the trigger, with the dart hitting the back of his hand.

Well, at least he was out.

Shaking the adrenaline off from the fright, I moved the car back until I nudged his swinging body with the open rear door. Maybe nudged was being nice with how hard he made contact, but in my defence he deserved it after scaring me.

With his body suspended, it was easy to swing him into the back, with his body landing heavily on top of Chris and Trent. I was consciously aware of one of them making a grunting sound before I slammed the door closed.

With the four men secure and unconscious, I navigated my way from the enclosure. With the use of the GPS and their previous location still in the system, I drove until I made it back to the property they called home—fighting off micro-sleeps the entire way.

Pulling the car to a stop, I didn't even get the car door open before passing out due to sheer exhaustion. My body decided it was safe to sleep.

Kira

47

I startled awake, throwing my arms out wildly in self-defence at the feeling of fingers at my throat.

"Woah there, precious. I was just making sure you were still breathing," Kyden reassured, holding his hands up in front of him in surrender, standing beside me in the open driver's side door.

I groaned, rubbing my hands down my face, wiping away drool, then turned over my shoulder to see my other three captives had already woken and vacated the rear of the vehicle.

How long had I been asleep?

"Where are the…"

"Right here, Little shadow." Trent appeared from the side of the car to push beside Kyden, elbowing him in the process.

Leaning in, he cupped my cheek and pressed his lips to mine. I melted into his kiss, leaning in to deepen it, but he pulled away with a soft chuckle, tucking a stray lock of hair behind my ear and staring at me as if I had handed him the moon on a golden platter.

"You are truly spectacular. I never doubted you for a moment."

His arms wrapped around me, pulling me awkwardly against his chest. I unbuckled the seatbelt and twisted, resting my head on his chest, letting his warmth envelop me—humming in contentment.

"Here." Kyden pushed a hand past Trent's bulking body that was blocking me and handed me a bottle of water and a muesli bar.

I squeaked as my stomach rolled, noting the olive branch being offered.

"Ah, thank you."

Trent kept a hold of me, but loosened his grip enough for me to gulp back half the bottle before ripping into the bar of oats and dried fruit. I chewed without tasting, swallowing it down quickly, then emptied the rest of the water from the bottle. Immediately, I felt better.

"What is it that you wish to claim, as you are the rightful victor in the challenge we posed?" Chris asked, his gaze steady as I blindly shoved my hand out past Trent, the empty bottle and wrapper in my grip, offering them to Kyden to take.

I looked around Trent's shoulder to where Chris stood

beside Grady, both standing with their arms crossed and the same neutral expression, looking more alike than I had seen yet.

"The deal is I get to walk free or do as I choose. I successfully apprehended you all and then safely returned you back here, so now I want to collect my prize."

"And what exactly is the prize you wish to collect?" Chris asked.

I smiled wide, looking at each of them slowly, enjoying the concerned glances between each of these men.

"I want you all at my mercy." I looked at Trent with a raised brow in question. "Want to remind them of your bondage skills?"

A mischievous grin spread across his face as he eyed each man, rubbing his hands together with glee. The sight was enough to make me burst into laughter.

"Is it too late to call for a do-over?" Grady asked hopefully. "Like best of three or some shit?"

Kyden let out a whine, dropping his head on Grady's shoulder. "Just accept defeat, Gray. We were all bested."

"You still haven't answered my question." Chris's voice was tight with irritation as he ground his teeth, clearly waiting for me to reveal my intentions.

I couldn't help but enjoy the moment. "You will find out," I said softly, walking through the front door behind Trent, with Chris, Grady, and Kyden following close behind.

"Now, if you three wouldn't mind stripping down to your underwear and making your way to…"

"My room," Trent called from the hall.

The three men following all baulked, halting their steps. "Did you say strip?" Chris asked hesitantly.

"To your underwear," I confirmed.

Grady let out a deep chuckle and dropped his pants where he stood, followed by his shirt, which he tossed in my face.

"I like where this is going," he smiled darkly.

"Oh, do you now?" I smirked.

"I wouldn't be so quick to assume you know where this is going," Kyden told Grady, assessing me closely with his tongue pressed into his cheek. He crossed an arm over his chest and grabbed his chin, rubbing it with his free hand. "She has already outsmarted us all once."

"We will not allow you to undermine and degrade us for your own perverse pleasure, little girl." Chris said sternly.

I gave Chris my best unbothered expression. "You are one to talk. Is that not what you all do with every woman you murder?"

"Touché," Kyden smirked.

"That is not the same, nor is it part of the agreement we set when…"

I rolled my eyes. "Fine, keep your clothes on. It doesn't really bother me either way."

I shrugged and walked past Grady, who lingered at the entrance of the hall, suddenly looking uncertain. His gaze shifted down to where he stood, having eagerly stripped, then back to Kyden and Chris, who had chosen to remain dressed, both with scowls on their faces. I trailed a finger across his bare chest, then prompted him to follow with a curl of my finger, walking into Trent's room where he was setting up the next phase of my plan.

"Line up against the wall," I told them, pointing to the blank wall, which now housed heavy-gauged wall shackles.

Trent was standing at the end of the bed facing the wall in question, with his hands behind his back, hiding what I had asked him to retrieve.

Chris breathed out heavily, flaring his nostrils, his jaw clenched tight as he made his way to the wall with his arms crossed, waiting patiently. Grady was all too eager to cooperate and see where this was going. Kyden lingered at the door, his eyes flicking to Trent, then to myself, and lastly, to the shackles on the wall.

He sighed and gave his head a brief shake. "I can see where this is going."

"Well, perhaps you want to be a good boy and show the other two what is going to happen."

Kyden huffed out an annoyed noise. "I am only agreeing to this because I am a man of my word, and you have proven yourself to have bested the four of us. Mark my words, precious, when I am free, I will be making certain you know *exactly* who is in control."

Chris shot Kyden a look that clearly said, *Oh really?*

I barked out a laugh, then approached Kyden with a length of rope Trent had passed me. Kyden ground his teeth together, his posture stiff as he extended his arms in front of him. I ran my fingers slowly along his forearm to his wrist, watching as his muscles relaxed beneath my touch. Slowly, I wrapped the rope around his wrist, tying it off before raising his arm toward the shackle on the wall and securing it there. Kyden gave the rope an experimental tug, then, with a heavy sigh, moved his other arm closer for me to repeat the process.

Grady was eagerly standing in only his tight-fitted trunks, with a very prominent erection, his arms held out waiting for his turn, with a slightly impatient bounce in his stance.

I chuckled and shook my head. He was different from what I expected. Goofy in a way, it was kind of adorable.

Once Grady was restrained, I made my way to Chris, who

stood as still as a statue, arms crossed over his chest. His jaw was clenched tight, and his brow was furrowed, casting a shadow over his narrowed eyes.

"Just so it's clear, I don't like any of this," he said, his voice low.

I batted my eyelashes innocently and flashed him my sweetest smile. "It's almost like you don't trust me, Chris." I gently took his bandaged hand from his chest and pressed a kiss to the wound I'd inflicted. "I would never intentionally hurt you."

Kyden and Grady both chuckled, the sound clearly saying they didn't take me at my word.

"Play along with me?" I asked, poking my bottom lip out in a pout. "After all, I did play your little game."

Chris harrumphed, lowering his other arm from his chest. "I'll reiterate my earlier statement: I do not like this. However, you're right. You played our game and outmatched us. I'll play along... for now."

Once Chris was secured to the shackle, I stepped back into Trent's embrace, admiring the sight of men bound at my behest. It was empowering, knowing the control I held over them in this moment. My captives. My personal trophies.

With the three men restrained and utterly subservient to my every whim, I decided it was time to unleash my retribution.

In Chris's defense, he was probably undeserving, and Trent should have been the one forced to submit in his place. But since I'd set this up with Trent as my victory, and he'd assisted me, I chose to overlook that.

"I never thought I'd see the day when the tables were turned and you three would be in this position," Trent mused.

"Why aren't you tied up, too?" Grady sneered, as if just now realizing the irony.

Trent beamed. "She just likes me more."

I elbowed him in the stomach, and he grunted in response.

"Behave or you will join them, and I'll make you watch while I get myself off."

Trent bit down on his lower lip, his eyes lowering down my body, and I had no doubt he was imagining just that.

"Tell me what part of that I wouldn't enjoy?"

I rolled my eyes at Trent. "I'm serious."

Turning back to Grady, I told him, "Trent could have won the hunt many times over, so this is his runners up prize."

"Oh, I am fully aware, little shadow." Trent ran a hand along my clavicle, moving it up to my neck, tilting my head to the side so he could kiss my neck.

"I quite like the idea of coming second to you," he murmured against my skin, continuing his teasing.

I closed my eyes, entranced by the sensation of his stubbled face and soft lips on my erogenous zone, a small mewl escaping me. His fingers tightened around my throat as he dragged me back a few steps with him, all while moving his mouth seductively along my neck to my shoulder. An appreciative moan fell from my lips, causing an irritated huff from one of my captors, who were forced to bear witness to my pleasure.

Trent laughed silently. Slowly, his hands ran down the front of my body, lifting the hem of the top I wore. He pulled it up, removing it completely from my body, leaving me exposed in my bra. Next, his fingers popped the button on my pants, and slowly he lowered the zipper.

I locked eyes with Kyden, his lips parted expectantly as he watched the strip show Trent was putting on for them. I let my eyes roam between the three men as Trent pushed down my pants, before letting me step out of them and moving to unhook my bra. He paused for effect, holding it undone against me, making eye contact with each of his friends, before letting it drop to the ground at my feet.

Chris grunted in approval when the bra fell from my body and Trent reached around and pinched my nipples firmly between his fingers.

I gasped in surprise, leaning my head back against his shoulder. "Harder," I breathed out.

Trent spun me so fast I nearly lost my footing. His hands held me steady digging into my hips. His mouth came crashing down on my breast, sinking his teeth into my flesh and causing a small scream to break free.

"Mark her," Chris ordered.

Excuse me? I pushed Trent's mouth away and glared over my shoulder at Chris. "You aren't in control here. Zip it before I gag you."

Chris's nostrils flared in annoyance, but like a good little captive, he snapped his jaw shut, shooting a glare in Trent's direction. Trent, on the other hand, was thoroughly amused by the unfolding events, clearly enjoying the chance to use me as a form of payback against his friends. Honestly, I had no problem with it. In the end, I would be the one benefiting from it.

The next thing I knew, Trent had thrown me onto the bed and was pulling my underwear down my legs, only after having learned that they didn't tear away easily. Kneeling between my thighs, he lowered his head, with his mouth latching onto my pussy before I could move up the bed, feasting on me like a starved man.

"Fuck!" I cried out, digging my hands into his silky hair and holding his head between my thighs.

A feral groan and guttural whine came from my unwilling

voyeurs. Although judging by the sounds they were making, there was nothing unwilling about what they were forced to watch. In fact, I'd hedge that they were quite enjoying the show.

Trent licked firmly through my slit, then sucked my clit into his mouth, nipping it with his teeth. My back arched up off the bed, an inhuman sound left my lips, and the first orgasm tore through me so suddenly, and so intensely, I almost blacked out. His assault on my pussy continued as I rode out the orgasm, grinding against his face while I held his head there with my hands clenched tight in his hair. He moaned against me; the vibration dragging out the pleasure in ways I never knew possible.

This man was going to be the death of me, in all the best ways possible.

I released my hands from Trent's head as I came down from the high. Breathless and in a happy daze, I looked down at the only thing to ever match my Satisfyer. Trent didn't just match it, he made it so I would never be *satisfied* by what it could offer again. He gave one last long, languid lick before rising to his knees. A smug grin plastered across his face in knowing how quickly he undid me.

"Arsehole," I muttered.

"If you are offering…" he flipped me onto my stomach

with one fluid motion and lifted my hips so I was on my knees.

I pushed myself down, back onto my stomach, and glared over my shoulder. "Not fucking happening Trent, this is my rodeo, and I don't want you in my arse. I want…"

Before I could finish my sentence, Trent dropped on top of me, straddling my thighs and thrust his cock straight into me until his body was flush with mine. The sudden force of him filling and stretching me almost brought me to orgasm again.

Trent groaned in pleasure, kissing my cheek. "Kira. God, you feel like heaven."

"Move or I'll make your life a living hell," I implored, when he didn't move. I tried to rock my hips, needing friction, but he was too heavy. "Trent, I'm serious," I snapped.

I heard Grady chuckle but ignored him, focused on my own needs.

A deep rumble fell from Trent as he sat back on his knees, bringing me up with him. "You could do anything to me, little shadow, and I would relish it."

The new position at least allowed me to move. Taking advantage of the friction I was craving, I rocked forward slightly, but Trent's fingers dug into my hips, halting my movements, causing me to let out a frustrated growl.

"Patience," he whispered over my shoulder, grinding his hips up and down slightly, forcing little whimpers from me. He was enjoying this too much, and I noticed that somewhere along the line he had flipped the tables so he was in charge.

Did I care? At that moment in time, nope.

He slid out slowly, the motion torturously arousing. I held my breath in anticipation of him filling me again. I was not as prepared as I thought when he then thrust into me, dragging my hips back against his forcefully and hitting my cervix. The sensation bordered on painful as he ravaged me with a brutal, propulsive force, morphing into a new kind of pleasure. I moved my hand between my thighs, rubbing frantically at my clitoris, matching Trent's pace. My orgasm building quickly, I was so close.

The sound of our heavily combined panting and wet slapping sounds were drowned out by the growls emitting from our three bound voyeurs. I had never pictured myself as an exhibitionist before, but hearing their responses only made the whole experience more thrilling.

"Yes. Yes. Yes. Fuck me harder."

Trent brought his hand down across my arse. It landed with a satisfying *thwack*! I squealed at the unexpected contact, followed by a groan as the sharp sting leached into a pleasurable burn. I lifted my head back, crying into the air as he brought his palm down again and again against my flesh, with punishing hits. I could feel the welts blooming into red marks, which would bruise on my skin. Something about him marking me that way was a huge turn-on.

"Oh, fuck!" Kyden groaned.

Taking advantage of my head being thrown back, Trent fisted my hair, yanking my head back even further at an angle so I could see his face as he rammed into me even harder with brutal thrusts. My scalp burned where his grip held my head steady, while my body was jolted forward with each punishing, pleasurable movement.

My eyes found the three men watching, with what can only be described as hunger and rage. Their erections all painfully throbbing against the confines of their pants, begging for contact, and their hips subtly moved as they humped the air.

I licked across my lips, eyeing each of them individually, taking them in from head to toe, whimpering in pleasure and pain. Something about having them watch me as Trent fucked me only made the whole experience more arousing.

"Does it turn you on knowing how much they want you? How badly they want to be buried inside your dripping cunt and are unable to do a fucking thing about it?" Trent asked, seeing where my eyes were trained.

When I didn't answer, he pulled my hair tighter, making my eyes water from the pain.

"Yes," I screamed out as my orgasm lingered just out of reach, frustrating me.

"I bet you could take all four of us at once, couldn't you? You greedy little whore. Just one of us isn't enough for you." Trent reached under me, pushing my hand away. He pinched my clit, bringing me to the point that had been slowly building. I screamed out, my body tightening around him, the tremors of my release rolling across me in an endless torrent. Trent mercilessly hammered harder into me. Fisting my hair in his grip like reins, he leaned back, his other hand still torturing me. As I peaked and rode through the last of my orgasm, he bellowed, finding his own release and filling me with cum.

Panting in short, sharp breaths, we both collapsed face down, Trent landing beside me with an arm and leg possessively wrapped around me.

The murmured grunts and curses from Grady earned a chuckle from Trent. Rolling onto his back, he looked down the end of the bed with a taunting smile to his friends—way too pleased with himself by what had happened. Recovering his erratic heart rate faster than I had, with his breathing already steady, Trent nestled his face into my neck and pressed a soft kiss to my shoulder. I hummed, savoring the blissful high I was still riding, the sensation only heightened by his gentle affection. Trent continued the path of kisses to my back. My body was sensitive to touch and was slightly ticklish, goosebumps flicked everywhere he touched. I giggled when Trent licked up my spine, unable to help the reaction. Before I could pull away, he sunk his teeth in. I screamed and tried to elbow him, but he rolled off before I made contact. My movements were still languid after being so thoroughly fucked.

I watched as Trent got to his feet and began striding naked, standing in front of his friends. He walked past each of them, flaunting what he had just done, with a cocky swagger, all while they remained tied up and unable to react.

Grady snarled at Trent, baring his teeth when he stepped in front of him. Trent whispered something to Grady too quiet for me to make out. Grady and Kyden's eyes flicked from Trent to me with a conspiratorial smile that unnerved me. Looking over at Chris, I found he was mirroring their expression.

Uh oh.

Trent turned back to me, pulling me to my feet and walking me to the end of the bed, so I faced our unwilling captives. Pressed up against my back, Trent rested his hands on my hips with his head against the side of mine.

What was going on?

"Oh, little girl," Chris clucked his tongue. "You have no idea what you've just done."

I smiled, proud of the hunger I had sparked in each of their eyes. Alarm bells rang in the back of my mind, but I shut them out, refusing to acknowledge them.

"It's not like you can do anything about it, anyway. You're entirely at my whim." I said confidently, loving the fact that these predatory men were in a reversed situation than what they were accustomed to.

Trent stifled a laugh behind me. Moving his hands to wrap around my waist, he pressed his lips to my shoulder.

"You will pay for that, pretty girl," Kyden threatened.

"If I were you, I would run, chocolate drop," Grady warned. "Because when we catch you, get our hands on you…"

"You will pay," Kyden finished with a growl.

"You have until the count of ten," Chris warned.

My smile faltered, taking in the sudden change of atmosphere in the room.

"What?" I asked in confusion

"Ten," Trent whispered in my ear.

I turned my head over my shoulder to look at him. He

raised his brows and then looked over to the others.

"Nine," Grady drew the word out slowly, with a devilish smile.

My head whipped back, and I saw Grady's left hand free from its restraint. He waved it at me tauntingly. I gasped, stepping back into Trent's chest.

"Eight," Kyden grinned, flexing his muscles and tearing the ropes free from the wall with ease.

"Fuck!" I exclaimed, pressing firmer into Trent, feeling his silent chuckle.

"Seven," Chris said, showing his hands free of restraints, rubbing his wrists.

"Run," Trent growled from behind me.

With a squeal, I took off, my heart in my throat. I laughed, excited by the thrill of the chase.

I must have run out of time because behind me I heard Chris's taunts, "I hope you're ready for your punishment, little girl."

"Because when we catch you, you're going to be taking four dicks at once," Grady yelled, sounding closer than I expected, behind me.

"That wasn't ten," I yelled as I was thrown forward, a heavy weight holding me down.

I attempted to throw whoever was on me off, but I was met

with a pair of boots in front of my face. Chris bent down to pull my arms out in front of me, holding them captive.

"Since when do we play by the rules?" Kyden said in my ear, yanking my head back by my hair painfully.

I bucked my hips, continuing to try to throw him off. Strong hands grasped my ankles, holding them stationary.

"I knew you'd be a wild ride." Kyden ground his hips into my arse, letting me feel just how turned on he was.

"Oh, for fucksake," I groaned and quit struggling.

I heard Trent tsk. "You gave up too easily, little shadow."

"And here I thought you were going to fight us," Grady sounded disappointed.

"Maybe spill some blood," Kyden added.

Chris released my hands with a sigh at the same time as both my ankles were released.

Seizing the opportunity, I swung my elbow back, catching Kyden in the face, and rolled him off me. Clambering to my feet, I punched Chris in the crotch before straightening and took off, smiling to myself. I heard Grady and Trent's bellows of laughter from behind me, edging me on.

"Kira!" My name was called out in warning, urging me to run faster. I didn't know who it had been, but something in the tone flooded me with anticipation.

Disappearing into the surrounding scrub, I ducked down

behind a large thicket of tall weeds. The coarse foliage itched against my bare skin, and I tried not to think about any bugs that might be lingering in the ground at my feet looking for a warm habitat. Squatting down was basically giving them open-door access, and the last thing I wanted was trying to explain to the emergency department how a family of insects had made their home in my passages.

My pulse thrumming loudly in my ears made it difficult to hear their approach. I was startled when Kyden passed me first, not seeing me hidden. It was a good thing they were all such large men, they were unmistakable as they ran past me, splitting in different directions through the scrub in search of me.

When my breath had slowed and there was enough distance between me and my predators, I stepped out from my hiding spot and ran back towards the house, fully prepared to enjoy a bath while they continued hunting for me. A long soak in a hot bath was exactly what I needed. I felt grimey and gross from the initial hunt still, and that wasn't even adding the aches of my body from Trent fucking me.

I should have known better.

Just as I reached the door handle, a hand covered my face, silencing my scream, with another arm wrapping around my middle, lifting me from the ground.

"Caught you, little girl," Chris growled. "Now you will pay."

"Don't call me little girl." I murmured behind his hand.

"I will call you whatever the fuck I want, and you will like it." Chris dropped his hand from my mouth to my throat, squeezing firmly.

I turned my head to see his face. "And I suppose you want me to call you *Daddy* too?" The heated look in his eyes told me he wouldn't be opposed to it. *Well damn!*

Forcing me forward on stumbling feet, he swung open the door. I was met with Grady, who was casually leaning against the wall, one foot crossed over his ankle, his arms crossed over his chest and a single brow raised as though he had simply been there waiting for me.

What the fuck?

"What's the matter, Chocolate drop? Thought you could really escape us?"

"You got your reward. Now it's time for ours," Chris warned.

I stupidly, just nodded. My mind had fallen victim to their charisma and wanted to play along with wherever this was going. What else was I supposed to do?

Kira

48

They dragged me into the bedroom, snapping cuffs onto my wrists before attaching them to the bedhead and spreading my arms wide above me. My breathing came in sharp and heavy, thrilled to be caught in the clutches of these dangerous men. There was something seriously wrong with me.

"Do I at least get a safe word?"

Four barks of laughter rang out around me. "Do we come across as the type to offer a safe word?" Chris asked, throwing his domineering tone at me, making me squirm.

"Well, no…."

"Then there's your answer. Now be a *good girl* and do exactly as you're told. We assure you it will be as pleasurable for you as it is for us."

Well shit. My pussy purred at being called a good girl, happy to keep going with this game.

"Do you understand?"

I nodded, yelping at the harsh bark from Chris.

"Words, Kira," he gritted out.

"Yes," I spat.

I was already feeling overheated and desperate. Being restrained, utterly defenceless against these predators while they did as they pleased to me, caught my stomach in knots. I squeezed my thighs together in an attempt to alleviate the throb that was crying out for friction just from their voices. My body betrayed me with lust when I knew I should fear these men. Instead, I was so turned on that their presence alone almost had me coming.

So much had changed in the short time from being abducted to now. I was so fucked in the head to be entertaining the idea of allowing them to do as they pleased—was my fantasy coming to reality? I hope these men were wealthy because I was going to need a lot of therapy after this.

Kyden stalked up to me with a small knife flicking in his hand. He sank his teeth into his lower lip, eyeing my body over hungrily.

My heartbeat galloped in my chest knowing he was going to slice me open and bleed me for his own pleasure. As if my body was recalling the last encounter with his blade from a few days ago, the cuts he had already inflicted began to sting—a reminder of what was to come.

A small whimper fell from my mouth, but it wasn't from fear, it was the thrill of the pain, the sensation, the high.

Kyden smiled, his eyes crinkling at the edges as if he knew what I was thinking.

"Oh, sweetness, I can practically smell your heightened arousal at the mere thought of me spilling your life essence from you." Kyden tutted. "I think I will make you earn it. What do you say, Chris?"

I looked over Kyden's shoulder to where Chris stood, looking more relaxed than I had ever seen him. Leaning against the wall with his legs crossed at the ankles. He had one arm cradling his elbow with his hand rubbing thoughtfully across his stubbled chin.

"I say we make her beg," he urged.

I narrowed my eyes. "Not happening, big man."

Grady chuckled creepily from near the side of my head, causing me to yelp and yank against the cuffs, which in turn only increased his laughter. "Oh yeah, she needs to be punished."

"Trent," Chris barked to my other side. "You know what to do."

Then, to Grady, he nodded. I turned my head to see what they were doing, but Grady caught my chin in a vice-like grip, holding my head still.

"Don't fucking move, Chocolate drop. You made your choice and fucked with us. Now it's our turn."

My chest heaved with short, fast breaths, as the thrill of events unfolding filled my veins with dopamine. I looked at Grady in peripherals, catching his smile a split second before my sight was stolen and a blindfold was placed over my eyes. I tried to shake my head free, but was met with a slap to my cheek, leaving a warm burn behind on my face.

"You were told not to move," Chris warned. "Another."

Another? Before I could question it, I was met with another slap. This one hitting straight at the apex of my thighs with more force than the one on my cheek.

I inhaled sharply, unsure what to make of the sensation.

"I think she enjoyed that too much," Trent commented. "Let's take it up a notch?"

"Kyden," Chris ordered, not needing to say more.

This was clearly a well-practised scenario between them. I couldn't help the pang of jealousy that rang through me knowing they had been this intimate together with other women before me. I gritted my teeth at the thought.

"Wha…" A hand slammed across my mouth, cutting off my words before I could speak.

"Tsk, tsk," Grady chastised.

"No talking unless you are being asked a question. Do you

understand?" Chris's deep voice sent shivers racing across my skin.

I nodded. A sharp sting landed across my breast where a hand connected, sending ripples of heat through me.

"*I said*, do you understand?" Chris repeated angrily.

"Yes," I snarled from behind Grady's hand. He snickered and removed his hand from my mouth.

"Yes, what?" Chris snarled.

I gritted my teeth, deciding to give him what he wanted, but making sure he was aware just how much I was going to fight him. "Yes, *sir.*"

Another whack came, again between my legs. This time I pulled my knees together because of the discomfort. I hissed between my teeth.

"Less attitude," he reprimanded.

The bed near my legs shifted as a weight settled beside me. I heard Kyden's small groans before I felt the cold pressure of his knife against my skin, just below my rib cage, not yet piercing me.

"We're going to play a little game," he murmured, increasing the pressure ever so slightly. A small nick grazed my flesh, breaking the skin, and a quiet squeak slipped from my lips. The pressure eased back just enough for me to breathe again.

"I want to see how still you can stay while Trent does everything he can to make you squirm. If you flinch, you will be cut, and I *will* make sure it hurts. But if you are a really good girl… then we will reward you."

"Do you think you can stay still for us, little shadow?" Trent purred.

I nodded my head, my voice coming out a breathy whisper, "yes."

"We will see," Chris sounded disbelieving.

I felt hands move to my thighs, and I jumped instinctively. A sharp sting caught my sternum, followed by a few drops of a liquid, causing the cut to burn painfully. I let out a small scream, locking my muscles so I didn't move again.

"Not a good start, Chocolate drop," Grady whispered in my ear, his fingers grazing across the side of my cheek with a feather-light touch.

When I felt the hands move higher, I forced myself to remain still. My thighs were forcefully pulled apart, bare legs settling between mine as their skin brushed against mine.

"Bend your knees," Trent encouraged, bringing his hands to my outer thighs and lifting them slightly.

I complied, allowing him to flex me how he saw fit, not wanting a repeat punishment from flinching.

I felt Trent's face against my inner thigh and had to resist the urge to raise my hips. The first swipe of his tongue made me gasp, but I remained still, despite wanting desperately to grind against his face. My body was aching for more. He licked again, more slowly, then sucked my clit before pulling away with a humm. I had no control over the sounds that fell from my lips as he continued to rile me up with torturously slow motions. His fingers then came into play, following his tongue, sliding back and forth before they were plunged deep inside my body. I moaned loudly, clenching my core around his fingers, with my hands balled into fists above my head where they were cuffed.

"Fuck, she's dripping," Trent ground out.

"Bring me your fingers, I want to taste," Chris ordered.

Trent moved off the bed. I heard his feet shuffle across the ground to where Chris stood. A low hum rolling from his chest made me whimper at the thought of him sucking both my arousal and any lingering release from Trent.

"You taste like heaven, little one. Seeing you splayed out before us like the perfect offering for us to use however we please without complaint, makes me think you deserve a reward. Would you like that?"

"Yes, sir," I replied automatically, my body desperate for more than the tiny amount of teasing so far.

"Hmm, I'm not convinced you really want it," Chris

dismissed. "Grady."

Grady's hand wrapped around my throat suddenly. His fingers pressed firmly at the sides, causing my vision to blur instantly. I pulled my hands against the cuffs instinctively.

A sharp sting followed by a scorching burn hit beside my navel, but my voice was stolen with my air, not allowing me to scream. Just as darkness closed in, I felt teeth latch onto my clit, biting down hard, and I was met with more cuts to my flesh, followed by blinding pain.

I was so overwhelmed by varied sensations that the unthinkable happened—I came. My back arched, and I screamed into the air as the pressure on my throat was released, only to be met with rough thrusts into my core by Trent's hand, as his mouth sucked and bit on my clitoris. I rode the high, bucking against Trent until my body gave out and the last of my orgasm faded away, leaving my limbs languid, and my breathing ragged.

"I did not give you permission to come," Chris snapped.

"Ss… sorry, sir," I answered, breathlessly.

"Roll over."

Forcing my sated body to move, I rolled with assistance, so my arms were crossed over above me. I was brought to my knees, with my legs slightly spread. A firm hand pushed down between my shoulder blades, forcing my chest into the mattress with my arse in the air and everything on display. If I had known I was going to be kidnapped and used sexually, I would have made a waxing appointment beforehand. Too late now, I suppose.

"Such a filthy little slut," Chris scorned. "I can see your needy cunt weeping down your thighs, begging to be filled with cock. But you haven't earned that right, have you?"

I shook my head.

A heavy hand came down firmly across the backs of my thighs, causing me to scream out.

"I said, you haven't earned that right, have you, little slut?"

"No, sir," I whimpered. A gentle hand rubbed across the sting of the slap, making me lean into the touch.

"Uh," Chris chastised. My clit was pinched between two fingers painfully. I gritted my teeth, my toes curling, so I didn't react.

"Good girl, you're learning," he praised. "But you still need to be punished for coming. Ten hits should be a good start."

"Count for me," Grady said a moment before my flesh was met with a sharp, blinding sting.

I cried out at the sudden flare that bit in. It was quickly followed by a sharp slash across my forearm, where I assumed Kyden had cut me.

"Count, or he starts again," Chris warned.

"One."

The next hit landed across my lower back, harder, and I arched against it.

"Two," I whimpered, preparing myself for the next cut, which met at my hip.

The following three came in fast succession across my arse cheeks, with barely enough time to count aloud, before the fourth hit landed in the same spot, making me scream out loud.

"SIX!" Three shallow, small nicks peppered my thigh.

How could I handle four more, when that last one all but crippled me?

Concentrating on the dull ache that remained after the sharp sting, I focused on that lingering warmth, allowing the pleasure of it to help me push through, as the next hit landed across my middle back. An agonisingly slow slice slid across the arch of my foot, being met with Kyden's deep moans as he bled me.

"Seven," I gritted out.

"Eight." When it landed across one thigh, it met with a stab in the exact same spot.

Fuck.

"Nine." The other thigh. A hit and a shallow stab.

I blindly waited for the final hit. Listening intently for the sound of whatever implement was being used to whistle through the air. Seconds stretched on, the anticipation building to the point that I felt like I was going to climb out of my skin if I didn't feel the sting soon. When I heard the air whip, relief flooded me knowing what to expect. I was eager for it, feeling desperate for my final punishment. When the blow finally landed, it was harder than any of the other hits. It caught perfectly in line where the majority of the others had fallen. The blinding agony of contact felt as though my skin had been torn. I let out a silent scream before I managed a whispered, "ten."

I waited for the press of the blade against my skin, panting heavily in anticipation. My hand was uncurled. The cold press of metal against my palm caused me to try to pull my hand away, but it was trapped by the cuffs. Kyden's larger hand curled around mine, pressing the edge of the knife into the soft tissue. Slowly he dragged the knife from my grasp with his hand curled around mine, holding my hand in a fist. I whimpered as it opened my palm, warm blood cascaded down my wrist, to my shoulder. Kyden released my hand and let out a deep, breathy groan. He kissed the wound on my palm, then his tongue traced the open flesh.

"You are my undoing, precious," he murmured, then pulled away.

My knees collapsed from under me while I chased the high from the stinging heat caused by the inflictions. I didn't know how it was possible to be so close to the verge of an orgasm after suffering through that. But my body obviously had other ideas as I throbbed uncomfortably between my thighs.

Soothing hands massaged the welts across my skin, the contact causing me to hiss in response.

"Such a good little girl. I think you deserve a reward for taking your punishment so well," Chris praised, making my stomach flutter.

I didn't know whether I could handle a reward. My body was exhausted from my punishment. Despite still feeling needy.

"Lift up." Trent placed hands on my hips, lifting them so I was on my knees again. I felt someone shift under me, and my legs were manoeuvred so I straddled wide hips. My pussy purred eagerly at finally getting the attention it was craving. I ground down, feeling an erection glide across my slit, sending a shudder rippling through me.

"Fuck, you're wet," Grady moaned, rocking against me. A body pressed in behind me, a hand grasping my throat and pulling me firmly against a hard chest.

"Hold still," Trent said into my ear. Moving his mouth to

the side of my face, he bit down on my jaw and then kissed the spot gently. "We are going to fill you up and have some fun."

Trent nudged his cock at my entrance and thrust in. We both cried out in unison. "You're so fucking tight, even after you've already been fucked. Why didn't I take advantage of your cunt before I fisted it?"

I let out a small laugh, unable to help myself. Trent pushed in two more times before withdrawing fully. Before I could protest, he pushed me forward onto Grady's chest, where he stole my mouth with his own. His kiss was rough and demanding. His tongue brutally lashing at mine, sucking on it then whipping it around his own. It was messy, uncoordinated and hot as hell.

I felt Trent adjust himself behind me, running his cock back and forth down my crack. He pushed into my arse without any prep, using my arousal as lubricant. His fingers grasped my hips painfully so I couldn't pull away, the burn lasting for the few seconds it took him to gather himself—with a few curse words— before he began slowly thrusting. I pulled my head back from Grady, whimpering, and grinding against him, desperate for more.

"What a greedy little slut. One cock isn't enough to satisfy you. Do you think you deserve more?" Chris asked, his voice coming out gravelly.

"Yes, sir, please." I wanted all of them; I needed them to fill me in every way.

"Hmm, you do beg so prettily," Chris mused.

Grady reached down and adjusted himself between us while Trent paused for him. I tried to lower myself, but Trent held me still, while Grady teased me with just the tip of his cock, dipping it in and out slowly.

"Please, I need more."

Chuckles from the men swarmed me from all directions.

Agonisingly slowly, I was lowered onto Grady. He was thick, and the combined feeling of his cock seated inside of me with Trent, was everything I could have hoped for. I rocked back and forth a few times between them, earning several curses.

"Hold still, pretty girl, there's room for one more cock in your greedy cunt." Chris spoke from somewhere near my face, halting my movements and causing me to gasp. I tried to wrap my head around the logistics of how that was going to work.

No, it wasn't possible. Surely not?

"Not in my arse, Ky," Trent growled, followed by an amused cackle from Kyden.

Trent pressed me flat against Grady, pushing his weight

down onto my back. Grady took advantage and began assaulting my mouth again, while I rocked my hips as much as I could to gain friction, despite hands trying to hold me still. I felt fingers at my entrance working their way in alongside Grady's cock. I whimpered into Grady's mouth as he groaned into mine. The hand at my hips digging in more firmly, holding me still. Then I felt the pressure of Kyden, forcing his cock against my entrance. My pussy began stretching uncomfortably as Ky forced his head in with a hiss. Grady moaned into my mouth as Kyden rubbed up against his cock, trying to squeeze in beside him.

"Shit. She's too tight," Ky gritted out.

Grady released my mouth, peppering kisses along my neck in an attempt to help me relax.

"Hurry up Ky, it's killing me not moving." Trent was losing restraint.

Grady laughed darkly, and moved his lips to my shoulder, then opened his mouth and sunk his teeth in hard. As I screamed, Kyden forced his cock in along Grady's.

It hurt—I felt like I was being ripped in half. Tears rolled down my cheeks. I was about to demand they all pull out, but the burn quickly faded, morphing into pleasure, as I was filled and stretched beautifully.

"Fuck!" All three men ground out at once and began

finding a rhythm. It was unlike anything I had experienced.

"I'm going to come," I warned, feeling it build quickly.

"No!" Chris snapped. "Not until I say, now open your mouth."

I whimpered and clenched my core, making the men grunt.

I opened my mouth and poked out my tongue. My body quaked as I fought back my orgasm. Chris's hand gripped my chin, turning my head further to the side. He ran his calloused thumb across my cheek. "Such a good little girl. Please me, and I'll let you come."

The silky tip of his cock sat on my tongue, touching my top lip. I opened my mouth wider, letting him guide it further into my mouth. He clenched a fistful of my hair, then thrust into the back of my throat so his balls slapped my chin and cut off my air.

"Fuck, I'm not going to last," Grady grunted, increasing his thrusts.

I hummed in agreement, not able to do more with a cock hitting the back of my throat, because I wasn't going to last much longer either.

Chris began jack hammering into my mouth, moaning his own pleasure when I did. I continued to humm as he hit my throat, sucking firmly each time he slid back.

"Fuck. Fuck. Fuck!" he stammered.

As if on queue, the three men mercilessly upped their tempo, cursing.

"Come for us," Chris hissed out.

At those words I allowed my body to free itself of the building orgasm I was keeping at bay, and came so hard, I blacked out for a second. Cum filled me as the men all came in unison, filling my ears with their satisfied release.

I swallowed back Chris, only gagging briefly as I fought between breathing and crying out. Chris slowly pulled himself free from my lips, wiping his spilled cum from the side of my mouth with his thumb and pushed it back between my lips. I sucked it off his thumb greedily, pleased when a low rumble fell from him.

The blindfold was pulled free, and I blinked away the light as my eyes adjusted.

Trent and Kyden pulled out and then rolled me to my side. My arms twisted further above my head, but I had zero cares. Out of breath and exhausted, I collapsed forward onto Grady and closed my eyes. For the first time in my life, I felt an inner peace.

A gentle kiss landed on my cheek. "You did spectacularly, little one."

I cracked an eyelid, smiling up at Chris. "Little one? What happened to little girl?"

He gave me a smirk. "I think you just proved you're not a little *girl*. You are one in a million. Our one."

"If that's the case, then no more killing innocents," I murmured. I closed my eyes, smiling with contentment.

My hands were uncuffed and brought down in front of me.

The silence was heavy for a moment. "Deal," they all said in unison.

"As long as you remain with us," Kyden said hopefully.

I hummed a small agreement.

"Come on, let's get you cleaned up." Trent tucked his hands under me, lifting me off of Grady and the bed and into his arms.

"Five more minutes, I just need a little nap first."

He snickered. "Liar, you will pass out. You will get cleaned up, then drink and eat. After that, you can sleep."

I whined, letting my head flop against his chest, not having the energy to protest while on the verge of sleep. But Trent wasn't perturbed as he walked me to the bathroom. The sound of the bath filling and the subtle scent of herbs roused me from my grogginess. I turned my head to see a massive square tub with steam rising from it. Trent stepped into the rising water with me in his arms, lowering us into the hot water as it filled. I hissed as the water met the various cuts on my skin, tensing until the stinging settled.

I finally relaxed, finding myself nestled between Trent's thighs, leaning back against his chest. He held an arm under my breasts, keeping my body close against him.

I could die happily right now. I let out a contented sigh as the warmth sank into my achy muscles.

"You do know we are never letting you go now?"

I nodded. "I gathered."

Trent ran a hand from my scalp down through my hair. I leaned into his hand, enjoying the sensation.

"Where did you come from?" he whispered to himself.

"I was lost before you found me," I murmured, not sure how much I made sense and not really caring. I was in a small bubble of bliss.

"Gray has Ky tucked up. I left him to take care of him, in his own way…" Chris's voice trailed off with a shudder as he entered the bathroom carrying an armful of water and fruit.

I tilted my head up to look at him, wondering what he meant by that, but my mind was too languid to press the question.

"You look relaxed," he chuffed, raising a brow.

I gave a sleepy smile. Chris and Trent both laughed. Chris placed the items on the ledge beside the bath and stepped into the oversized tub at my feet and turned off the water.

Then he reached down and grasped my calf, lifting it up and began rubbing his fingers into my muscles. I moaned happily, snuggling further back into Trent.

"At least you let us take care of you and don't fight us after we use your body however we please," Trent said as he reached over and grabbed a bottle of water.

"This is the best part," I murmured sleepily.

Unscrewing the lid, he brought it to my lips, making me drink. When he was satisfied I had drunk enough, he placed it back.

"I don't know if we should be offended by that statement." Chris narrowed his eyes on me, as he worked his way down my leg to the arch of my foot, forcing small sounds from me.

I smiled, lapping up the attention and care. "Trust me, that was the best sex I've ever had."

Trent scoffed, pulling back the grape from my mouth that he was about to feed me. "Well, now I'm offended."

I laughed, despite the lack of energy. "Believe me, Trent, I have no complaints there. Besides, there are plenty more opportunities for you to claim back first place."

Chris and Trent shared a conspiratorial look, making me wish I could take back those words.

"I think we need to up the game. What do you say?" Chris asked Trent.

I gulped. The silent communication that passed between them unnerved me. They looked at one another and then back at me.

Trent let out a small, amused snort. "Hide and seek? Or …"

Chris looked at me, smiling wide with a promise that I wasn't done paying for my little stunt earlier. *Oh shit!*

"Tag," they said darkly together.

Acknowledgements

Thank you to each and every one of you who takes a chance on an unknown Indie author. Every page and book you read makes a world of difference and encourages us to keep doing what we love – writing stories to share with you. You're the best! ❤

And to my family—thank you for your endless patience and understanding, especially when I became completely consumed by my characters and neglected everything else at home. You all encouraged me and offered constant reassurance when I was suffering from self-doubt. I love you all dearly.